"If I thought you completely untrustworthy, I wouldn't have allowed you in my house,"

Grace explained, regarding him steadily.

Elliot swallowed hard, trying to keep a rein on his emotions. Never before had any person's trust meant so much to him. It was ridiculous, really. She shouldn't be having this kind of effect on him. She had dragged him through the mud and forced him to remain in hiding like a criminal.

She also had the loveliest eyes in the world, and the most tempting lips. She had gone to considerable effort to rescue him from the rain. She was bravely doing her best to take care of her sister.

What had he ever done to deserve the trust she was placing in him?

Nothing.

Dear Reader,

The Rogue's Return is the next book in award-winning Margaret Moore's new MOST UNSUITABLE... series. Set in Victorian England, this story features Elliot Fitzwalter, (the villain of *The Dark Duke*). Wounded and on the run from his creditors, Elliot is taken in by a proper schoolteacher and discovers there is more to life than he ever thought possible. Although he still must convince himself that he is worthy of the love of such a fine woman. And keep an eye out for the author's story in our Christmas collection, *The Knights of Christmas,* which will be available in October.

Outlaw Wife by Ana Seymour is a bittersweet Western about the daughter of a notorious outlaw who loses her heart to the rancher who saves her from jail. And fleeing Britain and marriage to an elderly preacher, an English adventuress becomes involved with an American spy in *Nancy Whiskey* by Laurel Ames.

Quicksilver's Catch by *USA Today* bestselling author Mary McBride is a delightful story featuring a runaway heiress and the tough-as-nails bounty hunter who is determined to make as much money as he can from their association, if she doesn't drive him to drink first. Don't miss this warm and funny story of two people who *really* don't belong together.

Whatever your tastes in reading, we hope you'll keep a lookout for all of our books, wherever Harlequin Historicals are sold.

Sincerely,

Tracy Farrell
Senior Editor

Please address questions and book requests to:
Harlequin Reader Service
U.S.: 3010 Walden Ave., P.O. Box 1325, Buffalo, NY 14269
Canadian: P.O. Box 609, Fort Erie, Ont. L2A 5X3

Margaret Moore

The Rogue's Return

Harlequin Books

TORONTO • NEW YORK • LONDON
AMSTERDAM • PARIS • SYDNEY • HAMBURG
STOCKHOLM • ATHENS • TOKYO • MILAN
MADRID • WARSAW • BUDAPEST • AUCKLAND

ISBN 0-373-28976-6

THE ROGUE'S RETURN

This edition published by arrangement with Harlequin Books S.A.

® and TM are trademarks of the publisher. Trademarks indicated with ® are registered in the United States Patent and Trademark Office, the Canadian Trade Marks Office and in other countries.

Printed in U.S.A.

Books by Margaret Moore

MARGARET MOORE

confesses that her first "crush" was Errol Flynn. The second was "Mr. Spock." She thinks that it explains why her heroes tend to be either charming rogues or lean, inscrutable tough guys.

Margaret lives in Scarborough, Ontario, with her husband, two children and two cats. She used to sew and read for reasons other than research.

To my great-great-grandfather Moore,
the rogue who got sent to the colonies to reform,
or so I've been told.

Chapter One

Lincolnshire, 1868

"**O**h, Miss Barton, how wonderful to see you! Isn't it simply *dreadful?*" the unfortunately familiar female voice declared pleasantly.

Grace Barton smiled noncommittally as she turned to face Miss Myrtle Hurley and her silent twin sister, Miss Ethel, who were now blocking her way as formidably as any brick wall.

As always, the elderly women wore virtually identical black bombazine dresses, gray wool cloaks, ratty fur muffs they had apparently owned since the Regency, and corresponding black bonnets. Their thick white hair was dressed the same way, and to a stranger, they would look like mirror images of the same, sweet elderly woman.

Unfortunately, Grace knew from long experience that neither the brisk April breeze blowing from across the fens and tugging at her thin wool cloak and bell skirt, or the smell wafting toward them from the nearby fishmonger's, would cause them to move until they had said what they wanted to say.

"Good afternoon," she said evenly, wondering what particular piece of salacious gossip the Hurleys would regale her with today.

"Good afternoon," Miss Myrtle, the eldest of the twins by a full five minutes, said breathlessly. She always spoke breathlessly, and she always smiled, no matter how terrible the tale she was going to relate, or how damning her criticism.

Grace often felt that was how the Hurley girls— who had been "girls" for the past seventy-five years—managed to avoid criticism themselves. If any other person who did not look like the epitome of sweet seniority said the things they did and revealed the secrets they told, they would be shunned.

"It's just too *distressing!*" Miss Myrtle exclaimed. "Not for us, of course, but for so many others!"

"What has happened?" Grace asked, keeping her tone carefully neutral as she shifted her basket into her other kid-gloved hand, partly because she was impatient, but also because Miss Ethel was trying to peek inside, and Grace didn't want her to see the contents. It was none of the woman's business that the fish Grace had purchased was the cheapest she could find.

"It's the *rents,*" Miss Myrtle announced, not without a sense of importance. "Sir Donald *is* raising them—most definitely! I heard it from Mrs. Banks herself not two hours ago."

Grace swallowed hard. As well as the holder of the largest estate in the country, Sir Donald was also the landlord of Barton Farm. For once, the Hurleys' news *was* important and, if it came from his housekeeper, likely to be true.

"I do so *hate* to be the bearer of bad tidings," Myrtle Hurley said eagerly, a pleasant smile still on her round face. "But *everyone* will know sooner or later. Sir Donald came home yesterday, and he has already spoken with some of his tenants!"

How typical of the Hurleys to treat this news of a raise in rents as just another fascinating piece of gossip! Grace thought, keeping any sense of her displeasure from her face. The Hurleys had nothing to fear, for their parents had made quite a tidy fortune in the wool trade, which they had bequeathed to their daughters. Sir Donald could triple the rent, and they would not suffer.

Not so herself and Mercy. Her family had been the major landholders here for over three centuries—the village Barton-by-the-Fens was even named for them. Sadly, in her grandfather's time, a series of investments had turned out to be disasters. Her father had done his best to recoup, to no avail. Little by little, their land had gone to Sir Donald, until all they were left with upon their parents' deaths three years ago was one acre and their house, and all they had to live on was the interest from her mother's dowry, not very much at all.

"Do you know how high he intends to raise them?" Grace asked, her voice quite cool and calm in spite of her inner turmoil.

"No, I don't how much he intends to raise them,"

Miss Myrtle said rather primly. "It is improper for ladies to discuss business matters."

"Improper," Miss Ethel murmured.

Grace didn't point out that they were discussing business matters at that very moment, and as far as she was concerned, if the Hurleys wanted to be the unofficial town criers, they should expect to be interrogated. "Do you know when?"

"It's none of our business," Miss Myrtle answered affably. "Perhaps when he does, he will pay for more policing. The chief constable *claims* he is unable to do anything about the vagrancy problems unless he can hire more help."

She nodded in the general direction of The Three Crowns, one of the small brick establishments that lined the village square, where a group of ragged, ill-fed men lingered. Simultaneously all three women pulled their cloaks tighter, as if to ward off the men's unblinking stares.

"And just the other day, my dear, I heard that some travelers were *robbed* on the road to Grantham by a band of brigands. Even our countryside is not safe anymore!"

"Not safe," repeated Miss Ethel firmly and with an affable smile.

If the proposed rent increase would go to improvements in the county, Grace would have been less upset about it, even though the means to pay would still be a problem.

Unfortunately, she doubted Sir Donald had any intention of spending the extra income on anyone but himself. After his recent knighthood—which had come as a surprise to everyone in Barton—he had declared the house that had belonged to his family for three generations was not grand enough for a knight. Work on improving, or at least expanding, the stone structure had begun immediately.

"I should be going—" Grace began, hoping to get away from the Hurleys before they could impart any more bad news.

"They do say he's thinking of marrying," Miss Myrtle noted.

"A rich heiress," Miss Ethel announced.

"If he did marry well, then perhaps he wouldn't have to raise the rent," Grace observed hopefully, and not all that hope had to do with the proposed rent increase. "If you ladies will excuse me, I had better get home to Mercy."

"Oh, and how is dear little Mercy?" asked Miss Myrtle solicitously, as if Mercy were a child of six instead of a young woman of eighteen.

"Very well, thank you," Grace lied.

She lied because if the Hurley girls discovered Mercy was ill, they would arrive at the house at the most inconvenient times with soup, or medicines they bought from peddlers and Gypsies, or simply to "see how she is, poor dear." Afterward Grace would hear from those who thought she ought to know that the Hurleys considered their housekeeping faulty, their garden untidy, and their food undercooked.

At times such as these, Grace was relieved they had no servants to reveal that Mercy had been sick this morning.

"I hope she isn't too distraught over Adam's absence,'' Miss Myrtle said, coy as a fifteen-year-old as she spoke of her nephew.

''She has not mentioned him this past month,'' Grace replied evenly. ''They were merely acquaintances, after all.''

Or so Grace fervently hoped. Mercy had made no secret of her infatuation with the dashing young naval officer visiting his aunts on leave. He had been at his aunts' home in Barton for only a month, but in that time, he seemed to have quite captured Mercy's fancy.

''Mere acquaintances,'' Miss Ethel confirmed firmly.

No doubt the idea of their precious relative marrying a poor girl, no matter what her family background, gave them the vapors.

''Miss Mercy was simply being her charming self, nothing more, I'm sure,'' Miss Myrtle said. ''And Adam is such a fine young man, *anyone* of *any* discernment would wish to enjoy his company.''

Grace knew she intended that remark to be a rebuke, for Grace had not paid much attention to the young man. He had struck her as handsome, but little more, and rather too proud of himself. However, she calmly smiled her agreement.

''He has arrived in Gibraltar safely, and is already *quite* a favorite of the wardroom,'' Miss Myrtle continued.

''Quite a favorite,'' Miss Ethel repeated.

''I'm sure he is. Now, I really must beg to be excused. This wind is so very cold!'' Grace was shivering when she dipped them both a curtsy and turned to leave.

"Good afternoon, Miss Barton," Miss Myrtle called out cheerfully as Grace hurried on her way. "Try not to worry about the rent!"

With that parting shot rankling in her bosom, Grace barely caught Miss Ethel's "Afternoon!" as she crossed the square, for indeed, the breeze had picked up and was decidedly frigid.

They *would* shout about the rent, just in case the whole village didn't know of the Bartons' circumstances, Grace reflected sourly. Well, she shouldn't get annoyed about that. After all, everybody already knew they were not well off. There were few secrets in such a small place.

Few changes in the daily routine. Few new faces to make life interesting…

Not for the first time Grace tried to imagine leaving Barton-by-the-Fens, to begin again in a larger place, where no one knew who you were, or what difficulties you faced.

Where no one cared about you, or gave you respect because your ancestors had been lords and masters there time out of mind.

Grace sighed heavily. As always, her ruminations about leaving came to that point, and served to make her dread abandoning her home.

Besides, she had Mercy to think of, and Mercy would sooner lose a limb than leave Barton. She had said so often enough.

She said many things often enough, and emphatically enough that her feelings were an open book not only to her sister, but to the whole village, including, unfortunately, the Hurley twins.

Why wasn't Mercy more circumspect? Grace thought with an old, familiar frustration. Why couldn't she learn to keep her own counsel? Why did she have to be so blatant in her admiration of Lieutenant Brown?

Well, it would have been worse if *she* had expressed any admiration for the Hurleys' darling nephew. They would have told her every time they met why it would be an unsuitable match, although the simple fact of the matter was that the Hurley girls didn't like Grace.

They never had, not since she was a small child. It had taken her some time to realize why: the Hurleys lived for reactions, and Grace didn't give them any. She had always been quiet and rather shy and not given to showing how she felt.

The Hurleys much preferred the type of response Grace's sister gave them. Mercy was always emotional and sentimental, and their tales could move her to the heights of happiness or plunge her to the depths of despondency, seemingly within minutes.

As Grace reached the far side of the village green, she noticed the usual gathering inside the blacksmith's forge. No doubt they were discussing the future raise in the rents.

At least she would not be alone in her dismay over the increase. While the villagers had supposed Sir Donald had every right to be proud of his mysterious knighthood, there had been much speculation as to how the money for the planned renovations was to be obtained. Now they had their answer.

They were probably also discussing, again and with dissatisfaction, the labor Sir Donald had hired. He had imported carpenters and masons from London, and it was said the furniture was coming from there, too. Taken all in all, the villagers were in as disgruntled a frame of mind as Grace, she was sure.

A black barouche turned down the main road and, recognizing its occupant, Grace quickly stepped back into the shadow of the butcher's doorway, her basket clutched defensively to her chest. She had no wish to be seen by Sir Donald, any more than she wished to speak with him.

Fortunately, he seemed far too immersed in looking every inch the country gentleman to be peering into doorways, his large, heavy-lidded dark eyes staring straight ahead, his carriage erect—although his posture couldn't disguise his overly large stomach—his tall hat perched fashionably to one side on his round head, and an expression of haughty condescension on his fat features.

Grace subdued a shudder, remembering again the precise moment during the Christmas service when she had realized Donald Franklin was watching her with an interest she did not appreciate in the slightest. At first, she had wondered what was wrong with her attire to warrant his scrutiny. Later, when he had way-laid her at the church door with some inane observation about the holidays and how things had changed since her grandfather's time, it had slowly dawned upon her that he thought he was being charming.

Why charming, and more importantly, why to her? What had been the meaning of that supercilious little smile, and that look in his watery eyes? The only answers that came to her struck her as a form of insult, and she had been loath to encounter him ever since.

When he was safely gone, Grace stepped out of her hiding place, quickening her pace.

Once she left the village, the wind picked up even more. The stone hedgerows provided some protection, and the trees would have done more, if they had been in full leaf. However, they were not and Grace realized the wind had veered from the east to the north. She glanced anxiously at the sky. As if she didn't have enough to trouble her, the billowing clouds had grown darker and thicker, and it looked about to rain.

Her old cloak provided scant protection. If she didn't hurry, she would be not merely cold, but wet through before she could get home.

Thinking it was a good thing the Hurleys couldn't see her, Grace lifted her skirts, got a good grip on her basket, and disregarded any notion that it was unladylike to run.

The handsome young man cursed and gingerly felt the gash on his forehead. When he looked at his fingers, squinting not just because the sky had grown darker, but also because he was having difficulty focusing, he saw blood. Not a lot, though, and he supposed it could have been worse. "I could'a been sober," he mumbled with a wry smile.

His bleary gaze traveled to the offending limb of

the oak that loomed over the road. "Where did you come from, eh?" he demanded, only half in jest, because the branch had truly seemed to come from nowhere. He hadn't noticed that he had entered a small wood, or that the road took a sudden dip there.

"Maybe this is an enchanted forest," he continued, his enunciation less than precise. "Ogres and trolls—and Boffins, I shouldn't wonder. No beautiful princesses to help out a poor traveler, though."

His smile disappeared, to be replaced with a bitter frown as he looked around for his horse. Or rather, the nag he had "borrowed" from some unsuspecting innkeeper. "I suppose Adrian would say that if I wasn't drunk," he muttered bitterly, "I would have seen the damn thing, and if I hadn't cheated, Boffin wouldn't be after me. And he'd be right. Again. Damn him to hell."

Forcing all thoughts of his half brother from his mind, he contemplated using his last handkerchief for a bandage, then decided against it. The cut was minor; no need to ruin a perfectly good handkerchief, even if it did need a washing. Instead, he picked up his battered hat and placed it lightly upon his head. Then, having located the nag placidly munching grass at the side of the rutted road beside the mossy stone fence, he reached into his worn saddlebag and withdrew a bottle, which he tilted and put to his lips.

He lowered it after a moment. "Hardly enough to taste," he mumbled, tossing the bottle over the hedgerow. He scratched, wondering if he had picked up something more than a bottle of hock at the tavern. Gad, he needed a bath and new clothes. These garments had withstood the voyage from Lower Canada, but they couldn't take much more wear.

If any of his friends from London should see him, they would think he had indeed suffered these past five years. Adrian would say it was no more than he deserved—but he wasn't going to think about Adrian.

Then he looked back the way he had come. No. Nobody there. Thank God. He didn't have the strength of a baby at the moment.

The man shook his head. "Doesn't do to think about that," he murmured, staggering back toward the horse. "I couldn't have done anything else."

Then, with a soft curse, he clambered onto his mount. "How the mighty have fallen, eh, my Pegasus?" he said to the horse. "Let us away!"

The beast lurched into motion and started down the road, eventually coming out of the woods to what appeared to be the junction of this road and a farmer's lane. The man strained to see any kind of a sign, but either his eyes were going, or the light was fading, or he was just too drunk, because he couldn't find one. Not so much as a white cross.

Just where the devil was he? Why couldn't the local inhabitants have signposts, like other civilized people? He should have disembarked at Liverpool, or Dover, not Yarmouth.

He knew he must be somewhere to the southwest of Boston, still close enough to the fens to catch a marshy whiff of the breeze blowing over the plowed fields too often for his comfort. The land was getting less flat, though, and every now and then, he spied a sheep.

Lincolnshire was terrible country, he thought grumpily, and the roads were the most terrible thing about it. Once he got out of here, he'd never come back. *If* he got out of here. If he didn't keep going around in circles, and if Boffin and his gang didn't find him...

Surely there must be an inn somewhere in this god-forsaken countryside, where he could play a few card games and earn enough for a meal.

He pulled his soiled jacket tighter. The weather was damnably cold for England in April, but not nearly as cold as some of the places he had been since he had left the country. That was why he had come back, of course. The weather. Only the weather.

He still had no wish to see his family. Not his mother, who had betrayed him. Or his half brother, with his condescending self-righteousness. He could imagine the martyr's face and hear his admonishing words.

And certainly not his half brother's wife.

His mother would be glad to know he was alive, of course. His spoiled, indulgent, vain mother, who had given her son whatever he wanted, until he was as vain and spoiled as she.

No one had ever had to tell him such things; he had realized early in his school days what he was. It had never troubled him, and as for Adrian, he was jealous. Not just because of the mother who had come into his house to replace his own, but because their father had loved his second son, too. Which was only right.

He didn't need or want to see Adrian or anybody

else in his family. To live in anticipation of the condemnation sure to come his way. To see the disrespect in his sibling's eyes. To hear his mother sing his praises, and know that she did so only because he was her son, not for any merit she believed he possessed.

Suddenly, the nag stumbled on the mud-slick road. It quickly regained its footing, but not before the young man slipped from the saddle. He lay on his stomach, then tried to stand, too drunk to make much of a success of it. "I'll just rest a moment," he mumbled, lying down and laying his head on his arms.

In another moment, Lord Elliot Fitzwalter, second son of the fifth Duke of Barroughby, was fast asleep in a Lincolnshire ditch.

The indomitable old woman sat staring out the window, her back straight and her gaze fastened on the long, sweeping drive that led to Barroughby Hall before continuing to her habitation.

The Dower House stood on a low rise, and at one time, before the present dowager duchess's occupation, it had been screened from Barroughby Hall by a row of larch trees. The dowager duchess had ordered them cut down, the better to see over the large lawn past the ornate gardens to the drive and the front entrance of the hall.

As she looked out, she paid no heed to the young couple who had quietly entered the tastefully furnished drawing room. The man was dark haired, tall, handsome and serious; his wife was not a great beauty, but there was a calm serenity to her features that the duke considered far more lovely.

The Duke of Barroughby glanced at his wife, and then addressed his stepmother. "Good afternoon, Your Grace."

The dowager duchess did not turn to look at her visitors. She knew who they were; they came to the Dower House every day when they were in residence at the ducal seat. "Have you heard from him?" she demanded, as she did every time they called.

"No, Your Grace," the duke's wife replied softly.

"He will come tomorrow," the dowager duchess said firmly, as she always did, referring to her beloved son, who had stormed from Barroughby Hall nearly five years ago after a bitter and angry confrontation. "Leave me now."

Adrian and Hester looked at each other and obeyed, each of them silently wondering how long the dowager duchess could maintain her daily vigil before she gave up hope of ever seeing her cherished son again, for Elliot Fitzwalter had sworn that he would never set eyes on his family again.

Between themselves, they thought he must be dead. No one had heard from him. There had been no letters to his doting mother, and perhaps more surprisingly, no demands for money to his half brother. Every inquiry had been fruitless. There had not been even a whisper of a rumor concerning the handsome young nobleman.

It was as if Elliot, in his determination to be rid of his family, had disappeared from the face of the earth.

Chapter Two

Grace hurried along the road, no longer running, but walking as quickly as her laboring lungs would allow. A light rain had started to fall, and her high-top boots would be thick with mud if she was not home soon.

She was also mindful of the ruffians she had seen loitering outside The Three Crowns that afternoon. There had been many itinerant workers in Lincolnshire of late, causing some unrest, and certainly a sense of unease. Donald Franklin had brought over many poor Irish to work on his estate, and there were others, like those men today, who she suspected had never done an honest day's work in their lives. Why they were in Barton-by-the-Fens was a mystery, and Grace hoped they wouldn't linger, or, worse, come along this particular stretch of road.

She glanced back over her shoulder, then sighed with relief. Mercy would say it was only her imagination running away with her again, but Mercy had never understood how upsetting it could be when one's mind persisted in creating vivid pictures of possibilities, most of them bad.

Grace halted abruptly. There was a bundle of clothing in the ditch. Some poor soul was going to be the worse for that. Maybe she should take it to the vicar.

She went closer to investigate and let out a gasp of shocked surprise, for it wasn't an abandoned bundle of clothing: it was a man lying there, not moving.

For a moment Grace's heart seemed to stop beating, until she saw his back rise and fall as he breathed. "Not dead," she murmured with relief.

She regarded him from where she stood, nearly five feet away. His trousers and jacket were not clean, something not unexpected when one was lying in a ditch. His hat had tumbled off and lay on its side nearby, so she could see his rather unkempt blond hair. His shoulders were broad, his hips narrow, his legs long and lean. His clothes, while dirty, were not ragged or patched. Indeed, once they had been quite fine.

Despite his resting place, there was something almost elegant about him, as if he were a prince in disguise. His head was turned away from her, and she very much wanted to see his face.

"Sir?" she said quietly, setting down her basket and taking another step nearer. "Sir?"

He didn't stir, so she ventured even closer, moving slowly around his long, lean legs until she could see his face.

He was a young man, probably no older than she, and his profile revealed remarkably handsome features, including a shapely nose, strong chin, and long lashes, for a man. His complexion was quite brown, as if he spent time out-of-doors, and his blond hair clung to his brow. She wondered what color his eyes would be.

She bent down, prepared to rouse him with a slight shake, when the overpowering smell of wine drove her back.

Why, he was *drunk!* Handsome prince indeed! He was just a common...common...drunkard!

What a waste! she thought as she turned on her heel to leave, even as she wondered what had brought a young man to such a pass.

Then she told herself it didn't matter. She had enough troubles of her own without worrying about a drunkard who didn't even know enough to get out of the rain.

She grabbed her basket and started to march away, once again aware that she was far from physically comfortable herself. Her skirt was muddy, and her cloak getting wetter every moment.

Then she noticed the hoofprints fast dissolving in the mud. There was no sign of a horse nearby. None of their usual visitors had saddle horses, only the heavier draft animals. Had he been mounted?

If so, it was possible that he had been attacked. She recalled Miss Myrtle's tale of a band of brigands robbing travelers. His less-than-sober state would have made him an attractive target for thieves who could have robbed him of his horse and money, too. Perhaps this poor man was not asleep, but unconscious.

She glanced back at him again, noting that the rain was falling harder now. He would soon be soaked to the skin.

Victim or not, he was none of her concern, and if she were smart, she would leave well enough alone.

She started to walk again. She should be thinking about Mercy, who *was* her responsibility. Mercy had been unwell this morning. When questioned, she had dismissed Grace's fears and told her not to worry so much.

But it was Grace's nature to worry, about her sister, and the rent and the village and strange men lying on the side of the road....

She halted again. Perhaps the smell of wine was strong because he was damp. Maybe he had spilled some on himself the last time he had a meal, and his condition had another cause entirely.

Grace emitted a sound that was both a sigh of dismay and admission of acceptance. She couldn't leave him, or her conscience would give her no peace. At the very least, she could get him to shelter, someplace that wouldn't put Mercy or herself at risk. A good Samaritan she would be, but not a fool.

The cow shed. They had only one cow, and there were three empty stalls. Surely Daisy wouldn't mind a visitor, and there was nothing except Daisy he could steal, if he was a thief. But Daisy was better than any dog when it came to keeping watch. If someone other than Mercy tried to lead her—even Grace—she mooed so loudly and so long, it would wake the household.

Grace turned back and approached him again. "Sir?" She set her basket down on the driest patch she could find, reached out and shook his shoulder. "Can you hear me, sir?"

She continued to shake him, but with increasing urgency when he did not respond. "Sir!" she repeated loudly.

He moaned softly and rolled over, and she gasped again, for there was blood on his forehead. She carefully brushed back a lock of hair to reveal a very nasty gash.

He must have been attacked and robbed, and left to die on the side of the road. Thank heavens she had followed her conscience!

The stranger opened his eyes, which were a shade of blue so brilliant Grace drew back in astonishment. He looked about confusedly. "Where...?" he mumbled.

"You are—" Grace didn't finish, because by the time she had opened her mouth, he had closed his eyes again, apparently to relapse into an unconscious state.

Grace regarded the recumbent man and wondered how she was going to get him to the cow shed. He wasn't going to be much help.

Maybe she could get him to stand. Grace stood behind his head, leaned over and put her hands beneath his shoulders to try to hoist him to a standing position. The man was heavy and limp, and he did not wake up again.

She straightened and wrapped her arms around herself as she shivered from the cold and her rapidly dampening clothing. It was getting dark, too. Mercy would be very worried and, Grace thought ruefully, not without some cause. If she escaped this adventure with nothing more serious than a cold, it would be a miracle.

And wouldn't Mercy be surprised to see what Grace had brought home! Usually it was Mercy who collected strays and wounded animals, her tender heart making her particularly susceptible to such creatures. She would finally be able to make sport of Grace for an even more outrageously generous impulse.

Well, there was no help for it, and once Grace made a decision, it generally stayed made. She would just have to endure, and so she was going to have to drag him. With a determined frown, Grace tucked up the hem of her skirt into her belt to keep it out of the mud as much as possible—for at least there was no one here to see her immodesty—put the handle of her basket as far up her arm as she could, and taking hold of his shoulders again, she turned him around and began the slow process of dragging him home.

Bob Boffin took a long pull on his mug of ale, then wiped his wet lips with the back of his hand and surveyed his comrades as they sat together in the dimmest corner of The Three Crowns. "I say we stay another couple o' days," he growled.

A tall, thin man with a narrow scar on his cheek glanced around at the few other patrons who were enjoying an evening's repast. "What for?" Treeg muttered. "He's long gone by now. Probably in London. And your money with him!"

Boffin's gaze took in the other two men seated at the battered table, one young, one old, before coming to rest on Treeg. "He didn't get to Lincoln. Nor Stamford, neither. He couldn't 'a traveled that fast, not on that nag."

"That's true," confirmed young Skurch, whose face was ruined by smallpox scars.

"He could'a gone another route," Treeg said. "Or took the train."

"Or he could be dead," Boffin replied. "But I don't think either one's true. He's around here somewheres."

The old man, who looked as if he had spent several years at Her Majesty's pleasure, which was indeed the case, raised his eyes to Boffin. "It's only a matter o' ten pound," Wickham said in a low, hoarse voice. "I say, why hang about lookin' suspicious?" He nodded at the other people in the tavern. "They knows we ain't no sheep men."

"Aye!" Skurch said. "And there's no women worth lookin' at, neither."

"'Ceptin' that one we seen, eh?" Boffin said with a jovial gleam in his eye that made Skurch smile, until Boffin reached out to grab him by his thin throat. "You're goin' to get yourself in trouble agin if you don't keep it in your trousers," Boffin snarled. "I don't want nobody doin' nothin' that'd make folks more suspicious than they are."

He let go of Skurch, who coughed and rubbed his throat, while Boffin's eyes narrowed and he leaned toward the old man. "I'd be careful 'bout usin' the word *hang* if I was you, Jack Wickham. Might give people ideas."

Wickham's hand tightened on his mug, and his

other went toward his belt, where a knife's handle was barely visible. "I ain't gettin' hanged for no ten pound," he whispered forcefully. "Not on your say-so!"

"Quiet!" Boffin admonished. He looked around to make sure no one was paying more attention to them. "Listen to me, then, Jack, and I'll come straight wi' you. We're lookin' at considerable more than my ten pound."

"What d'you mean?" asked Treeg, leaning in to hear. Young Skurch also moved closer.

"Do you mind me asayin' how that bloke looked familiar, but I couldn't place 'im?"

"Aye," Wickham acknowledged. The others nodded.

"It come to me yesterday, when we was on the road, where I seen 'im before."

"How come you didn't say nothin' then?" Wickham demanded in a harsh whisper.

"'Cause I *thought* you was all with me, that's why," Boffin replied. "I knows who he is, I tell ya."

"So what?" Wickham said scornfully.

"So he's rich—leastways his family is. And they'll pay plenty for knowin' where he's at. Or he'll pay plenty for us to keep it quiet," Boffin finished triumphantly.

"Who is he then?" Treeg demanded.

"He's Lord Elliot Fitzwalter, that's who. Missin' these five years. When he up and did a bunk, his brother, the Duke of Barroughby, offered to pay a handsome price for news o' his brother."

The men's eyes widened, then Wickham scowled.

"Thinkin' you'll put the black on 'im? That was five years ago. Maybe the duke's changed his mind.''

"Maybe he hasn't," Boffin countered.

"P'rhaps they've patched up their quarrel," Skurch offered.

Boffin gave the lad a sarcastic look. "You must be off your chump. If they was friends, why'd he come back lookin' like he hadn't but two pennies to his name? Why did he tell us he was David Fitzgibbons? Why did he cheat me out o' ten pound? I tell you, he's hidin'.''

"So how's he goin' to pay for us to keep our gobs shut, if that's what he wants?''

"He's got to have friends. How else could a man disappear the way he did?''

"If he's gone to ground again," Wickham said, "then how d'ya expect us to find him when his own rich brother couldn't? Take out an advert in *The Times?*''

"No!" Treeg said excitedly. "If Boffin's right, and he's still around here, we'll find out soon enough. A good-lookin' toff like that's bound to stand out, and Lincolnshire's not exactly a popular spot with the aristocracy, now, is it?''

"With good cause," Wickham muttered.

"*Exactly!*" Boffin said, ignoring the ex-convict. "Now you're understandin' me. He's hidin,' all right, but probably some place 'round about here.''

"Now hold on," Wickham demanded. "How come you know a lord? Been to his club, have you? Gone to a few society balls and made his acquaintance?''

"This particular lord liked things 'sides gentlemen's clubs and assembly balls," Boffin said significantly. "I've seen 'em, and that's a fact. I say we start with the gentry 'round here."

"What, walk up to the front door and say, 'Scuse me, have you seen Lord Elliot Fitzwalter 'round about?" Wickham proposed with a cynical sneer.

"Yeah, right, that's exactly what I thought!" Boffin replied with an equally cynical sneer. "We'll keep an eye out on the fine houses nearby. And the village, too, and anybody else looks like they might have company." He smiled at the young man. "A good-lookin' bloke like him, I bet he's holed up with some woman. You can see about that.

"Either way, we'll find my fine lord."

With a relieved sigh, Grace opened the garden gate and tugged the man through. She would be a happy woman when this was over. She hadn't been this out of breath since the pig had gotten into the garden two summers ago.

She glanced down at her burden. The man's trousers were going to be in a terrible state, but she thought that a small enough price to pay for preventing illness and possibly death—if she didn't fall ill and die from the effort herself.

She closed the gate and began to pull him toward the cow shed, finally managing to get him inside. Brushing a damp, dangling lock of hair out of her eyes, she smiled at Daisy, who was placidly chewing and regarding her with large, bland brown eyes. Then, to Grace's considerable surprise and chagrin, she no-

ticed a fine black stallion comfortably lodged in the
stable she had intended to use as temporary accommodation for the stranger.

Only one man in the county had a stallion like that,
and that was Donald Franklin.

What was Sir Donald Franklin doing here? Had he
come to inform them of the rent increase personally?

Grace stifled a groan. She had hoped to keep that
particular difficulty from Mercy, at least until she had
thought of a solution to their problem. How was
Mercy coping with Sir Donald's unwelcome presence
and, more importantly, was she managing to act a
little polite? Now would hardly be the time to offend
their landlord.

Unfortunately, Mercy had never liked Sir Donald,
and if he told her what he intended to do, she would
surely burst into tears or angry denunciations.

Grace expelled some air, put her hand on her aching back as she straightened, regarded the horse and
then the stranger.

She could tell Sir Donald about the man, of course.
He might be able to offer assistance. The stranger and
his welfare would be out of her hands, and she and
Mercy need not have any fear of being attacked by a
runaway criminal, if he *was* a criminal.

Therein lay the problem, for Donald Franklin had
never been known for his merciful qualities. He
would be far more likely to have the stranger thrown
in the village lockup, a small, damp building little
better than the out-of-doors. He would probably never
entertain any possibility that the wretched man might
be a victim himself.

Grace could just see herself trying to convince Sir Donald of that notion. He would undoubtedly claim she was being a silly, sentimental young woman—and she could even envision him using his callous solution as an example of his fine leadership and concern for the safety of his tenants.

She was not about to have her efforts to help this man undone by the unsympathetic Donald Franklin.

Grace tugged the stranger into the farthest unused stall as quickly as she could, and piled some straw over him for warmth, as well as to hide him from Sir Donald, who would have to come to fetch his horse. Hopefully, the fellow would sleep quietly until Sir Donald was gone. Considering that he hadn't awakened again, and the mode of movement had not been very gentle, she felt there was little danger of that.

She would come back as soon as she could to see if he was awake, with her father's pistol tucked into her skirt for safety.

Giving the slumbering stranger a final glance, she went on her way, dashing through the farmyard and into the back door of their house, reflecting that it was a good thing the drawing room was at the front of the house and faced the main road.

When she entered the kitchen by the scullery, she called out a cheery "Mercy, I've come home!" as if she hadn't seen Sir Donald's horse. Under normal circumstances, she wouldn't have, and she certainly had no desire for Sir Donald to suspect that anything abnormal had happened today, beyond his surprise visit.

She removed her boots and cloak, surveyed the wreckage of her dress, which looked as if it might never come clean, set her basket on a sideboard, then grabbed a linen towel used to dry the dishes and wiped her face and neck.

As she did so, a quick survey of the small kitchen showed that Mercy must be feeling better, for a kettle was on the hearth, and the smell of beef stew emanated from the small iron pot dangling over the fire. If Mercy was still feeling ill, she wouldn't have bothered with a stew, for Grace had told her before going to the shops that morning that they could have cold meat for supper.

"I'm sorry I'm so late, Mercy," she said, still feigning an ordinary day as she proceeded into the drawing room, pausing to put on her shawl, which was laid over one of the Windsor chairs. "I fell in the mud. My cloak is quite a disaster—"

She halted on the threshold, taking in the scene before her quickly. Sir Donald was standing by the window, his face red, his chest puffed out like a pigeon, and his stance belligerent. As always, he was finely and extravagantly dressed, in the latest of fashion. The ensemble he wore would have looked rather odd on the most handsome of men, for even a sudden vision of the outfit on the stranger in the cow shed was not pleasing. On Sir Donald, the blue frock coat, green-and-yellow-striped vest and plaid, tight-fitting trousers looked utterly ridiculous.

Mercy sat beside her small work table, the fabric for her new green gown heaped negligently on the floor at her feet, her pretty face surrounded by its halo of blond curls pale and worried, and with her slender hands clasped together on her lap.

With dismay, Grace guessed that Sir Donald had told her about the rent. She hurried to her sister, taking her cold hand in her own, even colder one.

"What is it?" she demanded, although she knew very well what was the matter and she hated Donald Franklin even more. "What has happened?"

"Good afternoon, Miss Barton," Sir Donald said loftily, and there was an angry expression in his gray eyes which Grace couldn't help thinking was an improvement over that other, lustful look she had last seen there.

"Oh, Grace!" Mercy whispered. Then she pulled away from Grace's grasp, put her face in her hands and started to weep. "He's…he said…"

Grace cast an accusing look at Sir Donald before putting her arms around Mercy's slender shoulders. "I think I know what this is about," she said. "Don't cry, dear. It doesn't matter."

"Yes, it does!" Mercy wailed. "We'll be thrown out of our home! We'll have to go to a workhouse!"

In her mind's eye, Grace could see both of them lying on the side of the road the way the stranger had been—hurt, hungry and sick. Perhaps some kind unknown person would take pity on them, but perhaps others would assume that they were no more than tramps or, considering they were women, something worse.

Grace rose and looked steadily at Sir Donald. "You are raising our rent," she said flatly.

"There is no need for this emotional display," Sir Donald blustered, spreading his hands in a gesture of incomprehension. "It is a most unfortunate necessity—"

"Necessity?" Grace declared as her sister continued to sob. "It's greed!"

"Please, my dear Miss Barton!"

"I am not your 'dear Miss Barton,'" Grace answered, fighting to regain control. She wouldn't let this man upset her. He mustn't be able to dismiss her as simply an emotional female. "By how much do you intend to raise it?"

"Fifty pounds per annum."

"Oh, Grace!" Mercy whimpered.

"That's more than twice what we pay now," Grace replied, achieving a dispassionate tone with great effort. "You know we cannot afford that much."

Sir Donald flushed, and then shrugged his beefy shoulders. "I have a position to maintain."

Grace would have liked to ask exactly how he had come to be knighted—who he had bribed, or by what secret means he had managed to get it done.

"The increase will not come into effect for three months," Sir Donald said placatingly. "In that time, you may pursue other opportunities—"

"*Opportunities!*" Grace interrupted angrily. "What opportunities? You will take away our home and cast us out to—what?"

"You have no family to whom you could appeal?"

"No, we do not, or at least none close enough that we would beg of them," Grace retorted.

Sir Donald looked as if he were trying to appear sorry, but he couldn't quite manage the subterfuge. "I understand how difficult this must seem to you, because of your family's connection with the county, but I have been holding off raising your rent out of respect long enough." He smiled. She would have preferred an angry frown, for that, at least, would have looked natural. "I deeply regret the effect this must have upon you."

Liar! Grace thought angrily.

"I think it would be wise of me to take my leave of you," he said, glancing at Mercy.

"So do I," Grace retorted. "Good day."

She watched him turn on his heel and suddenly remembered that he must not find the stranger in the shed.

"No, wait!" she cried in a most undignified manner. "There is *much more* to be said!" She started to follow him to the door.

Mercy grabbed hold of her hand. "Oh, Grace," she pleaded softly. "Let him go. He won't change his mind. He's so mean and hateful!"

"I must speak with him," she replied hurriedly, freeing herself gently from Mercy's grasp and rushing after Sir Donald.

"But your cloak—!" she heard Mercy cry as she closed the front door behind her. It was still raining; nevertheless, Grace didn't have the time to fetch her cloak. Sir Donald was nearly at the cow shed.

Sir Donald paused at the entrance, looking back at her with an interrogative smile. "Yes, Miss Barton?" he inquired as she joined him at the door. "Please, come inside out of the wet."

He pushed open the door and gestured for her to enter, which she did, although that meant she had to push past him, her shoulders brushing his immovable chest. A quick glance around the cow shed revealed Daisy, still chewing, and the stallion, still waiting. There was no sign of any other human there, and for a moment, Grace wondered if the stranger had awakened and left.

"How can I help you, Miss Barton, who only moments ago was so anxious to have me gone?"

She whirled around to face her landlord, noting the smug amusement in his heavily lidded eyes.

"You must reconsider," she began. "You must be reasonable."

"Reasonable?" he countered. "I am being reasonable. I either need money from you, or from someone who can provide it."

Grace took a deep breath and struggled to remain composed. She wouldn't beg. Not of him, not even for Mercy's sake.

Sir Donald's smile grew broader, and his gaze more intense. "I could perhaps be *persuaded* to reconsider," he mused, his voice low and uncomfortably intimate. "You are a remarkable-looking young woman, Miss Barton."

Grace's eyes narrowed with suspicion and disgust. "I hope what you are about to propose is not going to insult me," she warned.

"Believe me, Miss Barton, when I tell you that nothing could be further from my mind."

This time, Grace did not try to hide her skepticism.

"Oh, do not frown so, sweet lady! It quite mars your loveliness."

"If you don't mind, Sir Donald, say what you have to say at once. I'm rather cold."

He ran his gaze over her in a way that reminded her of the damp clothes clinging to her body and she hugged herself. "I see that you are," he said. "Therefore, although I would much prefer to take my time about this, I will be brief and to the point."

Suddenly, and to Grace's utter amazement, Sir Donald Franklin dropped to one beefy knee. "Miss Barton, would you do me the honor of becoming my wife?"

Chapter Three

Utterly dumbfounded, Grace stared at Sir Donald, convinced she couldn't have heard him correctly. "I...I beg your pardon?" she gasped.

Sir Donald reached out and took her fingers in his large, damp hand. "My dear Miss Barton—and I do mean dear—I am asking you to marry me."

"But...I..."

"It's a surprise, I know," Sir Donald continued smoothly, stroking her hand as he laboriously got to his feet. "As much to me as to you, if I were to speak truly. It was only when I realized how devastated I would be if you were forced to leave Barton that I knew my own heart."

"Then do not raise the rent," Grace said, regaining her faculties and immediately snatching her hand from his.

Sir Donald shook his head. "I regret I cannot do that."

"Then allow me to say that while I appreciate the honor you do me with this proposal," she said, her shock giving way to a sarcasm she could not conceal, "I regret my answer must be no."

Sir Donald looked not a whit dismayed. "I would not be so hasty," he replied softly, his gaze still upon her. "What I offer is not to be dismissed lightly. Wealth, privilege, a fine home. I would see that your sister wants for nothing. Indeed, she would be most welcome to make her home with us. She would not have to leave her beloved Lincolnshire."

Somehow, Donald Franklin had discovered the one thing that could force Grace to hear him out without slapping his face: Mercy's ardent desire to remain in Barton.

Grace forced herself to think of something that would overrule Mercy's preference. "I don't love you."

"Perhaps not at present," Sir Donald replied. "I'm sure you'll see my merits soon enough."

She knew him to be a vain fellow, but his persistence was beyond imagining. "Surely you don't expect me to believe that you love me, either. You hardly know me."

"Really, Miss Barton, don't underestimate your charms." He ran his gaze over her body in a way that made her understand that he knew all he apparently wanted to about her. "And of course, there is the value of your family name. Don't you think you could appreciate being married to a member of parliament?"

That he was ambitious as well as vain was not beyond her expectation; nevertheless, it had not occurred to her—or even the Hurley twins—that he might aspire to political power.

Yet now, when she looked at him and thought of his vanity and ambition and sudden, unexpected desire to be connected to an old family name, she could easily believe it.

She could think of no one worse to represent her county than this conceited, arrogant and greedy man. "You suppose that by marrying me you will advance your own career?"

"I do, and so does Lord Denburton," he replied, naming a man who had been successful in fielding candidates who were sure to do his bidding for years.

"But I am penniless," she noted, wondering why this particular point hadn't stopped him before.

"You are also a very beautiful woman," he said in what she assumed he intended to be a romantic manner.

He looked like a fool.

"Do you think I could *ever* be so desperate—"

He held up his hand to silence her. "I would not be too impetuous, Miss Barton," he said harshly, with a spark of anger in his eyes. "Not when you have such limited alternatives, unless you quite fancy the idea of spending the rest of your life in a workhouse." He took hold of her hand again, so firmly that he hurt her. "I am making you an honorable offer in good faith. Will you not at least do me the courtesy of thinking about it before giving me your final answer?"

Whatever Grace thought of his offer—and at the very least, she considered it outrageous—her mind told her to be circumspect at present. After all, the three-month period he had set to raise the rent was arbitrary, to be extended or shortened at his whim. "Very well," she said. "I will think about your proposal."

"Excellent!" he declared, lifting her hand to his lips to kiss it.

She managed to subdue a shudder, yet she could not refrain from tugging her hand away as soon as possible.

He realized the meaning of her action, and a scowl darkened his features. "I have not taken offense at your manner because I knew my proposal would come as a shock to you," he said, his voice full of menace. "However, Miss Barton, you would do well to remember that I have a long reach. And an even longer memory."

With that final threat, he retrieved his horse and led it out of the shed.

Grace started to shiver and drew in a great, shuddering breath. She couldn't marry Sir Donald. Not if she had to become a beggar in the streets.

She heard a small sound, and instantly remembered the stranger sleeping not so far off. Her face flushed with shame at the thought that even an unknown person would have heard Sir Donald propose to her, and she quickly moved to the stall to look at her uninvited guest.

Still asleep, thank heavens, and his presence still a secret. She regarded him for a long moment, marveling that a man so handsome, who had apparently at one time been well-to-do, and who had, perhaps, had a home and a family, was now reduced to sleeping in a stranger's cow shed. This could be their fate, if Sir Donald would not lower the rent.

Then she realized with some surprise that she was also feeling a sense of relief. Surely Mercy would not be willing to stay in Barton if her sister's marriage to Donald Franklin was to be the price. She would still be loath to go, but Grace would not be to blame.

And if the only alternative was marriage to their landlord, she would far rather depend upon the compassion of strangers.

For now, her first duty was to Mercy, weeping in the house, so she quickly left the shed.

Lord Elliot Fitzwalter slowly opened his eyes and gazed at the roughly shingled roof over his head. He could hear rain hitting the wooden wall at his back. After a long moment, when his eyes had adjusted to the dimness, he realized he was in an outbuilding of some sort. He could glimpse dark sky through the slats, and supposed that meant it was evening.

Straw. He smelled straw, which wasn't unexpected since he was apparently lying on it, in a shed with a...cow, he thought, nearby. What had happened to the nag?

Hadn't he just heard voices? Where had the people gone?

He sat up and ran a hand over his face. His head ached, and so did his back. His shoulders felt as if somebody had been trying to rip them from the sockets.

Where the devil was he, and how had he gotten here?

He sneezed violently, from the straw, he thought, although his clothes were wet. God, he smelled like an old, wet sheep. No doubt he looked worse.

He stood up shakily, the movement making his head hurt even more, and stepped out of the stall. The cow in the next stall stared at him.

Nothing and nobody else present. Only a cow and himself.

Yet he knew he had heard voices, and *somebody* must have brought him here. He closed his eyes and tried to remember, focusing his efforts on the voices. There had been a woman and a man, talking in low, intense tones. Not friends, judging by the hostility in their voices.

Still, that didn't mean it hadn't been a farmer and his wife, perhaps one of whom did not relish the idea of giving a stranger shelter, not even in their shed. Country folk could be very suspicious of strangers, he knew, and a glance at his clothing confirmed that his appearance would not be in his favor.

It would probably be a good idea to expect hostility. It was an even better idea, he thought, to lie back down and rest. Surely after more sleep, when his clothes were a little drier and he was a little more himself, he would find a way to charm his rural Samaritans.

After all, he was a very charming young man.

Elliot started as the door of the cow shed opened again and, although he was cold, damp, very hungry and dry mouthed, he quickly lay back down as if still asleep. It would be wiser to feign such a condition until he knew exactly who had taken him in.

"Grace!" said a female voice. A young woman, he thought. Too mature for a child, but young yet.

"I told you I had an adventure today," another woman's voice responded. A little husky, but melodic. More mature and far more interesting that the too-soft, almost childlike first voice.

Not that he thought the second speaker an old woman. About his age, he would hazard to guess. More curiously, neither voice sounded like that of a Lincolnshire farmer's wife or daughter, he was quite sure. These women were educated, and their voices close enough in tone and timbre to suggest that they were related.

Which woman had been in here before, with the man? Not the first, he ventured. The second.

Perhaps the man was her husband.

A husband was always a problem. Or maybe he was her father—a far more congenial notion.

He heard the rustle of garments as they apparently moved closer, and then the scent of something hot and made of beef assaulted his starving stomach. Probably a good English stew. His mouth started to water and he almost opened his eyes, yet caution— something, he thought wryly, Adrian would believe he did not possess—told him to wait a little while more.

What kind of a man sent women out to tend a stranger? Either he was naive or stupid.

Maybe they had slipped out here without his knowledge. It could be the fellow didn't even know there was an unknown man in his shed. Now *that* was a very interesting idea.

Adventurous young women always thrilled Elliot, and as he waited for the women to speak again, he wanted very much to open his eyes and see what faces and forms accompanied the voices. Perhaps they were wholesome, pretty country girls. That would be a welcome relief from the colonials of Muddy York always seeking to impress him with their version of fine manners, or the haughty noblewomen of his former acquaintance, whose cool masks quickly slipped when they had him alone.

"Who is he?" the younger woman asked quietly.

"I don't know."

"You don't know?"

"He didn't wake up."

"Didn't he walk here with you?"

"I had to drag him."

That was an unexpected admission. Perhaps she *was* a farmer's wife after all, with brawny arms, wide hips and double chin. And what had happened to the nag?

"His trousers are thick with mud, but there was nothing else I could do."

Probably the horse wandered off, the stupid beast— with his few belongings, too.

"You should have come home and fetched me to help you," the younger voice said.

Why didn't she suggest asking the man for help? Why fetch another woman for assistance?

"It was getting late and the rain was worsening."

Maybe he hadn't heard a man's voice, after all. In

his previous state, he might have mistaken the older woman's deeper tones for that of a man.

"Perhaps we should wake him," the younger one said in a tentative tone. "The supper will be cold if we don't."

"Rest might be the best thing for him," the other replied. "We could leave the food here for him to eat when he wakes up. I daresay he's had worse."

She sounded practical and matter-of-fact. Like Adrian.

"Don't you think we should invite him inside the—"

"No, I don't. He must not come into the house," the huskier voice said, and Elliot was suddenly sure she must be an elder sister, by domineering manner as much as tone. What was it about older siblings that made them think they had the right to order others about? "We don't know anything about him, who he is or where he's from. Not only would allowing him inside our home be a foolish and risky thing to do, Mercy, but think how bad it would be if somebody were to discover we had taken a complete stranger into our house! Why, imagine what the Hurley twins would say!"

Another older sibling also worried about gossip.

"But Grace, they wouldn't have to know, would they?"

"You would have us harbor this man in secret? For how long? A few hours? A day? Mercy, you have to stop letting your tender heart overrule your intelligence."

The woman named Grace might have the more fascinating voice, but it was obvious Mercy would be the more sympathetic.

Then the full realization of his situation hit home, and Elliot subdued a smile. Apparently he had been rescued by young women who lived alone. To be sure, the older one was suspicious, but he could surely win her over. Why, if he worked this right, he could stay here for a while, safe from Boffin and probably very well fed.

He couldn't have asked for anything better, and he dismissed Grace's distrust. Young women always liked him, and often rather more, and it would surely not be difficult to charm a country lass, even a skeptical one.

"Didn't Sir Donald see him?"

"No, thank goodness."

So, there *had* been a man—a Sir Donald. Not a relative, Elliot gathered, and not a lover, or even very well liked, to judge from the slight alteration in Grace's tone.

He heard one of them move closer. "What's that smell?" Mercy asked.

"Wine."

"Is he...is he...?"

"Drunk? He may have been, but he's hurt, too."

One of them came close enough for him to discern the slight scent of lavender, and to feel her warm breath on his cheek. "It's not terribly serious. The cut is not deep, and there's no bump."

It was Grace, and her soft and surprisingly gentle words made him want to open his eyes more than ever.

He was about to, when Mercy spoke. "We should not leave him in those damp garments."

As tempted as he was to see the women who were discussing him with such tender concern, Elliot thought it would be more amusing to wait and see if they were going to try to strip him. As he did so, it occurred to him that he was feeling somewhat better.

"I suppose you're right," Grace said reluctantly. "I wouldn't want him to become ill. I'll take off his boots. You loosen his cravat."

He thought both of the women had come near him.

"My, doesn't he smell?" Mercy whispered with obvious disgust. "Maybe we shouldn't touch him."

Elliot decided it was time he woke up. He moaned softly and opened his eyes, to behold a pair of surprised and worried gray eyes in a very pretty, almost childlike face topped with a tousle of blond curls. The young woman wore a lace shawl over a pink dress of plain, albeit good quality fabric.

He gave her a wan smile, and then looked behind her to the person who was obviously the older sister. Both women had fine and delicate features, as well as smooth, satiny complexions and blond hair. Yet while the girl kneeling beside him looked like a concerned cherub, the older one, with her smooth, golden hair, ringlets, suspicious brown eyes, frowning full lips, and severely plain navy blue dress looked more like a judgmental angel.

A strikingly lovely judgmental angel. Her form was astonishingly fine, quite as shapely as any Elliot had ever seen, even in that hideous dress that looked like something the leader of a strict religious sect would design. Her features were flawless, and her complexion such as one only found in England. Indeed, she had the potential to be a rare beauty, if she had the proper clothes and hairstyle, whereas the younger one would never be anything more than wholesomely pretty.

Nevertheless, Elliot realized that it was going to require considerably more effort and charm to secure the older sister's aid, and he was absolutely certain she would be the one to decide his fate.

"Where...where am I?" he murmured, putting a hand to his head and contriving to make it sound as if the very act of speaking was an incredible ordeal.

"Barton Farm, Lincolnshire," the elder sister said warily. "I am Grace Barton, and this is my sister. Who are you? How did you come to be lying in the road?"

"The...road?" Elliot repeated.

"Grace, perhaps we shouldn't press him with questions now. Can you sit, sir?" Mercy Barton asked, bending down and putting her slender arms around him.

Elliot allowed her to assist him, secretly enjoying the sensation of her embrace before he glanced at the older woman to see what she thought of this activity. He expected outright disapproval; to his chagrin, he realized her expression was one of the most inscrutable he had ever seen on a woman's face.

Nevertheless, she was obviously a cautious creature, so in all likelihood she did not approve.

"I think he can sit without your help," Grace Barton said to her sister evenly before addressing him again. "Where do you wish to go?"

"Grace, please!" the kindhearted Mercy pleaded. "Can't you see he's hurt?"

Elliot thought Grace Barton's expression softened a little, so he gave her a winsome smile, a thing that had stood him in good stead many a time. Several woman had confided that his lopsided grin had been instrumental in making them fall in love with him.

"I hope you will understand, sir," she said as calmly as if they were discussing the weather, "that this shed is all we can offer by way of accommodation."

Grace Barton seemed singularly immune to the power of his grin.

Elliot nodded, then decided that it might be wise to indicate that he had not been without some means before Grace Barton had found him. "My horse...?"

"Gone, I'm afraid," Miss Barton answered, and he thought she thawed a little more.

He saw that slight change with unmitigated triumph, his natural optimism and confidence in his attractiveness to the opposite sex reasserting itself.

His delight was short-lived, as a sudden draft blew in through a large crack in the wall near him. When he shivered, it was not playacting.

"Oh, Grace!" Mercy cried. "He cannot stay out here all night. He'll be too cold."

Elliot quite agreed. He would much prefer the warmth of a house, and the company of these two lovely women. Therefore, with every effort to sound weak and helpless, he began to cough.

"Oh, Grace, we must let him come into the kitchen!"

Elliot watched the two sisters and suddenly realized that if he was adept at manipulation, his skill was nothing compared to the way Mercy Barton was using her large gray eyes to compel her sister to agree. She contrived to create an expression in their depths that was both begging and accusatory. Why, even the most hard-hearted of men would find it difficult to resist.

And then, just as suddenly, he felt that her efforts on his behalf were somewhat misplaced, and that expression was aimed at someone who didn't deserve it. Grace Barton had already helped him, and with considerable personal effort. Why, her slender arms looked barely strong enough to drag a ten-pound sack of flour any distance, let alone *him*, and in the rain and through the mud, too. If she now saw fit to refuse a stranger entrance to her house, that was not weakness or cruelty. It was only wise.

Nevertheless, he felt quite pleased when Grace Barton finally spoke. "Very well. This one night."

As the handsome young man struggled to his feet, Grace tried to convince herself that they were not taking a foolish risk. Her rational mind told her she was, but she had never been able to resist Mercy's pleading looks—not when her sister had gotten into innocent mischief, or when she had brought home yet another wounded animal, or when she saw a particularly lovely bonnet, or even now, when they might be putting themselves in danger by inviting a stranger into their home.

Grace consoled herself with the observation that he seemed too weak to cause any trouble, even if he wanted to. Her hand went to the pocket of her skirt, where she could feel the cold steel of her father's old pistol, and she felt a little more confident. She wasn't a good shot, but she felt safer knowing the weapon was there. Just in case.

Mercy hurried to help the young man, yet it was not to Mercy he looked. His bright blue eyes narrowed for the briefest of moments as his gaze followed Grace's movement, then he smiled, and in those eyes, she saw that he not only realized that she was concealing something, and that he could tell what it might be, but also that he didn't begrudge her the caution. Surprisingly, she also saw a kind of respect there, which made her blush.

Don't get silly or stupid, Grace reminded herself. Mercy was the sentimental one, not her, and she had best remember that.

It was also abundantly clear that Mercy's assistance alone would not be enough, so she, too, put her shoulder beneath his and slipped her arm under his jacket and around his waist, which was slim, like his hips.

With her body up against his, his chin beside her cheek and his damp shirt offering the thinnest of barriers to his skin, her heart started to beat wildly in a most unfamiliar rhythm.

I must be fatigued from the effort of dragging him here, she told herself, especially when a quick glance at Mercy showed that her younger sister was apparently quite unaffected by her proximity to the stranger.

She gave him a sidelong look, to catch him regarding her with gratitude in his eyes, and that amazingly attractive lopsided grin on his face.

Grace blushed again and told herself to concentrate on the task at hand, which was getting him inside the house.

"Just for tonight," she said firmly, as much to herself as the company. "And he must remain in the kitchen."

Chapter Four

The next morning, Elliot was awakened by the sunlight streaming into the bedroom window. Regardless of his aching shoulders and sore back, he put his hands behind his head and took a deep breath, reveling in the scent of the lavender sheets and quite satisfied with himself to think he had so easily convinced the Barton sisters to allow him to sleep in their spare bedroom.

Well, he had easily convinced the cherubic, innocent and possibly foolishly naive Mercy. Her sister had been much more resistant to the idea, no matter how much he coughed and shivered. He had put on his most pathetic-yet-not-wanting-to-be-a-nuisance face and kept his voice to a whisper as he told them his name was John Elliot and that he had been journeying to Lincoln when he was attacked. After that, he had apparently been too weary to speak. He hadn't found it necessary, for Mercy had begged her sister to allow him a "proper bed."

"You wouldn't want him to get seriously ill, would you?" she had demanded.

Gad, and he thought *he* knew how to sway a sibling! Perhaps the most surprising thing was that Grace Barton gave in, despite the stern, determined look in her eye.

So now he was here, comfortable in this narrow but clean bed, and in a nightshirt that had belonged to their father. He breathed a luxurious sigh as he snuggled beneath the covers.

He looked around the small upstairs room. The walls were whitewashed, yet adorned with several watercolors, painted by the Bartons, no doubt, and the ceiling sloped with the pitch of the thatched roof, exposing ancient beams of sturdy oak. Small leaded windows looked out over the farmyard and garden. In many ways, it was a typical farm house, if rather large. The kitchen had been roomy and comfortable, too, and blessedly warm.

He was surprised that there had been no servants, nor had any been mentioned.

It was also a pity he was alone under the covers. How long had he been without a woman? It seemed an age.

Mercy—or Grace? Which one would he prefer to make love with? Mercy was pretty, but clearly full of sentimental, romantic notions. Seducing her would be no challenge at all.

Grace Barton, though. *She* would be worth the effort, provided he wanted to be bothered.

Provided Boffin and his gang didn't find him.

Elliot sat up a little straighter, sucking in his breath as a pain shot through his back. When it subsided, he noticed that his trousers, free of the worst of the mud, were now neatly laid on a small and spindly chair. His shirt was nowhere to be seen, but his vest and jacket, now also mud-free, hung on a nearby hook. All he needed was his shirt, and he could be on his way.

Even as he thought that, he felt a definite reluctance to do so. It was probably fatigue, he reflected, and the realization that his accommodation here was better than that to be had at many an inn.

On the other hand, Boffin might be nearby, and it would be poor recompense to his hostesses to put them in any kind of jeopardy from the likes of that man and his cronies.

However, this was a secluded farm, on a little-used road. Boffin would surely never think to look for him here. He would go to Nottingham, Lincoln, or south to Grantham; he would never expect his quarry to remain in this godforsaken country.

Why not stay here a few days until he was rested and refreshed, and then make his way to London?

He rose slowly and went to the window. Unlike yesterday, it looked to be a fine spring day. The fields in the distance were green and inviting, and he could hear the pleasant bleating of sheep in the distance. The Barton sisters seemed to enjoy flowers, for every spare portion of the yard was filled with the green beginnings of plants.

To one side of the yard he could see the shed where Grace had taken him, and on the other, a line where a row of white sheets bobbed in the breeze. There was a kitchen garden just behind it, cordoned with what would likely be marigolds to keep out the rabbits. Some chickens scratched in the dirt, and a rooster strutted about majestically.

Then, on the far side of the yard, he caught sight of Grace Barton, walking purposefully toward the house from another stone outbuilding with what looked like an egg basket over her arm. She wore the same plain blue dress she had on before, and now sported a straw bonnet, equally plain. Nevertheless, she possessed a fresh loveliness that owed much to the healthy, rosy bloom on her smooth cheeks, and even the determined set to her full, pink lips.

She reminded him of Adrian, striding along as if completely and utterly sure not only of his destination, but of his right to decide that destination for everyone else.

What was it about elder siblings that they felt they had to rule the family? he wondered as he watched her progress. Grace Barton probably never stopped to notice the beauty of a spring morning—

As if she had heard his thoughts and sought to contradict them, Grace Barton suddenly halted and surveyed the series of tender green shoots pushing through the dirt in pots on the kitchen windowsill, a small, pleased smile on her face.

In the right garments, she would be absolutely, breathtakingly stunning, Elliot realized. If he were to appear in London with her, he would cause a sensation. She would be admired, sought after, courted under his very nose, talked about.

She might grow to enjoy such attentions, even to crave them. She would become demanding and petulant, and when he tired of the monster he had helped create, she would denounce him for a cad and a libertine.

He shook his head and rubbed his sore neck. He wouldn't think about the past. It was over and done with, and there was nothing he could do about it anyway.

Suddenly he had heard a light step on the stair and climbed back into bed as quickly as he could, biting back a curse as his aching body protested the rapidity of his movements.

Mercy Barton timidly peered into the room. "Oh, you're awake, Mr. Elliot," she said, coming inside shyly, carrying a tray covered with a linen towel. "I hope you're feeling better."

In truth, except for that unfortunate lapse into memories best forgotten, Elliot was feeling much better, and the delicious smells accompanying Mercy, highly suggestive of bacon and eggs, revived him even more.

Nevertheless, he smiled wanly, as if trying to put a good face on a terrible situation. "Oh, yes, I am," he murmured. "A little tired, perhaps, but I shall not trespass on your kindness anymore. If you will bring me my shirt..."

He let his words trail off, to imply that he found even the simple act of talking fatiguing.

"Grace and I have washed your things, and your shirt is drying in the kitchen," Mercy replied.

She came closer, and he thought he could detect a small teapot and cream pitcher under the cloth. "It won't be dry for a while yet, I'm afraid. In the meantime, I've brought you some breakfast."

"You've been...so very kind...."

"Oh, think nothing of it," Mercy said, setting the tray across his lap, with her curly head near enough to kiss, if he had felt even a modicum of desire for her. Which he did not.

Which was not at all like himself, really. Perhaps the blow to his head had affected him more than he realized.

And perhaps he looked worse than he realized, for when she drew back, there was no sign that she felt anything at all for him except pity. Not embarrassment by their proximity, or admiration or desire. Just pity.

He smiled as winningly as he could. "I should go," he whispered.

She continued to regard him with a worried little frown that wrinkled her smooth brow. "Please don't think harshly of Grace," she said, clasping her hands together as if she were a supplicant. "She isn't mean spirited, really. She is very good and very kind. It's just that yesterday... We are having some troubles with our landlord...."

Mercy chewed her lip delicately and then there was a rather surprising flash of spirit in her gray eyes. "And Grace worries so. I wish she wouldn't, but she does!"

He knew exactly how Mercy Barton must be feeling. He, too, had chafed at an older sibling's constant fretting. In his case, however, he had done far more than complain about it.

"You mustn't think about leaving until you are *quite* well," Mercy protested with an almost fierce insistence that startled him. He regarded her with a look of puzzlement and wondered if he had missed some sign of admiration, after all.

"Not until you've eaten something, at any rate." She leaned over and lifted the cloth with something of a flourish. She smiled sweetly. "We would both feel terrible if we sent you away before you were fully recovered."

Elliot's nose had not led him astray as to the contents of the breakfast, and he was suddenly extremely hungry. He leaned forward to begin and halted abruptly, sucking in his breath.

"What is it?"

"My back." He moved more slowly, and the pain lessened.

Mercy colored. "Grace did her best to be gentle, but I'm afraid she had rather a trying time getting you here."

Oh, yes, she had dragged him. No wonder his body ached as if he had been tied to the back of a chariot and dragged around the Circus Maximus like some kind of Christian martyr.

"You were too heavy for her to manage otherwise."

Hardly a flattering remark. However, he had been flattered so often, Mercy's blunt observation was almost refreshing. Almost.

"Very far?" he inquired weakly.

He had no idea where he had gotten off the horse, which he gathered had returned to its place of origin and was, therefore, out of his reach.

Maybe if the horse returned riderless, Boffin would

assume "David Fitzgibbon" had come to a bad end, and leave off the chase.

Then he recalled the anger in Boffin's beet-red, beefy face and realized that was far from likely. The man would want his ten pounds, and would probably be willing to seek it for months.

"It was over a mile," Mercy said.

"Over a mile?" Elliot repeated, with genuine incredulity. Grace Barton didn't seem strong enough to drag a man of his size more than twenty feet.

Then he thought of her slender, graceful arms, and wondered if it was more strength of character than muscular strength. Perhaps she was the kind of woman who, having decided upon a course of action, would see it through, no matter what.

"In the rain, too," Mercy continued. "Later she said she was glad of the mud. It made things easier, but I fear her cloak is quite ruined!"

Elliot wished he had the money to replace it, with one as fine as money could buy. "I hope...she didn't... hurt herself?"

"She says not," Mercy answered. She swallowed hard, and her eyes began to glisten with unshed tears.

He sat up in the bed, mindful to appear weak and sore. Something was wrong, and he was curious to discover what it might be. Before he spoke, though, he reminded himself that their troubles were none of his, and he had enough of his own.

"I shouldn't be telling you all this, but you seem so sympathetic," Mercy said, which puzzled him. He wasn't trying to appear sympathetic. Maybe all that mattered to her was that someone was available to whom she could unburden her soul.

Elliot Fitzwalter as Father Confessor. Interesting notion—and something very new to him, that was certain.

"Sir Donald is going to raise our rent, you see, and we don't have very much money." Mercy paused expectantly.

"Oh?" Elliot said. He was going to say, *Is that all?* when it occurred to him that perhaps that was more than enough. Money had never been a trouble in his life until very recently, but he was certainly learning the difficulties poverty caused rapidly enough now.

As the son of a duke, he had been born into wealth, and his mother had been very generous to her son. Later, when he had left home, his charm and his looks had insured him easy access to the upper levels of the society in British North America, and he had no difficulty obtaining easy credit. He was a lucky and skillful gambler, too. Only since he had had his wallet stolen and he had lost to Boffin had he known more precisely how it was to be in serious need of funds.

"Oh, here you are," Grace Barton said calmly, appearing in the doorway with his shirt over her arm and taking in the scene before her with an expression so enigmatic, Elliot began to wonder if she often found her sister alone with unknown gentlemen.

In truth, Grace was profoundly and deeply shocked to discover Mercy in the spare bedroom with the man who had identified himself as Mr. Elliot. They had already reached soaring heights of impropriety and recklessness by taking a man totally unfamiliar to them into their home, but to venture into his room and stand so close beside him—with him clad only in a nightshirt, too! What on earth was Mercy thinking?

Or, more precisely, Grace thought as she briskly entered the room and placed the shirt on the chair with his other clothing, not thinking. She was feeling, only feeling, with no regard for anything but a wounded, handsome young man who apparently needed her help.

Mercy had to be made to see that sentimentality was not the only possible response!

Despite her anxiety, Grace forced a noncommittal smile onto her face. ''Mr. Elliot, you're awake and—'' she glanced down at the empty plate ''—feeling better, I see.''

He returned her smile with his grin, and she instinctively avoided meeting his gaze. ''Somewhat,'' he murmured.

''He's not at all well,'' Mercy observed plaintively.

Grace didn't reply. She had little patience with Mercy's pleading voice and anxious eyes this morning. She had lain awake half the night contemplating their financial difficulties without coming to any conclusions, and always with the haunting specter of marrying Sir Donald as a final resort. If she hadn't been worn-out from dragging Mr. Elliot, she probably wouldn't have slept at all.

''If he leaves now, he may not even be able to walk into the village!'' Mercy continued.

''Mercy,'' Grace warned, uncomfortably realizing

that the mysterious Mr. Elliot's blue-eyed gaze was turned upon her. "You know he *cannot* remain here."

"What if he gets terribly ill?" her sister pleaded. "Would that not be on your conscience? It would be on *mine*."

Grace certainly had no wish to discuss their most unsuitable guest with him in the same room. "Mercy, we should leave Mr. Elliot to get dressed."

She went to the bed and bent down to retrieve the tray, then realized that her hands were shaking.

Which was absolutely absurd, and probably merely because he was a handsome young man, and she had never been so near a handsome young man, lying in bed and wearing only a nightshirt.

She couldn't help it. She had to glance at his face, to encounter his eyes regarding her steadily, with such a strange, unexpected expression....

He needs me. The thought came to her suddenly, vivid and unbidden.

Not as Mercy needed her, as parent and guide. Not as Sir Donald needed her, as an object to display and to warm his bed.

This man needed her because he needed a friend.

She moved back quickly, almost dropping the tray.

That had to be the most foolish notion she had ever had in her life. This man, with such manners and looks, surely had many friends.

Even if there was a haunting look of loneliness in the depths of his eyes.

"Grace!" Mercy protested again. "He isn't well. Are you, Mr. Elliot?"

"No," he replied softly.

"There. He *cannot* leave yet! We mustn't make him."

Grace didn't answer as she carried the tray to the doorway, where she turned back.

"Grace...?" Mercy implored urgently, for her sister's face betrayed nothing.

"He may stay."

Elliot watched them leave the room, then stared at the closed door for several minutes. Something odd had just transpired, and he wasn't quite sure what to make of it.

Or how to interpret his own feelings.

His intention had been merely to try to stay another day or two in the Bartons' home. It still was, he tried to tell himself. Nothing more than that, no matter how Grace Barton looked at him with her shrewd brown eyes that made him feel that she saw beyond his lopsided grin to...what? The man beneath?

That had been a frightening thought, because of the unfamiliar shame that had suddenly coursed through his body the way a river rushes at the flood.

No, no, he was being ridiculous. She couldn't see into his mind, his heart, his past. She couldn't know the things he had done, the people he had hurt, or the need...

Not need. He didn't need anything or anyone. He would be all right on his own. He was the charming, the handsome, the clever Lord Elliot Fitzwalter, and whether he called himself by that name or another, he was still the same.

He couldn't be anything else, not even for a woman

with deep brown eyes that seemed to say she would
help.

Especially for a woman with eyes like that.

Therefore, he would stay another day or two, until
he was recovered and well rested, and then he would
go.

In full, resplendent majesty, Mrs. Banks sailed
through the Hurleys' drawing-room door behind their
timid little maid. The housekeeper of Franklin Hall
wore a new bonnet and cape of the finest gray alpaca.

That was not all that gave her such an air, however.
She knew she had a piece of news that would make
the Hurleys nearly faint.

Nevertheless, she took several minutes to traverse
the midsize room, which held a dizzying array of
heavy, dark oak furniture, three sofas covered in worn
blue brocade with very large antimacassars, six otto-
mans, a piano, a harp, several small tables cluttered
with numerous statuettes on gleaming white crocheted
doilies and a glass-fronted bookcase that looked as if
the books inside hadn't been disturbed this century.

"Good afternoon, Miss Myrtle, Miss Ethel," she
said in her very best imitation of upper-class tones—
which would have quite impressed her family, who
resided in East London lodgings—to the two sisters,
who rose slightly from the sofa when she entered.

"Good afternoon," they replied while she, in response to their gestured invitation, sat in her customary chair on the sofa opposite the one occupied by
the Hurley twins.

"A fine Saturday," Miss Myrtle Hurley remarked.

Mrs. Banks smiled, determined to take her time relaying her astonishing news. "Indeed, very fine," she said. The sisters smiled, too.

Euphenia Banks tried to restrain herself, but it was no use. "You'll never *guess* what has happened!" she declared, and it was obvious by her tone that her news was both shocking and bad.

"Shall I bring the tea now?" the maid asked nervously as she edged toward the door, nearly upsetting a spindly table bearing a particularly ugly statuette.

"No! Yes, Becky, yes, of course—and be quick about it," Miss Myrtle replied impatiently before returning her avid interest to their guest. "Now, do go on, Mrs. Banks."

Mrs. Banks took a deep breath. "Sir Donald is going to be married!" she exclaimed triumphantly.

"What?" the Hurleys cried unanimously, their shock making them blunt as they fell back against the sofa in one motion.

"Yes, it's quite true. I'm absolutely sure of it!"

"Well, I've heard this sort of thing before," Miss Myrtle said when she recovered. "To whom is he said to be affianced this time?"

The hypersensitive Mrs. Banks sat up even straighter. "I'm surprised you don't believe me."

"Oh, but we do, we do!" Miss Myrtle hastened to say.

"We do!" Miss Ethel confirmed.

"Of course we *couldn't* be as *familiar* with Sir Donald as *you* are, Euphenia," said Miss Myrtle sweetly. "Did he actually say he was getting married?"

Slightly mollified by Myrtle's placating tone, Mrs. Banks settled more comfortably on the sofa. "No, he didn't—but he returned home yesterday in *quite* a jovial mood, and when I remarked upon it, he said that he hoped I could accommodate myself *to a new mistress at Franklin Hall.*"

"Oh, how delightful! A wedding!" Miss Myrtle said, and she was quite sincere. A wedding of any kind offered a fascinating source of discussion for several weeks.

"Who is to be the bride?" Miss Ethel asked abruptly, her full sentence momentarily stunning Mrs. Banks.

"Is she someone he met in London?" Miss Myrtle inquired eagerly.

"I *think* it's someone who lives in our county," Mrs. Banks replied. "He wasn't gone for very long yesterday."

"He might not have *proposed* yesterday," Miss Myrtle observed. "I'm surprised you haven't heard him mention any particular lady."

"I think he *did* propose yesterday," the housekeeper said firmly. "When he left Franklin Hall yesterday, he was quite matter-of-fact, even rather glum, with all this trouble over raising the rents. Yet, as I said, when he returned he was *very* jovial. Very jovial indeed—and *then* he remarked upon a new mistress at Franklin Hall!"

Before the Hurley girls could respond, Becky returned with the tea, setting it and a plate of delicacies on the wide, round table near Miss Myrtle, who began to pour.

"Do you suppose it could be Lady Hermione Huntington-Smith?" she asked, after Becky had departed and as she handed a filled teacup to Mrs. Banks. "No, it couldn't be," she said, answering her own question. "She's too old. He'll want to have children, and Hermione Huntington-Smith is closer to our age than his, try as she might to act otherwise."

"Not Hermione," Miss Ethel agreed.

"If I were a gambler," Mrs. Banks said significantly as she reached for a delicate cucumber sandwich, causing the other ladies to lean forward. "I would put my money on one of the Barton sisters."

If Euphenia Banks was expecting the Hurleys to agree, she was soon set right.

"Absolutely impossible!" Miss Myrtle declared. "They are too poor for him."

"Too poor," Miss Ethel echoed emphatically.

"Poor they may be, but they are *beautiful,*" Mrs. Banks said huffily. "And either one is certainly young enough to provide him with *several* heirs."

Miss Myrtle and Miss Ethel each reached for a sandwich, simultaneously took a bite and chewed synchronously.

"It could be Grace, I suppose," Miss Myrtle acquiesced doubtfully after she had swallowed.

"I should think she would be grateful to marry him," Mrs. Banks observed sternly, rising to the defense of her employer, who, while not the kindest of men, still paid a good wage and was amazingly easy to hoodwink in the matter of small discrepancies in the household accounts. "It would be quite a rise for her to marry a knight."

"It would be more of an achievement for him to marry a Barton," Miss Myrtle explained with a pleasant smile. "You are relatively new here, Mrs. Banks, so we can excuse your ignorance."

Mrs. Banks's lips pursed sourly, until Miss Myrtle continued agreeably. "The social attributes of small villages and counties are surely difficult for a woman of your London sophistication to understand.

"You see, the Bartons are descended from one of the county's oldest families. Their ancestor was Guy de Barreton, who came from Normandy with William the Conqueror. While it is a sad commentary on our times, it is nevertheless true that the family has fallen on hard times."

"Hard times," Miss Ethel murmured.

"However, theirs is a most respected name. Since Sir Donald is something of a—how should I say this?—a *newcomer* in Lincolnshire society, he would be wise to marry into one of our established families."

Never let it be said that Euphenia Banks would bite, or too openly disagree, with the hand that fed her so often and with such a nice tea. She nodded companionably.

"Did he say when this happy occasion might occur?" Miss Myrtle asked.

"No, but if your assumption about Grace Barton being the object of his affection is right—for I was never one to hold on to an opinion unnecessarily and I do believe you are on to something, Miss Hurley— I would have to guess that he would wish the wedding to be before the election."

"Ah!" Both the Hurleys sighed simultaneously.

Mrs. Banks wiped her fingers one by one on a napkin. "I really must be going. It's a busy day, and always busier when Sir Donald is at home. I only came today because I knew you take such interest in the doings of the gentry."

"We do our best to keep abreast of all the latest news of our *friends*," Miss Myrtle said affably and incidentally reminding Euphenia that they were nearly on the same social plane as the gentry. She rang for Becky to show Mrs. Banks to the door.

When their guest had departed, Myrtle fastened a keen and gleaming eye on her sister. "What did I tell you, Ethel?" she said with a sweetly malevolent smile. "I knew there was something between those two, and I have *never* trusted Grace Barton."

"Very wise, sister, very wise," Miss Ethel agreed.

"Quiet women are always sly. Untrustworthy and sly! Still, I suppose she'll do very well for an upstart like Donald Franklin."

Chapter Five

Grace had never known a more consistently and intensely dreadful time than she experienced in church the next morning.

To begin with, she was completely exhausted and more than half convinced she had acted like a simpleton by allowing a man they had never met to stay in their house.

Fortunately, he had slept all the rest of the day and all night, while she had spent the day in a state of nervous anticipation, constantly listening for any noise from the upstairs bedroom.

Not that she feared he would creep down the stairs and attack them, because she had locked him inside the room. She simply couldn't have left a stranger free to roam about their house, no matter how harmless he seemed. The doors of their house were stout oak, too, so he was as secure as a prisoner in the Tower of London, unless he tried to climb down the ivy. That would surely result in a broken neck.

There wasn't any noise, however—no voice calling, no knocking on the door, no sound of feet walking around. He didn't even wake up when she took him some supper. Indeed, he had been slumbering so peacefully, she hadn't even tried to wake him, but had left the bread, cheese and water on the bedside table.

He had still been sleeping this morning when she had brought another tray bearing fresher food. With one muscular arm thrown over his forehead, he looked like a slumbering god from one of the Greek myths, Apollo or Cupid, his long lashes brushing his undoubtedly masculine cheeks with their blond stubble, his longish hair covering his ears, and his full lips drawn up in what might have been a smile.

As she sat anxiously in church, she hoped Mr. Elliot would continue to sleep, until they could get home, at any rate. It was going to be awkward if he woke up while they were absent and discovered that he was a prisoner. Still, it couldn't be helped, and if he demanded an explanation when they returned, she would tell him that she had temporarily lost the key.

Grace sighed and slipped her cold hand into her worn velvet muff, where she could feel the iron solidarity of the house keys without making them jingle.

As for her belief that Mr. Elliot needed her…what a foolish conceit! He knew nothing about her; she knew nothing about him.

If she wasn't careful, she would soon be as sentimental as Mercy!

The ancient Reverend Percy-Pembleton began his sermon, and Grace quickly realized he had made something of an unfortunate choice of text, for he spoke about rendering unto Caesar the things that were Caesar's.

Sir Donald, sitting in the pew directly beneath the pulpit, was probably quite delighted by the choice.

Today he had managed to dress with a hint of restraint. Instead of his usual garish attire, he was wearing a subdued gray coat, plain black vest and trousers, and unembellished white shirt.

Unfortunately, his clothing did not lessen his bulk, or hide his smug, self-satisfied face. No doubt he had a sympathetic admiration for the conquering Roman emperors.

Not so the villagers. Around her, she could hear several people shifting on the hard wooden pews, and it sounded as if a sudden plague of colds and coughs had afflicted the congregation. They evidently felt as one with the conquered.

She was also sure that everyone sitting in the church around her was aware something was afoot between herself and Donald Franklin.

When she and Mercy had arrived for morning prayer, their neighbors had regarded them with the same fascination one might reserve for witnessing a train wreck, and a kind of understanding pity, although nobody said anything other than kind hellos or innocuous remarks about the weather.

However, the Hurley girls were particularly lacking in subtlety, as usual. They had not spoken to the Bartons, but had stared at Grace, then the arriving Sir Donald, then Grace, then Sir Donald as if they were figures in a clock keeping time, until Grace had wanted to scream. Even now, she could feel their scrutiny.

She tried to ignore them. After all, they *knew* nothing, or they would have said something to her. As it was, she would betray nothing of what had passed between Donald Franklin and herself. Miraculously he, too, seemed in no frame of mind to end any speculation, for although he continually glanced her way, he had not spoken to her, perhaps because he wasn't sure of her answer to his proposal and wanted to spare himself any humiliation on the slight chance that she would refuse.

She let her mind envision what the Hurleys would do if she accepted Sir Donald. They would be all sweetness and light, while making it abundantly clear that they suspected her motives.

As well they might.

Mercy shifted beside her, drawing Grace's avid attention at once. Mercy saw her sudden scrutiny and smiled.

That did not assuage Grace's growing dread that Mercy was far more ill than she was letting on. Indeed, she had looked so pale and tired this morning, Grace had proposed she not attend the service, only to have Mercy insist upon going in a most determined manner. She did seem better once they were outside and in the fresh air, and Grace hoped she was worried for nothing.

Nevertheless, Mercy's state reminded Grace of the greater ramifications if they were dispossessed. Then, even a simple illness could mean death.

She vaguely wondered what it would be like never to worry. To have the ability or the security to welcome the future, instead of fearing what new troubles it might bring.

Grace sighed again. She would likely never know, for as her mother often said, she seemed born to worry. No matter how she tried to stifle her thoughts and fears, she rarely could, for she was cursed with a far too active imagination.

Without conscious effort, Grace's gaze was drawn to the marble tablet dedicated to their late parents near her, which said, "George Barton, Esq. and his beloved wife, Alice," and the dates of their deaths.

Then, as if her mother were somehow offering her eldest daughter comfort, Grace recalled her mother telling her not to let her imagination get carried away.

Determined to do just that, Grace read some of the other memorial tablets around her in the old church, which had been built during the early years of the eighteenth century in the perpendicular style, which meant its square stone tower was suggestive of a castle rather than a house of worship. The covered church porch led into a building remarkable more for its perpetual chill than any architectural marvels, and for the combined stocks and whipping post, removed from the green, which stood inside the entrance as if they were necessary reminders of retribution other than divine.

Farther inside, the wooden pews were hard as rocks, the light poor, the stone floor frigid. Nevertheless, everything was cosily familiar to those born and baptized in Barton, and even Grace would have felt worshiping in a more comfortable and decorative church something of a luxurious sin.

She perused the tablet dedicated to Reverend Albertus Ezekiel Jones, born 1759, died 1843, adorned with a grinning death's head. The late Reverend Jones had so upset some members of the congregation upon his arrival in Barton that they had actually decided to blow him up, like a gang of religious Guy Fawkes. Thankfully for Reverend Jones, the gunpowder had proved to be prohibitively expensive, and by the time the malcontents had gotten enough money to buy it, they had grown used to the new minister.

Another tablet was devoted to Rafe Walters's sheepdog, who had drowned saving Rafe's youngest child during a flood. The small memorial was down near the floor and somewhat hidden in the corner. The Hurley sisters had almost left the congregation over that, claiming that the church had no business giving Christian burial to an animal. Rafe Walters had rather too pointedly claimed that his dog was more of a Christian than *some* people he could name.

In the end, however, Rafe had triumphed, and if it was because he somehow gave a substitute preacher the impression that Kip Walters was a child, well, nobody minded except the Hurleys, who were conveniently visiting a relative in Grantham that day. They never followed through on their threat to abandon the congregation, perhaps because Reverend Percy-Pembleton did not respond as if that meant impending doom.

On the opposite wall was the inscription to Meridith Wyton, noting that she had died of consumption in 1623. She was something of a local legend, for her lover had fallen from his horse and died while riding to Barton on the day of their wedding. Merry Wyton had died within six months, and despite the inscription, it was held that she had died of a broken heart. Mercy, in her sentimental way, always put a posy of spring flowers near the tablet on the date of Merry's death.

While Grace couldn't imagine wasting away and dying because of a broken heart, she certainly could imagine wasting away and dying of hunger, which brought her thoughts once again to the dilemma all too well represented by Sir Donald's visible and corpulent form.

As if on cue, Donald Franklin looked at her again over his fat shoulder.

She had to fight an urge to groan with frustration. *Why don't I just stand up and announce to the entire congregation that he's proposed to me?* she thought bitterly.

Then, giving her imagination free rein while the vicar droned on, she envisioned refusing Donald Franklin's proposal in public, in the presence of the Hurley twins and everybody else.

It was a most satisfactory idea, except that she knew she would never have the nerve. Nor could she rid herself of the fear that perhaps she *couldn't* refuse him, not unless she thought of some way to earn a considerable sum of money in three short months.

Mercy lowered her head, and Grace darted another sidelong glance at her sister.

"Are you feeling ill?" she whispered urgently, too concerned for her sister's welfare to consider the impropriety of whispering in church. "We can leave—"

Mercy shook her head slightly. "I shall be fine

once we are outside. I simply need some fresh air. It's nothing, Grace, nothing.''

Grace didn't think Mercy's trouble was "nothing," but short of making a spectacle of themselves by forcing Mercy to go, there was little Grace could do but trust Mercy's prognosis and wait for the service to be over.

She glanced again at Mercy, who lifted her head and returned Grace's look with a wan smile.

What if Mercy was seriously ill? She was the only family Grace had, and if anything happened to her—

Suddenly, from a pew approximately halfway down the chancel, she heard the distinctive sound of the Hurley sisters sighing loudly and simultaneously. The minister understood that message and quickly concluded his sermon, although whether he was quite through or not, Grace wasn't sure.

The service proceeded apace, and it was finally time for the recessional hymn. As the congregation stood, Grace turned anxiously toward Mercy, who looked in danger of swooning.

"I shall be fine in a little while," Mercy whispered, but this time, Grace didn't believe her. Mercy's face was deathly white, and she had to hold on to the back of the pew in front of them to steady herself.

"Come, we must leave!" Grace said insistently as the choir slowly made its way down the center aisle.

"No! I don't want the Hurley sisters to speak to me!" Mercy's voice was still an urgent whisper, but there were tears lurking her eyes, and her lower lip trembled.

Grace stared at her, dread filling her so that she felt almost faint herself, yet she did as Mercy asked.

The moment the final notes sounded, and the choir was dismissed, Grace took hold of her sister's arm to help her outside.

"No, wait. Let me sit a moment," Mercy protested, nearly falling down onto the pew. "Talk to me. Of the weather. Anything."

"First I shall open a window," Grace replied. When she turned back from that task, she saw Donald Franklin coming toward them, his hat in his hand and a friendly expression on his round, shiny face.

Grace thought he looked like a peddler who was contemplating cheating on his prices.

"My dear Miss Barton!" he said, looking at Grace before studying Mercy. "Miss Mercy."

Grace dipped a curtsy, and Mercy nodded.

Sir Donald continued to scrutinize Mercy gravely and Grace saw the Hurley sisters hovering near the back of the church, their inquisitive eyes trained on them as if they were bloodhounds on the scent.

"I should have eaten breakfast!" Mercy said with a brightness that Grace knew was forced. "I felt quite faint during the last hymn. Silly of me, wasn't it?"

Sir Donald's expression became an indulgent smile, and then he returned his unwelcome attention to Grace. "You must allow me the honor of taking you home in my carriage."

If it weren't for Mercy, Grace would have refused immediately, and unequivocally. The very last thing she wanted was to be seen in his carriage. However,

Mercy was obviously not well enough to walk home. "We shall be delighted," she answered.

"Oh, I can walk," Mercy said cheerfully, and quite firmly, demonstrating a rather astonishing recuperation.

"I think it is most kind of Sir Donald to offer us his carriage," Grace replied, giving Mercy a look that insisted her sister accept. She knew as well as anyone that Mercy didn't like Sir Donald; however, at the moment, that was immaterial.

"Oh, very well," her sister grudgingly conceded.

After Mercy's less than gracious response, Grace thought she had best make amends with their benefactor—odious word!—so she smiled at him.

She immediately regretted that, for his eyes shone with triumph, and his lips curled up into an answering smile that bespoke pleasure—and something else.

Something that made Grace feel soiled.

That was not important right now. What was important was getting Mercy home and getting her well.

"Allow me," Sir Donald said, holding out his arm for Mercy. She looked about to protest, but a glance at Grace told her not to refuse that, either.

Sir Donald and Mercy proceeded from the church, with Grace following along behind, mindful of the surreptitious looks of the rest of the congregation, and especially of the Hurley sisters. If there was anything to be thankful for at present, it was that nobody spoke to them, although tongues would surely wag once they were gone.

Even this much of a connection between herself and Donald Franklin was enough to make Grace want to get on a train and leave forever, even though she had no place to go, no money and had never been on a train in her life.

But she couldn't. Not now, and certainly not if Mercy was sick.

Mercy seemed to be walking without having to lean on Sir Donald's arm, but whether that meant she wasn't ill was not clear. She might simply be reluctant to be any closer to him than necessary, a feeling Grace shared.

Grace, who could hear the whispers of certain females, kept her gaze on Mercy as Sir Donald handed her into his barouche, and quickly took her seat beside her sister.

"I'm so sorry to cause such a commotion," Mercy whispered sorrowfully. "I am not very sick, really."

Grace paid less attention to Mercy's words and the whispered voices than the color of her sister's complexion, which seemed to be reviving in the brisk breeze.

Perhaps Mercy had been right all along. Perhaps she wasn't very sick, after all. Or so Grace fervently hoped.

From his hiding place in an alley between the tavern and the livery stable, Boffin watched the parade of parishioners and suddenly nudged Skurch sharply in the ribs.

"What the devil—?" the young man cried out sharply.

"Hold your noise!" Boffin admonished. He nodded toward the road around the green. "Look yonder at that carriage."

"What about it?" Skurch mumbled.

He wished he was inside the tavern with the others, instead of standing outside shivering, watching a bunch of villagers mosey along the green.

"Look at them women."

"Oh." Skurch obeyed, and slowly smiled. "Pretty, ain't they?"

"Now that I've got your attention," Boffin continued sarcastically, "what else did I tell ya? Find a pretty woman, and you'd find my fine lord!"

"So now what do we do?"

"We finds out where they live, and keep our eyes on the house. And on the women, too."

Skurch's pale, watery eyes began to gleam greedily. "I'm your man for that detail."

"I thought you might be."

Elliot stretched luxuriously between the lavender-scented sheets and sighed. If only he could stay here for a month, he would be as well rested as he had ever been! Here there were no worries to plague him and no doubts to darken his mood. To be sure, there was the slight strain of having to keep his identity a secret, but that was nothing, not after keeping that secret for five long years.

There was the worry that Boffin might show his ugly face and demand his money, but surely that fellow wouldn't linger in a place like this for very long. His kind needed busier places, where there were plenty of people to swindle and dupe and rob.

All things considered, Elliot thought, he couldn't have picked a better place to stay if he had tried.

He vaguely wondered what time of day it was, and a glance outside revealed a blustery sky whose slate-colored clouds gave no indication of the hour. Late afternoon or evening, perhaps.

A quick survey of the room showed him his clothes laid upon the chair, his shirt included. Someone had put shaving implements on the washstand, too.

He must have been completely exhausted to sleep so long.

He decided he would stay beneath the warm covers, and wait for pretty Mercy to see what he required.

That was something pleasant to contemplate, her seeing to his requirements.

He considered attempting to seduce Mercy Barton and found the idea rather curiously unappealing. In the past, he would have been able to come up with several different ploys to win her heart and tempt her into his bed; today, he couldn't think of anything at all. Indeed, he felt no desire for her, not in a sexual way. She seemed merely a pleasant enough girl who made a fine, if not overly intelligent, nurse. Her touch did not warm him; her presence didn't cause any familiar spark of heat.

Gad! Maybe that blow to his head *had* been more serious than he had thought. Surely he wasn't becoming some sort of monkish fellow who didn't find women appealing, or interesting or challenging....

Challenging. Grace Barton would be challenging, and when he thought of her, he knew that he wasn't in any danger of becoming celibate. *She* was far more tempting than her sister, with the beauty that she seemed completely unaware of, and the shrewd skepticism in her eyes. Why, to win her trust and regard would be no simple thing. A man would have to take some time seducing her—and even then, not without some danger to his own heart. But the reward...the reward would probably be worth it.

The notion that he would find *himself* drawn to a woman who was a challenge struck Elliot. He preferred the easily seduced, or, to be precise, the women who were more than half seducing him.

Elliot pushed himself up, then put his feet on the floor.

Such thoughts were all useless speculation. He was not going to play games with the naive Mercy, nor was he going to try to seduce his benefactress. He wasn't that complete a cad.

He looked around the clean, comfortable small room, reassuring himself that the decision to return to England had been a proper one. Where in Canada could he find such simple, familiar surroundings, albeit on a far less grand scale than he had enjoyed at home? Nobody in Canada knew how to cook bacon properly, for one thing. And as for the cold—he shivered at the memory.

He saw a jug covered with a cloth and a small loaf of bread on a table set beside the chair. Supper, or dinner?

No, breakfast, he realized when he went closer, for the milk in the jug was fresh, and the bread was still slightly warm. He must have slept right through the day and night. That was not impossible, for he had been tired and the worse for drink.

And this morning, no charming young lady to wait upon him. Obviously the time had come to go.

He dressed quickly, leaving his top few shirt buttons comfortably undone, and hurriedly ate his bread and milk. The bread was excellent, as had been the other food he had eaten here.

If he truly regretted anything when it came to bidding this place adieu, it would be the loss of such good cooking. Still, it couldn't be helped.

When he was finished eating, he put his hand on the latch of the door and pulled. It didn't move. He tried again, with more force, thinking it might be stuck, and still nothing.

He tried pushing on the door, then pulling it, but it didn't budge. "Miss Barton?" he called out.

No response.

"Miss Barton!" he shouted.

Still nothing. No answer at all. Where the devil were they?

He banged his foot on the floor, in case they couldn't hear him through the thick oak door, then waited.

All was silence. Muttering a curse, Elliot tried the handle again.

Then he realized what the trouble was. The door was locked from the other side.

They had locked him in!

Don't they know who I am? he thought angrily, and just as quickly remembered that they *didn't* know who he was. Nobody had known exactly who he was for the past five years.

Why had they done this? They had seemed friendly enough before, although Grace had still been wary.

A scowl darkened Elliot's face. No matter how he was dressed, surely he didn't look or behave like a fugitive from Botany Bay.

Had they finally decided to turn him over to some local constabulary? Had they suddenly grown afraid he would rob them? Or hurt them? Or worse?

Couldn't they tell…? Of course not. You couldn't tell anything about a person just from their looks, unless, he thought sardonically, they looked like Boffin and his boys, who resembled everyone's idea of the criminal element.

Obviously, the Bartons—especially, he thought, Grace—were not fools, and he had to admire her wisdom, although he didn't particularly enjoy being held prisoner, not even by two attractive young ladies.

Where were they now? He opened the window and leaned out, trying to see into every corner of the yard. The breeze carried the sounds of bells chiming in the distance, and Elliot drew his head back inside.

He recognized the tune, which continued for some minutes. He also knew what it indicated: church was over, which meant today was Sunday.

Sunday—the Bartons must have gone to morning services, as dutiful young ladies should, whether or not they were harboring young men in secret.

Perhaps *especially* if they were harboring unknown young men. He grinned, for given his experience of the secretive nature of women, that was the most likely explanation.

He also smiled at the predictability of English country folk. No doubt the Barton sisters were ensconced in the family pew, where their worthy ancestors had warmed the seats for generations before them. The building would be old, and made of mossy stone. Inside one would find memorial tablets to those bygone ancestors, who would be commemorated in awful majesty, with no hint of the scandals and stories that were likely still told about them as the current members of the congregation sat around their respective hearths on winter nights.

Quite different from the family chapel at Barroughby Hall, where he had been forced to endure Sunday and holiday services.

He rose abruptly and tried the door again before beginning to pace like a restless animal.

Apparently there was nothing he could do about getting free until they returned, unless he tried to break down the door, which looked thick enough to do serious damage to his shoulder, or to squeeze through the narrow windows and climb down the ivy, which would probably result in grievous bodily harm. He would simply have to wait for them to let him out.

Then he heard the sound of a carriage approaching and hurried to the window, where he beheld a very fine open barouche drawn by two marvelous horses driven by a liveried servant. Seated inside were two women, who were facing toward the window, and a man behind the driver.

Judging by their size and build, the women were the Barton sisters, attired in their Sunday best, their faces obscured by their bonnets. Elliot quickly drew back from the window, not wanting to be seen, although he remained close enough to observe them below.

He scrutinized the man carefully, for there was something familiar in the way the fellow tilted his head when he leaned toward one of the women seated across from him. Because of the wind, Elliot couldn't catch his words, or her reply.

The coachman halted the barouche, then got down to assist the ladies as they disembarked. They seemed in something of a rush, which showed they found no pleasure in the man's company, a thought that brought a pleased smile to Elliot's lips—even if these women would never be anything more to him than momentary benefactors.

Then the gentleman turned and raised his hat to bid them farewell, exposing his face—and Elliot gasped, shocked to think that the Barton sisters knew that particular man.

For when Elliot had begun his descent into a life of less than sterling accomplishments, there had been one man who led him on that downward path and soon surpassed him; one man whose activities soon so disgusted Elliot, he gave up all acquaintance with him; one man who came to serve as a milestone against which Elliot could measure his own decadence.

One man who collected young and beautiful women too poor or too naive to see him for what he was, who used them, abused them and abandoned them as if they were baubles created solely for his own amusement, who, unlike Elliot, never felt remorse.

No matter what terrible things Elliot had done, he had never, ever approached that man's reckless disregard for others.

And that man was Donald Franklin.

Chapter Six

Elliot wondered if Franklin was going to come into the house, which would indicate that he was on neighborly terms with the Bartons. That would have been distressing to see, no matter who the women were. Such a relationship wouldn't impugn the Bartons' intelligence; he had seen Franklin in social situations, and the man was as smooth as a snake sliding through wet grass.

Thankfully, however, Franklin didn't get out of the carriage, but contented himself with a farewell from within—which was received with a definitely lackluster acknowledgment from Grace Barton and none at all from her sister—before the carriage turned in the yard and returned down the lane.

This boded well for their safety from Franklin's lascivious machinations, Elliot thought with some relief.

His relief only lasted a moment as a sudden horrible idea struck him. Franklin had made no secret of his desire to be knighted. Indeed, he had bored everyone within earshot by grumbling every time anyone else received that honor. Was it possible that the "Sir Donald" Mercy had named as the Bartons' greedy landlord was the same Donald Franklin he had just seen? That Franklin had somehow connived to achieve his goal?

Elliot racked his brain, trying to remember anything Franklin had said about living in Lincolnshire. At the time he had been acquainted with him, Elliot had only been concerned about his own entertainment, not with listening to the other man's interminable bragging.

Yes, one night when Franklin was typically drunk and surly, he had mentioned a manor in Lincolnshire, and that he hated it. He had also said something about his tenants and the ridiculously low rents. He was going to raise them one day, he had vowed, when somebody he was currently "teaching" about gambling lost enough, and Franklin got what he wanted.

Had a knighthood been that prize? Probably. Having obtained that prize, had he decided upon a new one, and was that one of the Barton sisters?

How exactly did they come to be in this financial difficulty? Gambling debts? A father or brother who fell into Franklin's snare? It wouldn't be the first time female relatives were made to suffer under such circumstances.

And Franklin, that despicable villain, would no doubt make it sound as if he were coming to their rescue. Indeed, the fact that there were two lovely young women involved would surely enhance his desires.

All of them.

Perhaps Franklin wasn't their landlord, Elliot thought, his natural optimism reasserting itself. Perhaps he was only their neighbor, coincidentally named Donald.

Only their neighbor? What did it matter if he was *only* their neighbor? He knew what Franklin was, and he could well imagine that the Bartons would be perfect targets for his infamy. If he wasn't their landlord, he would still find a way to use their troubles to his own ends, either by loaning them money or some other means.

They couldn't be indebted to that man, for there was but one way he would want to be paid. Whatever Donald Franklin's relationship with them was, whether he was landlord or neighbor, didn't matter. He was near, they were pretty, they were in a perilous strait—that was all that Franklin would need to pursue them with the most dishonorable of intentions.

Did Grace Barton and her sister have any idea of the kind of man Donald Franklin was? If they didn't, they should be warned. He should tell them—

What? All the sordid stories, and how he came to know them? That he had seen some things himself, and enough to believe the rest? That his sources were the type of people who frequented the same brothels, taverns and watering places he had?

Why not? They were nothing to him, and their judgment of him unimportant. Once he left here, he would never see them again.

Why not tell them what he knew, and how? No reason, except for an undeniable reluctance to have Grace Barton think ill of him.

Which was ridiculous, really. What influence could a Lincolnshire lass's opinion have on his life?

Nevertheless, the thought of her reaction—the horror, dismay and distaste that would surely show itself, despite her unusual self-control—was enough to make him try to think of another way to warn them.

Then he realized that Franklin's possible habitation in the area presented another problem. If *he* recognized Franklin, Franklin could recognize *him*. Franklin would probably rush to tell Adrian, in the hopes of getting some kind of reward, and then Adrian would know his prodigal half brother had come home. Eventually Adrian would track Elliot down. There would be another confrontation and more recriminations...a meeting to be avoided at all costs.

If he was smart, he would stop worrying about the Bartons and get out of this place at once, before his past confronted him in all its forms and torments.

If he was smart, and if he was as totally selfish as everyone believed him to be.

Grace frowned anxiously as Mercy sat beside the table and sighed. "Is it your stomach?" she asked her younger sister. "Does your head ache?"

"No, truly, Grace, I'm much better," Mercy replied. "It is as I said to Sir Donald. I should have eaten breakfast. I'm only hungry and tired. I'm sorry to make you so upset."

"Mercy," Grace said firmly, sitting in the chair opposite Mercy and reaching out to take her sister's two slender hands in her own. "You are not well, and don't try to pretend otherwise. Your face is much too pale. And you were sick this morning before I got up, weren't you? Then you nearly swooned in church.''

Mercy rose agitatedly and began to remove her hat. Her hands were trembling, and Grace felt almost sick with worry herself to see it. ''My stomach is a little upset, that's all,'' Mercy said quietly. ''And I'm tired.''

''Why?''

Mercy faced her. ''I haven't been sleeping very well. Neither have you.''

''Were you sick to your stomach this morning?''

''Maybe it was something I ate.''

''I ate everything you did,'' Grace persisted remorselessly. She feared more than ever that Mercy was seriously ill, and foolishly trying to ease her sister's worries by pretending she was not.

''Then perhaps it is just from being worried about the rent. I'm sure things are worse than you are telling me, Grace, and you know I have a nervous stomach.''

With some relief, Grace realized that was true enough, and she managed to smile. ''You shouldn't be so worried about the rent. I told you, I will think of something.''

Mercy did not return Grace's smile. Instead, her eyes suddenly narrowed in an uncharacteristically suspicious expression. ''Tell me that you would never think of throwing yourself away in marriage because of any financial troubles,'' she said with a new and unexpectedly resolute manner.

''Whatever gave you that idea?'' Grace said, although she simultaneously wished Sir Donald to perdition. Must he have been so obvious in his attentions at church?

"Does Sir Donald want to marry you?"

"I have no desire to marry Sir Donald Franklin," Grace replied, and with conviction, while at the same time telling herself it would never come to that.

"That's not what I asked," Mercy pressed. "Does *he* want to marry *you?*"

"Why would he want to marry me?" Grace asked, noting that her own hands were trembling. She clasped them together to keep them still.

"He has no wife, you are beautiful and he knows exactly the problem we face, which I am certain he will use to his advantage."

Grace couldn't disagree with that, for she thought much the same thing. "Do you think Donald Franklin capable of being in love with anyone other than himself?" she said, still prevaricating.

"He doesn't love you," Mercy replied with complete certainty. "I know he doesn't."

"Nor I him," Grace countered. "Therefore, I think we can assume there is little chance Sir Donald and I will be married. Besides, we are not discussing Sir Donald's feelings for me, or anyone else. We are talking about *you.*"

"There is nothing to talk about. I'm merely tired and hungry. Has he proposed to you?"

Grace rose. "I will get our supper."

"I'll help."

"No. You sit and rest."

"I keep telling you, Grace, I'm *not* sick!" Mercy declared with what sounded like a choked sob. "Is

that why Donald Franklin came here the other day—
to propose?''

"Sit down, Mercy. He came to inform us of the
rent increase.''

"Is that all?'' Mercy demanded, putting her hands
on her hips, her face flushed.

"I keep telling you, Sir Donald and I are nothing
to each other!'' Grace declared angrily. "Stop talking
about him!''

Mercy's hands dropped to her sides and her eyes
filled with tears. "Oh, Grace,'' she said mournfully.
"I'm sorry. Don't be angry with me.''

"I'm not, dear,'' Grace said at once, meaning it.
She sighed raggedly and ran a hand over her brow.
"Sit and let me make the tea.''

Then, with no apparent provocation, the color
drained from Mercy's face and she swayed, clutching
at the table to keep from falling. Grace was at her
side in an instant, helping her to sit again. Tears came
to her own eyes as she said, "You are sick, Mercy,
and I'm going to send to Lincoln for a doctor.''

"We haven't got the money,'' Mercy said weakly.
"And I'm not terribly ill.''

Distraught, Grace lost all patience. "Hang the
money! You *are* terribly ill!''

Mercy shook her head. "No, I'm not.'' She reached
out and grabbed Grace's hand, then lifted her im-
ploring eyes to her sister. "I was trying so hard not
to upset you, and I fear I've done the opposite.

"But I haven't anything seriously wrong with me,
Grace. Truly,'' she explained quietly. Then her gaze
faltered. "I'm...I'm going to have a baby.''

Getting struck by a lightning bolt might have rendered Grace as immobile and stunned as Mercy's pronouncement. For a long moment she simply stood and stared at her sister's face as a battery of responses tore through her: disbelief and shock the most prevalent, but also relief that Mercy was not dying.

"You're...what?" she finally muttered as she felt for a chair and collapsed into it.

"I'm having a baby," Mercy replied with a weak smile.

"That's...that's not possible!" Grace whispered, willing that it be so.

Mercy nodded her head. "Yes, it is," she answered softly, and there was a confirmation in her eyes. "I'm sorry," she repeated, holding her hands out in a gesture of contrition. "I meant to tell you in a better way."

"A better way?" Grace said, still so dumbfounded she felt as if this had to be a dream.

Mercy...pregnant? Sweet, pretty, young *unmarried* Mercy? It *had* to be impossible. "Who...when...?" she whispered.

"Adam Brown, of course," Mercy replied with more confidence. "We're going to be married, the next time he's on leave."

The charming, the dashing Lieutenant Brown—of course.

Nevertheless, Grace didn't see how it was possible for them to have...shared such intimacy. She had kept a close watch on Mercy when she saw her sister's apparent fascination with the young man, although all she had feared was that he was going to break Mercy's heart.

Never, in her wildest fancies, had she imagined any result like this. Why, they had never even been alone together....

Then Grace recalled that day she had come home from the village to find Mercy and Lieutenant Brown in the drawing room shortly before he went away. Mercy had been somewhat flushed and flustered, but Grace had put that down simply to Lieutenant Brown's presence in the house. *He* had been cool, casual and polite. The whole scene assumed a new dimension as Grace considered it and wondered if there had been other trysts, too. Obviously she had been far too trusting of her sister's moral virtue.

"He never spoke to me about marrying you," Grace said pensively, hoping that although it was somewhat discourteous, Lieutenant Brown had assumed that since there was no male head of the household, he need ask no one's permission to marry Mercy.

"I suppose there wasn't time. Everything happened so quickly!"

This excuse did not comfort Grace. "When did he propose to you?"

To her dismay, Mercy colored deeply and said nothing.

"He *did* propose, didn't he?" Grace demanded, Mercy's reaction filling her with new dread and making her curt.

"He said I shouldn't fall in love with anyone else while he was away, and that he would come to me as soon as he returned to England,'' Mercy explained, her voice quavering.

"Mercy!" Grace gasped. A secret engagement would have been bad enough, given Mercy's pregnancy, but to learn that there might not even be *that*....

Mercy straightened her slender shoulders and a tenacity such as Grace had never seen in her sister's eyes appeared. "When you fall in love, Grace, you will understand. I have complete faith in Adam's devotion to me."

Grace wished she could have the same unwavering faith, for as she recalled Lieutenant Brown's manner that day, she thought his behavior did not bode well for Mercy. And why, if he truly loved her, did he *not* ask Mercy for her hand? It could be that he had never even thought of proposing marriage, and Mercy's own romantic nature had let her get swept away by his persuasive charm until she believed what she wanted to believe.

Oh, Grace chastised herself, how could she have been so blind and stupid and trusting! How could she have let down her parents, especially her mother who, on her deathbed, had made Grace promise to always look after Mercy?

Now there would be scandal and disgrace, as well as poverty.

Even if Lieutenant Brown had been sincere in his declaration of love, a host of things could prevent his return before the baby arrived. He could be lost at sea, or die of illness.

"Please don't hate me, Grace. I know I deserve it for being so weak and immoral—"

"I could never *hate* you," Grace said truthfully. "It's just that I'm…I'm…"

Unfortunately, she couldn't find any comforting words before the full force of the scandal that was about to erupt in their lives overwhelmed her. "Oh, Mercy! How *could* you?" she said, no longer able to hide her dismay. "Did you never consider what might happen? Did it never occur to either of you that you might become pregnant?"

Mercy blushed beet red. "I…I love him, Grace, and when we were together, it seemed only natural to—"

"*Natural* it might have been, but you are not dumb beasts," Grace interrupted. "He's left you in this state and—"

"And he's going to marry me!" Mercy wailed.

"How can you be so certain?" Grace demanded.

"Because I love him!"

"Love!" Grace declared skeptically. "Love it may be, but I still do not understand how you could indulge your passion without benefit of marriage. It is weak, it is foolish—and now *you* are going to pay the price, while Lieutenant Brown is far and conveniently away!"

"I don't mind the price, as you call it," Mercy answered just as forcefully. "I knew what might happen. It's *you* I'm worried about. I know as well as you, Grace, that my perceived disgrace will fall on you, too, and it is for *that* I am truly sorry."

Tears began to spill over onto her cheeks. "I

shouldn't have been so selfish, I know. But I love him so much, and he was going away so soon...."

Her words dissolved into incoherent sobs as Grace embraced her, stroking her curly head, all her exasperation and dismay gone in an instant.

Perhaps, in a way, Mercy and Lieutenant Brown were not completely liable for their weakness. Both had been indulged, by parents, aunts and even a sibling trying to protect a young woman from harsh realities. Maybe this coddling had been the greater error.

There could be no protection from this reality, unfortunately. Mercy's shame would be known to all, and she would have to bear the consequences.

But not alone. Never alone, as long as Grace had breath in her body.

"It's all right," Grace crooned softly. "It's all right."

Upstairs, Elliot wondered what the devil the Bartons were doing. He heard their voices and had gone to the rather preposterous length of trying to hear what they were saying through the keyhole. Regrettably, the door was thick, and their words were indistinguishable.

He ran his hand over his chin in frustration and, as he did so, noted that it had been some time since he had last shaved.

He couldn't do much until they released him. He might as well be presentable, he thought as he removed his shirt.

But if they didn't come soon, he would start shouting.

When Mercy's sobs subsided, Grace drew back and regarded her sister tenderly. "Lieutenant Brown's been gone over two months. When was the last time you had word from him?"

Clandestine though it would have been, Grace wanted to hear a different response than the one Mercy provided. "Oh, he couldn't write to me."

"Lieutenant Brown is stationed in Gibraltar, which is hardly the end of the world," Grace remarked, trying to keep her tone nonjudgmental.

"He couldn't write to me, even if he was only in the next county," Mercy said mournfully as she wiped the tears from her cheeks, "because we are not officially engaged."

"At this particular juncture, I think that is rather beside the point, don't you?" Grace asked, a hint of frustration in her voice.

Then she thought of how little privacy there was in the village. Everyone would know if Mercy received a letter from Lieutenant Brown, especially his aunts.

She could easily imagine *their* reaction. They would blame Mercy alone for her condition, and all their previous approval of her sister would dissolve like snow in the spring. They would never believe their beloved nephew was but all too human, and of somewhat less than sterling characteristics.

"I'm sure that was all for the best, since you are not *officially* engaged," she agreed.

"Grace, please say you forgive me," Mercy whispered.

"Of course I forgive you," Grace said sincerely.

It might even come to pass as Mercy fondly believed. It was possible that Lieutenant Brown fully intended to return and marry Mercy, perhaps before the child was born.

Grace commanded herself to share Mercy's faith, at least for the present. "This is what comes of allowing you to indulge in your taste for novels!" she chided ruefully.

Mercy smiled feebly. "It had nothing to do with literature. I assure you, Grace, what Adam and I feel for each other is good and right. He loves me, and I love him."

How many other young women had clung to such hopes? Grace thought, but she subdued her skepticism and returned to the essential situation. "You're absolutely *certain* you're with child?" This time, she put her questions with more gentleness, and Mercy answered just as calmly. "Yes."

"Were you in that condition before Lieutenant Brown went away?"

"It was too early to be sure. I think I am only a bit over two months gone."

Grace nodded. "Thank goodness, it will be a few months before the baby will be born. We shall have some time to make plans before your...predicament...becomes obvious."

Mercy reached out and once again took Grace's hand in hers. "I'm sorry for the disgrace to *you*," she repeated gently, "but I'm happy to be having Adam's child."

Suddenly there came a rapid thudding on the ceiling about them. "Miss Barton?" The familiar voice of Mr. Elliot, albeit muffled, drifted down into the kitchen like the voice of some impatient celestial being. "Miss Mercy? Is *anybody* there?"

"Oh, my goodness!" Grace cried, her gaze darting upward.

"I forgot all about him!" Mercy exclaimed.

"So did I," Grace confessed. "I had better let him out."

"He sounds upset. I think he knows he was locked in," Mercy said worriedly. "Maybe I should go with you."

"No. You stay here and rest. I wouldn't want you fainting. I would likely swoon myself. Nor do I think you should be going up and down those narrow stairs—"

"Grace, I'm having a baby, not dying," Mercy said.

"Nevertheless, I won't have you ill again. Leave Mr. Elliot to me."

Chapter Seven

"I'm coming, Mr. Elliot," Grace called as she headed for the stairs, Mercy anxiously watching her go.

Grace had no fear of Mr. Elliot's possibly angry reaction to being locked in his room. She was far more concerned about Mercy, and he would soon be gone, to trouble them no more.

Lifting her skirt in one hand, she went up the narrow stairs to the upper level, cursing herself for a blind fool not to have realized Mercy's state, although her rational mind knew that to have guessed her sister's condition would have taken a leap of imagination of which even she was incapable.

How could Mercy have behaved in such an immoral manner? How could she have been so... intimate...with a man without benefit of marriage, even if she *had* fancied herself in love? Did that not indicate a shocking want of morality, and a failure on Grace's part?

Before this, Grace would have confidently assumed that of all the young women of their acquaintance and social class—and granted there were very few of them—there was only one woman less likely than Mercy to be guilty of such a shameful thing, and that was herself.

A pregnancy out of wedlock was certainly not a rare event in a country village and, indeed, up until fifty years ago had seemed to be an accepted part of the courting process, forgiven once the couple were wed; no wedding, and it was something of a different story.

Well, she and Mercy would have to leave before her condition became obvious. Mercy would have to understand the necessity of going, and Grace would be spared many a scene of begging to stay and bemoaning Grace's decision. If anything, Mercy had made the decision when she had allowed Lieutenant Brown to take liberties with her.

If Mercy's romantic notion became reality and Lieutenant Brown returned, they would have to think of a way to leave word of their location that would not arouse suspicion.

Grace couldn't think of a single soul to whom she could trust that information who would not want to know why, not even the Reverend Percy-Pembleton. After all, Mercy and Lieutenant Brown had not been acquainted very long.

Where could they go, anyway? Their father's brother, the only relation she would consider imposing upon, had moved to the United States last year.

Even supposing they could afford to pay for passage, Grace had heard enough terrible stories of cramped ship's quarters, illness and death to make her wish to avoid such a thing under the best of circumstances; Mercy's pregnancy made a long sea voyage impractical, if not impossible.

How would they live when they left Barton? They had very little money and no relatives to appeal to. She could be a teacher, if someone would hire her, or a governess or even a lady's companion—but where would Mercy live? Who would hire a teacher, governess or companion whose sister was of questionable moral virtue, much less offer them a place of residence?

It would be easier if they had money of their own. Or she had no one to look after but herself. No duty. No responsibility.

As tempting as that thought was, Grace dismissed it immediately. She did have a duty and responsibility to a sister she loved very much, and she would never shirk them.

"Is that you, Miss Barton?" Mr. Elliot called from behind his door.

"Yes. I shall be just a minute."

Grace reached into her pocket for the key, then unlocked the door, pocketed the key, and entered, ready to tell Mr. Elliot about the sticking door.

Until she saw him standing in a casual pose beside the bed, dressed in his perfectly fitting trousers and with his white shirt open at his bronzed neck, his angular cheeks and chin clean shaven and damp, his arms crossed over his broad chest, and his mouth drawn into that breathtakingly charming grin.

He was obviously completely recovered. Indeed, he radiated a healthy vitality. And something else that she had never experienced before, but thought Mercy could probably name as a reason to forget every dictate of civilized society when it came to the relationship between men and women.

Her heart began to beat erratically, her body to grow unaccountably warm, her breathing shallow and rapid, and she felt the most incredible compulsion to run from the room before she did something wildly impulsive, like kiss him.

Disturbed by her primitive reaction, she looked at the floor and gathered her wits, until she felt able to regard him with a modicum of tranquillity.

If only her heart would settle down to its normal, natural rhythm!

"I take it the door sticks?" Mr. Elliot inquired calmly, one eyebrow rising eloquently as he finished buttoning his shirt. He tied his cravat with a few quick, economical movements, drawing her attention to the natural grace of his movements.

Grace nodded mutely, then, telling herself the interview below had to be the cause of her bizarre behavior, cleared her throat. "Yes, yes, it does," she answered. "I see you're feeling better."

"I have some bruises and my back is still a little sore. Nothing of any significance, I assure you," he answered. "I understand I owe my rescue to your efforts," he continued softly, his tone intimate and strangely thrilling.

So intimate and thrilling, Grace felt herself blushing. Yet even as Grace chided herself for being ridiculous, she thought it was probably patently impossible for any woman to remain calm in this man's presence, and she was a fool to attempt it. "I daresay your family will be anxious about you," she said, trying to sound perfectly matter-of-fact.

He hesitated a moment before replying. "I daresay."

"Your wife must be terribly worried."

Grace didn't know what had possessed her to mention a wife, other than the continuing sense of unreality that had come upon her when she had entered the bedroom.

"I am not fortunate enough to have a wife," he answered, and Grace tried to tell herself his personal life was none of her business. She never should have spoken of a wife, and she shouldn't feel so absurdly pleased to discover he was unmarried.

"I really must thank you for your kindness and generosity," he said softly. "Others might have left me on the road, supposing they had found me. This seems to be a singularly uninhabited corner of the nation."

"Oh, I'm sure anyone would have helped," Grace said quickly. "And we are not so isolated as you might imagine. I gather you took the wrong road."

"Apparently, although I cannot complain about that, or even the reprobates who robbed me, for their criminal act has allowed me to make the acquaintance of two such charming young ladies."

Grace Barton's expression remained remarkably inscrutable, and Elliot cursed himself for a dunderheaded fool. He had been far too fulsome in his praise to such a woman. She was no easily flattered miss, but a sensible, responsible female.

Despite her remarkable ability to hide her emotions, he had also realized the moment she had entered the room that something was wrong. He didn't think his supposition had anything to do with her surprise at his less than fully attired state, although he had forgotten how a proper young lady might react.

He wondered if the two women had had an argument—not something unexpected where siblings were involved, given his own experience—or perhaps he might find more of an explanation for her state in her recent time in the company of the odious Donald Franklin.

If she was upset because of him, which would argue that she had some grasp of the man's true and vile nature, he need have no concern for the Bartons' fate. They would require no warning from him, and he could go with no fear that he was leaving his benefactors in jeopardy.

But first, he would make certain that his assumption was a valid one.

"The local landlord keeps the roads in rather poor trim, I must say," he remarked. "I am not looking forward to walking to Grantham."

"Sir Donald does what he considers adequate," Miss Barton replied flatly.

"Your sister tells me you are having some trouble with him," he said, continuing to probe.

He detected a flash of ire in her usually calm brown eyes. "She shouldn't have mentioned him. It doesn't matter. It's nothing serious."

If Elliot was any judge of a woman's reactions—and he was—and although Grace Barton was definitely not an open book when it came to revealing her feelings, he thought he saw enough to surmise that she certainly did not like Franklin.

While that was a relief, he began to wonder how serious their financial troubles were.

He had known more than one case where a woman had gone against her inclinations because of money troubles.

"I'm sorry I was robbed, or I could have repaid you for your expenditures on my behalf."

"I wouldn't have taken it," she replied somewhat haughtily, and Elliot recognized the voice of stubborn pride.

"Well, it must be rather trying for you, looking after this place and your sister, too. The responsibility alone would send some people running."

She gave him a strange look. "Then some people are weak and unworthy of being entrusted with responsibility."

With difficulty, Elliot continued to meet her steadfast regard as that unfamiliar sense of shame invaded him again.

Then he reminded himself that she knew nothing about him, or what he had done, or why he had done it.

It was all very well for a country lass to spout talk of responsibility and strength; wait until she found herself connected to a young person who was clearly mad, and see how she dealt with responsibility then. She would probably fly to Europe, too, despite her fine words.

He was wrong. As he looked at her, he knew he

was wrong. Her moral strength was there in every aspect of her features, from her steadfast brown eyes that would not shrink from looking at things realistically, to her determined mouth, to her resolute chin. Grace Barton would never desert her duty.

Just as suddenly, he knew he was right to be ashamed in her presence, because he was a coward who had never accepted responsibility and who always fled his troubles, leaving them behind for his brother to correct.

Which was all the more reason he should go.

She cleared her throat again. "Mr. Elliot, I'm sorry, but I really must insist that you leave here today. It is highly improper for us to allow you to remain under our roof."

"I understand completely. I've trespassed on your goodness too much as it is."

"Since you seem so much improved, perhaps you would prefer to eat downstairs."

"I would be delighted."

She turned toward the door.

He couldn't bring himself to let her go so easily, despite the recrimination he felt in her presence, so he put his hand on her slender arm to make her halt.

Elliot Fitzwalter was not inexperienced when it came to women. He had touched many of them in far more intimate ways. How, then, to account for the thrill that went through him when his fingers wrapped around Grace Barton's forearm? Did it have something to do with the questioning look that appeared in her luminous brown eyes as she looked at him? Did she feel a similar thrill of pleasure?

"Mr. Elliot?" she queried in a whisper.

He scrutinized her face, and he knew what he saw there. He had seen it often enough in Adrian's face— an overwhelming desire to keep emotions in check.

What emotions? Desire? Anger? Pleasure? Frustration?

Or perhaps he was seeing characteristics that were not there. Not every older sibling was like Adrian, surely. It could be that there were no deep, troublesome emotions to be kept in check.

Yet he couldn't rid himself of a yearning to know if she liked him, at the very least.

He smiled his most winning smile, surprisingly determined to *make* her like him, if she did not already. "This Sir Donald, then—he is not a kind and generous man?" he asked in a very sympathetic tone, and one that would have worked marvels on many women of his past acquaintance.

Grace Barton was obviously not of their ilk. "There is no point discussing this matter," she said bluntly. "If you will come downstairs, we will gladly give you a meal before you go on your way."

It didn't matter anyway. He would eat, and then he would leave.

He followed Grace as she began to go down the stairs, and as he did so, he tried to ignore her graceful carriage and the tempting flesh at the back of her neck, which he wanted to kiss. No doubt she would slap him if he did, and unlike some, she would not be feigning her dismay. She was the very model of a dutiful, moral young woman, and the wonder of it was that he hadn't fled from her sooner.

"Grace!"

Mercy's agitated voice interrupted his thoughts and made Grace halt so abruptly he collided with her, nearly knocking her over. He reached out to steady her, and drew her back against himself.

The contact was astonishingly potent. This close together, all he was aware of was that Grace Barton was an attractive woman whose body was pressed provocatively against his.

He thought she swallowed hard, and the idea that she found their proximity unnerving pleased him immensely.

"What...what is it?" she called.

"It's the Hurleys!" Mercy answered. "They're coming up the lane this very moment!"

Grace half turned toward him, her face red with a blush, and her breasts rising and falling either in agitation or something rather more delightful to contemplate. "You must go back!" she said urgently.

He didn't respond at once, but took a moment to enjoy the responding excitement in his own body. "Upstairs?" he inquired softly.

"Yes, yes!" she answered. "Please! They mustn't see you. They are the most notorious gossips in Lincolnshire!"

"And you must not be found with an unknown man in the house. I quite understand."

"Yes! Now, please, hurry!"

The scenario would have been comic, if she hadn't been so truly alarmed.

He turned, but apparently he wasn't moving quickly enough for Grace Barton, because he felt her palms on his back, and she gave him a shove, which made him stumble on the stairs. His foot twisted.

"Damn it!" he exclaimed at the sudden pain.

"Precisely!" Grace cried. "They will be here all too soon!"

"Grace, they're in the yard! What are you doing?" Mercy exclaimed below.

"I'll be down in a moment! Wash your face and try to look calm," Grace called back.

Elliot glared at the eldest Barton as he straightened, not putting any weight on that foot, but she was oblivious to his injury.

"Please hurry, Mr. Elliot, and don't make any noise," she said, starting down the stairs again.

"If you're worried, you could always lock me in," he muttered under his breath.

She didn't hear him, but hurried on her way, pausing at the bottom to look back at him with a pleading expression in her lovely brown eyes.

"You had best go head off the worst gossips in Lincolnshire," he said with better grace.

"Yes, yes, I must," she said with a thankful smile before she disappeared around the corner.

Elliot bit back another curse as he tried his ankle again. Definitely sprained.

He certainly couldn't walk twenty feet, let alone twenty miles with such an injury. He would have to stay here at least one more night, no matter how trying that might be for Grace Barton.

After all, she had only herself to blame. There had been no need to push him.

Who were these Hurleys that they could panic

Grace Barton? Village gossips of the worse sort, obviously, and the type who barged in any time, without an invitation.

They would surely know the situation between the Bartons and their landlord, and perhaps, if he knew his gossips, the drive in Donald Franklin's carriage was the reason for this call. They would be curious about it, and what it portended, just as he had been.

If he really wanted to understand the Bartons' relationship with Franklin, this might be the perfect opportunity to learn the truth.

It would mean limping as far down the stairs as he dared, which wouldn't help his injury.

Grace Barton had gone to considerable effort to get him out of the rain and the mud; could he not limp down a few stairs to make absolutely certain that he need not warn them about Sir Donald?

As for transgression of eavesdropping...well, he was guilty of worse sins.

Chapter Eight

"Where is Mr. Elliot?" Mercy asked anxiously as Grace joined her near the front entrance.

Through the small window beside the door, Grace could see the Hurleys bustling up the lane, looking like startled ducks. Miss Myrtle's ample silhouette was broadened by a large basket she carried over one arm.

"He has returned to his room, where I sincerely hope he stays." Grace took a deep breath and told herself not to get so overwrought, a condition she was experiencing with more frequency, not surprising given the events of this day and Mr. Elliot's rather overwhelming presence.

"You go to the drawing room and sit on the sofa," she ordered briskly. "Get out your sewing. If they ask what was wrong at church, by all means stay with your tale of no breakfast."

Mercy gave her sister a slightly affronted look. "I know what I should say."

"Good. Now go," Grace whispered urgently.

Mercy obediently hurried off just as there was a

soft scratching at the door, as if a mouse were begging admittance, which was the Hurleys' usual method of announcing their presence.

"Good afternoon, Miss Barton," Myrtle Hurley simpered, her face wreathed with a pleasant smile as Grace opened the front door. "I do hope we're not disturbing you and your sister, but we were both very concerned—"

"Very concerned," Miss Ethel echoed behind her.

"About dear little Mercy and thought we should come right away—"

"Right away," quoth Miss Ethel.

"With some of our dandelion wine."

Miss Myrtle patted the basket, which looked as if it held enough dandelion wine to take care of the medicinal needs of a small army.

Grace wished there was some excuse she could give that would deny them entrance, but she could think of nothing that wouldn't increase their suspicions. It was obvious they were here to discover why Sir Donald had offered them a drive home from church that morning, and Grace knew, from long experience, that they wouldn't leave until they got what they considered to be a satisfactory answer. "Won't you please come in?"

"Oh, yes, thank you, Miss Barton," said Miss Myrtle, pushing past her into the house. "So kind of you to offer. It is *such* a walk from the village, but we simply couldn't rest until we knew how dear Mercy was."

"So kind," Miss Ethel murmured as she, too, went past Grace, her skirts forcing Grace against the wall.

"She was only temporarily—" Grace began, but by that time, the Hurleys had already entered the drawing room.

"Hello, my dear!" Miss Myrtle cried enthusiastically. "How are you, Miss Mercy? You gave us *such* a turn, I must say."

"Such a turn," Miss Ethel repeated, following her sister to the sofa, where the two of them sat like a matched pair of china dolls.

"You looked so very ghastly in church!" Miss Myrtle noted with a beaming smile.

"Very ghastly, indeed."

"I was a little indisposed. I am quite fine now," Mercy answered with more calm composure than Grace could have anticipated.

"I do think you are looking *much* better. Don't you agree, sister?" Miss Myrtle remarked.

"*Much* better," Miss Ethel agreed.

"Still, a little of our dandelion wine will soothe any ailment." Miss Myrtle again patted the basket she had set on the floor at her feet.

"Any ailment," Miss Ethel confirmed.

"Dear Adam claims it's the *best* medicine he's ever had, although he's so *rarely* ill, I don't suppose we could take his word for it," Miss Myrtle continued.

Miss Ethel nodded.

Grace realized it might have been better to have sent Mercy to "rest" upstairs, and not just because the Hurley twins gave every indication of preparing to remain for several minutes. When their nephew was mentioned, Mercy's face lightened as if she were beholding paradise, something even those less discerning than the Hurley sisters would have noted.

"Is he well?" Mercy asked eagerly.

The Hurleys' smiles broadened simultaneously. "Very well," Miss Myrtle replied. "It seems he is already a favorite in the wardroom, as we knew he must be."

They smiled very sweetly at Grace, but she felt their disapproval nonetheless.

"He is going to get another promotion," Miss Myrtle announced proudly. "Just as soon as some letter or other is despatched to the admiralty. I do hope they move a little more quickly than they are wont to do. Still, it should not take overlong."

Miss Ethel sighed softly and shook her head at the unconscionable delay while Mercy looked delighted.

If only she could remind her sister to be more circumspect!

"He is such a *favorite* of the admiral!" Miss Myrtle declared. "*And* the admiral's daughter! Oh dear me, such times they have! Balls and parties and fetes. It is wearing simply to read of them."

Grace darted a surreptitious glance at her sister, fearing some outward sign of agitation. To her surprise, Mercy registered very little change of expression.

Then she realized that the Hurleys had followed her gaze. Clearly Mercy was not the only one who needed to be more circumspect.

"Lieutenant Brown is sure to be an addition to any social gathering," Mercy observed quietly, and Grace was impressed with her calm tone.

She couldn't help wondering if she had managed to sound so calm in Mr. Elliot's presence, and rather doubted it.

"Have you any word as to his possible return?" Mercy inquired.

"None, I'm afraid. That is the drawback to his abilities," Miss Myrtle replied, smiling and sighing at the same time. "The admiral finds him *indispensable*."

"Indispensable," Miss Ether confirmed.

A swift and subtle glance at Mercy showed that her composure was crumbling at this dismaying news.

"Would you care for some tea?" Grace offered, determined to send Mercy from the room in a way that would not arouse any suspicions.

"Very much, my dear," Miss Myrtle said. "How kind of you to think of it."

Again they smiled very amiably at Grace, and she saw the censure they intended. No doubt they thought her offer rather late.

"It is such a *long* walk for us," Miss Myrtle noted virtuously.

"Mercy, would you please make it?" Grace asked.

"Of course. Excuse me, please," Mercy said, rising and leaving the room.

The Hurleys' brows furrowed ever so slightly, indicating very great criticism.

But Grace didn't care. It was more important to spare Mercy their unwelcome pronouncements, even though it meant she would be left alone with them.

Their onslaught was not long in coming.

"It was *most* kind of Sir Donald to provide you

with transportation," Miss Myrtle remarked with another genial smile. "So very *unexpected* of him."

"Unexpected," said Miss Ethel.

Grace wasn't surprised by her comment; nevertheless, it took considerable effort to hide her reaction. "It was indeed generous of him," she replied.

"*Such* a mark of regard," Miss Myrtle declared affably.

"*Such* regard," Miss Ethel likewise noted.

"He saw that Mercy was unwell," Grace explained.

"Unexpectedly perceptive of him, was it not?" Miss Myrtle observed. "I think there was more to it than *that*."

"More than that," Miss Ethel added with a decisive nod of her white-haired head.

"I must disagree," Grace said through clenched teeth, trying not to sound as frustrated with their genial inquisition as she was.

Then she decided to draw the one weapon in her arsenal that might cause them to change the subject.

"He was glad to offer his assistance to another gentleman's family," she remarked blandly, reminding them that she and Sir Donald could be classed as gentry. Although Sir Donald's claim was somewhat tenuous, it was still better than having parents who had been in trade, like the Hurleys.

"Yes, well, it was good he did, my dear," Miss Myrtle said, faltering slightly but recovering with amazing speed. "Do you recall those horrible men that were outside the tavern the other day?" she continued as eagerly as ever.

"Horrible!" Miss Ethel interjected, apparently not at all nonplussed by Grace's comment.

"They are still loitering about, and something *must* be done about them. Really, they are *quite* ill mannered and most *outlandishly* dressed—like something out of a *ragbag,* my dear!"

"Outlandish!"

"We asked the innkeeper who they might be, and he had no idea. As I said to my sister, *What* is Barton coming to?"

"Perhaps they were merely passing through," Grace said, deciding it was pointless to try to humiliate the Hurleys into keeping quiet.

"But they are *still there!*" Myrtle Hurley exclaimed. "They *claim* to be sheep breeders, but *I* don't believe them. Sir Donald *must* begin to show some *leadership* and not go galavanting off to London every chance he gets!"

"Galavanting!" Miss Ethel added in her most condemning tones, which meant she sounded like a slightly irate nanny.

"We fear we're going to be murdered in our beds!"

Miss Ethel, obviously too overwrought to speak, nodded zealously.

"Has anyone spoken to the constable about them?" Grace asked. "I'm sure Mr. Edwards—"

Miss Myrtle shook her head so rapidly her bonnet looked as if it were affected with palsy. "Of course not," she said, as if addressing a rather slow child, although still with a pleasant smile on her face. "He's too *busy* keeping an eye on that *wife* of his, although he never seems to see all he *should*."

Miss Ethel likewise smiled and nodded. "Never sees," she repeated.

Grace didn't believe the rumors about Mrs. Edwards any more than she believed that the Hurleys had arrived for any reason other than pure inquisitiveness. "What about Sir Donald, then? He is the justice of the peace, is he not?"

"That is just what *I* said, didn't I, sister?" Miss Myrtle answered excitedly.

Miss Ethel smiled and nodded.

"But *who* should speak to him?" Miss Myrtle asked innocently. "It must be someone whose *opinion* he *values*. Whom do *you* suggest, my dear?" Miss Myrtle inquired rather too pointedly.

"Perhaps Mr. Walters," Grace replied swiftly. "He owns the largest shop, and he wouldn't want his customers too frightened to come into the village. Or Mr. Reems. His tavern could get a bad reputation, so that travelers are afraid to stop there."

"Oh? We thought *you*—" Miss Myrtle began.

"Yes, you."

"Would have some influence with him."

"Me?" Grace exclaimed, doing her very best to sound absolutely stunned and surprised. "I do not think *I* could have much influence with him."

"Your modesty does you credit," Miss Myrtle declared in a dulcet tone that nonetheless implied she didn't believe a word of Grace's denial.

"It was for Mercy's sake he offered to drive us

home," Grace declared, trying not to sound defensive.

"Because she is *your* sister," Miss Myrtle countered with a benign countenance. "He is bound to be kind to the sister of the woman he hopes to marry."

"Yes, indeed!" Miss Ethel concurred softly.

Grace stared at them, appalled at what they had surmised, and angry, too. Her business was none of theirs! If ever she needed a reason to leave Barton, here was one—the obvious indication that no business was private!

As for their prying—it was very tempting to tell them that yes, she was going to be Sir Donald Franklin's wife, just to see their reaction. It would be even more interesting to watch their faces as she told them of the handsome young man currently residing in their upstairs bedroom. Not that she would dare, of course—

Suddenly Grace realized that Mercy had returned. She was standing on the threshold, the tea tray in her hands, and with a look of horror on her face.

"I knew it!" she cried, her voice strained, and her hands shaking. "I knew that was why you were so long in the cow shed! And why he told you all his plans for Franklin Hall when we were in the carriage."

The Hurleys' eyes grew nearly as large as their basket.

Grace had no more desire to discuss this matter in front of the Hurleys than she did to announce Mercy's condition. "We are not engaged," she answered firmly, marching toward Mercy and taking the tray from her trembling hands. "I was merely attempting to reason with him in the cow shed, about the raise in the rent. As for the plans for his house—why should he not discuss them in the carriage? You were there, too."

"Well, this comes as something of a *relief,* I must say," Miss Myrtle said. "I didn't want to believe that you could be so *mercenary,* Miss Barton, although that is often the way of the gentry."

"Mercenary gentry!" Miss Ethel affirmed, still smiling.

Grace regarded them with a feeling between anger and dismay. She never should have tried to embarrass them, and more than that, she didn't want to believe she could be so mercenary, either.

"Grace would never agree to marry that man!" Mercy cried passionately.

"No, of course not," Miss Myrtle agreed affably. "Then we can assume you were able to persuade him not to raise the rent when you discussed the matter with him? Alone? In the cow shed?"

"Alone," Miss Ethel repeated significantly.

Good heavens! Grace wanted to shout. *What do you think I did with him?* The very idea of being alone with him was repugnant.

Yet she had actually considered marriage to him as a means to save herself and her sister. She must have been mad, and she would never, ever agree to be his wife!

As if her own revulsion was not enough, there was the evidence of how the Hurleys and others in the village would regard the marriage—as well they should!

"He will not reconsider the rent," Grace told them, "but we shall manage, nonetheless."

"Of *course* you will, my dear," Miss Myrtle said, her words of comfort bringing none.

"He wants to double the amount," Mercy announced woefully.

Grace tried to catch Mercy's eye. Their financial predicament was not something she wanted common knowledge, especially given Mercy's other predicament.

She did not succeed.

"I don't know what we're going to do," Mercy said pitiably.

"This is truly a *terrible* situation," Miss Myrtle replied.

"You mustn't think of leaving Barton," Miss Ethel said, her complete sentence catching Grace as off guard as her apparent sincerity.

"Mercy, dear, you *must* come and stay with *us,*" Miss Myrtle declared.

"Yes, indeed!" Miss Ethel confirmed. "Stay with us."

"Thank you for your generous offer," Mercy gasped, obviously as taken aback as Grace by this near-command. "However, that is quite impossible."

"We could use the companionship of such a *fine* young woman," Miss Myrtle declared.

"I cannot go anywhere without my sister," Mercy said firmly. "Thank you all the same."

If it were not for Mercy's condition, Grace might

have counseled Mercy to accept their offer. The sisters liked her, they had plenty of servants, they set a good table, and she would not lack for anything.

Indeed, it was very easy to picture the sisters shopping for her. They would undoubtedly enjoy dressing Mercy up and showing her off as if she were some kind of doll, and patronizing her into the bargain.

As Sir Donald would display and patronize his wife.

"I'm sure Grace will manage, even if this talk of a marriage to Sir Donald proves to be merely a *rumor*," Miss Myrtle said. "Someone will offer her room and board."

As if she were an old mare ready to be put out to pasture! Grace thought angrily as she rose. "If you will pardon us, I have many things to do about the house today."

"On the Sabbath, my dear?" Miss Myrtle inquired with a friendly smile. "Surely not."

"Surely not," Miss Ethel echoed, a small furrow appearing between her snow-white brows while she continued to smile.

"Regrettably, I do," Grace replied firmly.

Mercy also stood and picked up the tray. "It was so very sweet of you both to come," she said, dipping a respectful curtsey.

She exited the room, and finally the Hurleys seemed to grasp that they had no alternative but to leave.

"You *must* let us know if we can be of any assistance to you," Miss Myrtle said, standing, and Miss

Ethel followed suit. "There is a valise we no longer require."

"Thank you very much, but I don't think we'll need it," Grace said frostily.

"Well, we had best be on our way. Come, sister," Miss Myrtle said. "We wouldn't want to be out at dusk, not with those men in the vicinity." Both the sisters turned baleful gazes onto Grace. "You had best be careful, too, my dear."

"I shall," Grace said, wondering what they were really warning her against, and barely resisting the urge to shoo them toward the door.

Thankfully they needed no further urging, and in another moment, they were blessedly gone.

When the Hurleys were halfway down the lane, Myrtle glanced at her sister. "It's true," she noted calmly. "She is going to marry him."

"Absolutely," Ethel agreed firmly.

"When?" Myrtle mused.

"Very soon, I should think," Ethel replied. "He will not want to wait."

"I believe you are right, sister."

"Of course I am," Miss Ethel said smugly.

Mercy joined Grace as she watched the two women bustle down the lane.

"You are certain you want to be married into their family?" Grace asked dubiously. "They try my patience to the utmost."

"They mean well," Mercy replied.

Had Grace needed any confirmation that Mercy

was too innocent of the ways of the world, this would have provided it. The Hurleys were inquisitive and nosy, and they meant only to satisfy their own curiosity.

"Besides, I am most certainly going to marry Adam, so there is little choice," she finished.

Grace gave her sister a wary glance. "You didn't believe all that about the admiral's daughter?"

Mercy shook her head. "Oh, I can believe any admiral's daughter—indeed, any woman—would *want* to marry him, but Adam's heart belongs to me." Then she faced Grace, a very determined expression on her pretty face. "You must promise me that you won't marry Sir Donald."

"Mercy, I have not accepted him."

"Promise me you never will!"

"Forgive me for interrupting," Mr. Elliot drawled from the stairs, "but would I be wrong in assuming that the most notorious gossips in Lincolnshire have finally taken their leave?"

Chapter Nine

"Oh, Mr. Elliot!" Grace and Mercy Barton cried together, as they simultaneously turned to stare at him.

He scrutinized them carefully. They were both flustered and, he surmised, upset—and not just with the shock of his appearance. Shameful eavesdropper that he was, he now knew for certain they were beset with troubles: the raise in the rent, the absent Lieutenant Brown who had obviously captured Mercy Barton's fancy, the men who might be Boffin and his gang lingering in the village—although he tried to dismiss that worry—and last but not least, Donald Franklin and Grace's relationship with him.

Franklin was definitely up to no good, and Grace was his object. Elliot was as sure of that as he had ever been about anything.

"I'll...I'll make some supper," Mercy said softly, glancing up at him shyly. "You must be very hungry." She hurried off toward the kitchen.

"I'm sorry to have kept you waiting all this time," Grace Barton said, moving to the bottom of the stairs and placing her slender hand on the banister. "We'll give you something to eat and then—"

"And then I should go," Elliot replied, without making a move, for his ankle hurt like the devil. "I understand, and I could certainly do justice to whatever your sister is cooking."

"You must understand why I couldn't allow you downstairs," she said, not meeting his gaze.

"Absolutely."

"And why you have to leave."

"Of course."

"But you can come down now," she said softly. "The Hurleys won't return."

"What about your other visitor?"

"He should not, either."

"Good," he replied, telling himself it would be better not to get too involved in this family's troubles.

Better for whom? his conscience demanded as he started to limp down the stairs.

"What's the matter with your foot?" Grace asked.

"As you can see, and as much as I would dearly love to accommodate your request, I regret that I have met with an accident that makes it impossible for me to venture very far today," he remarked sincerely.

"I...I don't understand," she said helplessly.

"Unfortunately, in my zeal to escape the notorious gossips, I have sprained my ankle rather badly."

"I beg your pardon?"

He continued slowly toward her. "When a man is pushed on a staircase and as a result, stumbles, an injury such as this is not to be unexpected."

"Oh. I'm sorry. I...it was necessary that they not see you."

She came to his aid, putting her shoulder beneath his and her arm around his waist, and he thought the very delightful sensations her actions engendered gave some compensation for his injury. "I understand. Naturally one wouldn't want to give the harpies more stories to spread, eh?"

"They are not harpies," Grace murmured, lowering her eyelids demurely so that her lashes fanned her satiny cheeks.

It was a charming gesture, all the more so because of its unexpectedness and her proximity.

"Gossips, then," he muttered absently, his mind on a far more interesting subject than gossips.

He wanted to kiss her. On her full and luscious lips, on her eyelids, on the curve of her cheek, on the lobe of her shapely ear, on the tip of her fine nose—anywhere and everywhere. "Well, I am not offended."

Grace raised blazing eyes to him and stepped away so quickly, he nearly stumbled on the last step. "How happy I am that you are not offended when it is *our* reputation that would be damaged!" she declared.

Instinctively he reached out and took her hand. "Please, I misspoke," he said frankly, surprised by her outburst. Those two old ladies must have upset her more than he knew. "I meant to imply that you could lock me in the darkest dungeon, and I would not complain. After all, you saved my life the other day."

"Oh." She regarded him warily, then sighed softly and relaxed slightly. "We don't have a dungeon."

He grinned, feeling as if he had won a major battle when she did not withdraw her hand from his. "I know. It is a sanctuary—even if you did feel it necessary to lock me up."

Grace Barton flushed, and took a step back as he took one forward, off the stairs. "I thought it best," she explained.

"It was very wise of you. You don't know me, so I cannot expect you to trust me."

"If I thought you completely untrustworthy," she said, regarding him steadily, "I wouldn't have allowed you in the house."

Elliot swallowed hard, trying to keep a rein on his emotions and to command himself to be in control of this charged situation. But never before had any person's trust meant so much to him.

This was too ridiculous, really. She shouldn't be having this kind of powerful effect on him. Why, she had locked him in a room and made him sprain his ankle. She had forced him into hiding like a criminal and dragged him through the mud. She dominated her sister as Adrian had tried to dominate him.

She also had the loveliest eyes in the world, and the most tempting lips. She had gone to considerable effort to rescue him from the rain. She was bravely doing her best to take care of her sister.

What had he ever done to deserve the trust she was placing in him?

Nothing.

He was not worthy so much as to touch the hem of her gown, and if he was an honorable man, he would warn her about Franklin and get away from her.

Yet even as he thought this, another emotion blossomed in his heart, and that was hope.

Hope that he could change. That she could show him how to lead an honorable life.

Elliot actually took a step back, overwhelmed by the force of that emotion. Then he lost his balance, only to feel Grace's strong grip as she quickly reached out and steadied him.

"Are you absolutely certain that you cannot walk?" she asked doubtfully.

He was tempted to tell her he could, regardless of his very real agony, so that he would appear as intrepid as she. Before he could frame a reply, however, Mercy appeared in the door leading to the kitchen.

"Supper is ready," she announced.

She smiled with a charming innocence that was not nearly as fascinating as the intensity of her sister's steadfast gaze, and Elliot marveled that he had ever wanted any other woman, for anything.

"Mr. Elliot has hurt his foot," Grace answered, facing Mercy. "He thinks he is unable to go into the village tonight."

Mercy's eyes widened with alarm as she looked at Mr. Elliot. Grace's gaze followed her sister's, to see him grinning his lopsided grin at her.

Suddenly Grace felt a very curious sensation, one she had never experienced before and so was not sure what name to ascribe to it.

"I'm afraid I may have to impose upon you yet more," he said quietly, and he was most certainly not talking to Grace. His soft, tender words were addressed to Mercy alone. "If your sister will allow it."

"Whatever Grace decides," Mercy murmured.

Why did Mercy have to make it sound as if Grace were being unreasonable? Mercy had to understand that they couldn't continue to harbor a young male stranger, no matter how sore his ankle, or handsome his face. He was no sick puppy in need of tender care.

He must have family who were anxious about him, too, even if he wasn't married.

He wasn't married.

If Mercy was safely married, Grace could tell Sir Donald to go to the devil.

Now here was Mr. Elliot, whom she had found most providentially by the side of the road, almost like the answer to a prayer.

And perhaps a well-to-do answer to a prayer, if his clothes were anything to go by.

Grace's gaze darted between the two of them as they smiled at each other. Mercy obviously liked him, for she was certainly loath to see him go.

Mr. Elliot liked Mercy. Why should he not, for Mercy was a good, sweet, gentle young woman, and pretty, too.

But then Grace realized what she felt.

Jealousy. She was jealous of Mercy, because of the way Mr. Elliot had looked at her and spoken so tenderly to her.

She must be losing her mind. All their troubles must have temporarily addled her brain. How else to account for the unaccountable?

Yet wouldn't it be wonderful to know that Mercy

was safely married, and not to a naval officer, who might take her very far away?

While it appeared that Mercy still harbored an attachment to the dashing, departed Lieutenant Brown, Mr. Elliot was more handsome than Lieutenant Brown, his manner decidedly more polished—and he was *here*. Mercy had apparently fallen in love with Lieutenant Brown over the space of a fortnight; such a rapid development of emotional attachment might occur again, given Mercy's romantic disposition.

But to manipulate her sister so callously, and Mr. Elliot, too! It was one thing to offer herself to save her family from scandal and poverty; it was another to try to make them the agents of defense.

Besides, as her own condition was currently demonstrating, emotions could be wildly unpredictable. Why, *she* was just as likely to fall in love with Mr. Elliot as Mercy—

Which was the most foolish notion she had ever entertained in her life!

She gave Mr. Elliot a sidelong glance. After all, what did they know of him, except for his manners and his clothing and the little he had told them?

Oh, of all the ridiculous ideas her mind had ever conjured up, this was surely the most preposterous. Or selfish, born of a desire to avoid marrying Sir Donald.

She realized Mercy was speaking. "Grace," she said softly, "you can see he cannot walk. He cannot leave today!"

Grace cleared her throat, trying to think and to buy herself a few more moments to consider what to do.

First and foremost, it was highly improper for two young ladies to harbor an unmarried man. If anybody found out, their reputations would be destroyed. Add to that the scandal that would ensue if Mercy's condition became common knowledge. Why, people might think Mercy *promiscuous,* and perhaps Grace, too, for seeming to condone her sister's immoral activities.

She would have no chance of finding employment without moving very far away, if then.

Of course, a scandal would also mean that Sir Donald would not want to marry her anymore—tempting thought, but hardly the way out of that predicament.

Mr. Elliot's ankle *was* troubling him, and she was to blame for it, shoving him in that most unladylike fashion. It would be a pity if she had gone to all that trouble to help him, only to have him hurt more badly because she insisted he go when he was not able.

Perhaps it would be possible to keep Mr. Elliot's presence a secret. No one was likely to visit them for the rest of the day, and if by chance someone did, they certainly wouldn't come upstairs.

One more day, and she could find out more about him, although for what purpose was subject to debate.

"Grace?" Mercy repeated softly, looking at her with her large, pleading gray eyes.

"I regret causing any further inconvenience, but could I possibly trouble you to continue our discussion elsewhere? I am not sure how long I can remain in this position."

Grace realized that Mr. Elliot's hand was gripping the banister tightly as he held his foot slightly off the step. "Oh, of course, yes. Let us go to the kitchen. Mercy, perhaps you could assist Mr. Elliot."

Grace watched Mercy take her place at Mr. Elliot's side and the pair made their way to the kitchen.

Then Grace decided that if Mr. Elliot showed the least sign of falling in love with Mercy, no matter what danger of scandal there might be, he would not be leaving that night, and perhaps not for several days.

The important thing was to insure Mercy's happiness and security.

Not hers.

The Duke of Barroughby stood in his study and pulled out the letter to read yet again, although he knew the contents by heart.

With a muttered curse and a heavy sigh, he crumpled it in his long, strong fingers. He was about to toss it in the grate when his wife entered, as always bringing with her a sense of calm peace that soothed whatever troubles plagued him.

Tonight, it was an old trouble.

"How is the little viscount?" he asked with a smile, deciding to ignore the letter's information.

"Your stubborn little son is finally asleep," Hester said as he turned away and flicked the paper into the hearth. He watched as it caught fire and burned.

"What's the matter?" his wife asked, coming up behind him and putting her arms about his waist. She laid her cheek against his broad back.

"Nothing of importance."

"You do not fool me, Adrian," she reminded him. "I know something is wrong."

He turned around in her arms and slipped his own about her waist, so that he was embracing her gently. "I should know better than to try to hide anything from you, my angel," he said gently. "Elliot is in England."

Hester drew back, her eyes wide as her steadfast gaze searched his face. "In England?"

"Perhaps. Maybe." Adrian stepped out of her loving arms and ran a hand through his dark hair anxiously. "That letter was from a shipping agent in Yarmouth. He thought he recognized Elliot getting off a ship from Montreal."

"Montreal? He's been in Canada?"

"That would explain why we couldn't find him in England."

"Why would he come back? Why now?"

Adrian shrugged, then gestured for her to sit. When she did, he joined her on the worn brocade sofa, the same sofa Elliot had so often draped himself upon when Adrian tried to have a serious discussion with his younger brother. He might just as well have tried to talk sense to the sofa.

"How did he look?" Hester asked, resting her hand on her slightly rounded stomach. "Was he well?"

"The agent's not even certain it *was* Elliot. He only says the man resembled the description we gave all the shipping offices before."

"It's been so long—he might have changed."

Adrian gave her a sardonic grin. "If I get a letter

requesting money, I'll have all the confirmation I need that Elliot has returned.''

Hester didn't smile. ''I wonder how he's managed all this time.''

''Well enough, I daresay. Women were always keen to assist him, in any way possible.''

''What are you going to do? Will you tell the duchess?''

With his elbows on his knees, Adrian ran both his hands through his hair. ''I don't know. If it *is* Elliot, and he has come back, maybe I should just let him go his own way.'' He glanced at his wife. ''That's what you thought I should do once upon a time.''

''I wanted you to make him accountable for his own deeds,'' she replied softly. ''I didn't mean for you to disown him entirely.''

Her husband smiled ruefully and lifted her hand to press a kiss to the back of it. ''I know, my own good conscience. I will send a man to Yarmouth to see what more we can find out about this potential Elliot.'' He frowned slightly. ''I don't think we should tell the duchess. I wouldn't want to raise her hopes.''

''Her hopes are always high,'' Hester said, stroking his muscular arm. ''As are mine, that we will find him someday.''

''Mine, too,'' Adrian said, his loving gaze upon his pregnant wife, the woman Elliot had wanted to marry, and who had chosen *him* instead. ''Mine, too.''

His expression a disgruntled frown, Jack Wickham stirred the waning flames of the fire he had built at the entrance to the cave. It wasn't even a proper cave, but more a space hollowed out at the base of a ridge.

The only thing his efforts to revive the fire achieved was to increase the smoke blowing into his face, for the wood was as damp as the ground. Skurch, also crouched beside the fire, moved farther away.

"Sit still!" Wickham ordered the younger man.

"I'm only tryin' to keep out o' the smoke," Skurch whined.

"Thinks we're bloody Robin Hood and his bloody Merry Men," Wickham muttered. He gestured toward the trees with his stick. "Hangin' about in a wood! Bah! I tells you, Skurch, this is barmy. All this talk about a lord in hidin'—well, it's just cackle, if you ask me."

"Boffin knows what he's about," Skurch said defensively.

Wickham snorted with disgust. "You think so only 'cause he's got you watchin' them women. Seen anything interestin'?" he finished sarcastically.

Skurch pulled his ragged coat a little tighter. "Not yet."

"Nor will ya! If'n this Lord Elliot *was* here, he's done a bunk and fooled us good. I tell ya, I'm sick o' freezin' meself on Boffin's say-so."

"Is that a fact?" Boffin demanded, appearing like a genie beside the cave. "Why don't you cut and run then?"

Wickham scowled as Boffin and Treeg also squatted by the remains of the fire. "I oughter."

"Go ahead," Boffin jeered. "I ain't stoppin' ya."

"I will, then." Wickham rose slowly.

Skurch nervously got to his feet. "Maybe we better think about this, Bob. I ain't seen hide nor hair of any gents 'round that place."

"You wanta clear off, too? Go ahead, the pair of ya. He's here, though. I feel it in me bones."

"Hear that?" Treeg said to Wickham.

"Yeah, and I feel the rheumatism in me bones from sleeping in this here cave like I'm some kind of badger. I'm clearin' out, and good riddance!"

With purposeful movements, Wickham grabbed his bundle of belongings, most of them stolen, and began to march away.

Before he had gone three paces, Boffin swiftly drew a knife from his boot and threw it.

Wickham's arms flew out as if he were beholding glory and he stumbled, falling to the ground. He tried to feel for the knife protruding from his back, but it was no use. He fell facedown in the dirt.

And when Jack Wickham breathed his last, the only benediction he had came from Boffin.

"Anybody else thinkin' o' desertin' me?"

Chapter Ten

As Elliot sat in the Bartons' drawing room two evenings later, he tried once again to think of some way to broach the subject of Donald Franklin. It had been his intention to do so ever since Grace Barton had allowed him to stay, provided he agreed to abide by a form of house arrest, which meant never sticking so much as the tip of his nose outside.

He was still determined to warn them about Donald Franklin, although he was unsure as to the exact nature of Grace Barton's feelings for the man. Nevertheless, he feared that she might indeed marry the villain if it meant keeping her sister in comfort.

During his sojourn in their household, he had seen the many subtle ways Grace sacrificed her own comfort for Mercy's sake, and enough to surmise that she routinely thought of Mercy's needs before her own. Mercy always got the choicest selection of food, the softest rolls, the freshest milk. Mercy had worn a different, fashionable dress every day of his residence; Grace seemingly had but one other than the gown he had helped ruin. Grace was always the first person

awake in the morning and the last one to bed at night.
She did the heaviest work, too, as if she were nothing
more than Mercy's servant.

Grace didn't seem to mind being Mercy's lackey;
however, during the course of his stay he *thought* he
detected an increasing tension between them that had
not been present the day he had arrived. That could,
of course, be attributed to his continuing presence in
their house.

Whatever was between the two young women,
Grace never complained or spoke impatiently, or indeed indicated any displeasure at all toward her sibling, not even by so much as a look. It was as if she
thought this was the way things *ought* to be.

As for Mercy, he was beginning to consider her an
ungrateful, selfish creature—rather like himself, if
truth be told—for she seemed to accept all Grace's
efforts as no more than her due. Never had he ever
considered Adrian's assistance as anything but right
and proper, either, and only now, as he watched the
interplay between the Barton sisters, was he starting
to realize just how ungrateful and selfish he had been.

How would Grace react to an offer of marriage if
it ended her drudgery? Would she not be tempted to
accept, as he had been tempted to lead a shameful life
to escape Adrian's overbearing custody?

The continuing trouble was, how could he warn her
against Franklin without admitting how he came by
his intimate knowledge of Franklin's decadence?

That was what he should be thinking about, he reminded himself, not uselessly trying to make sense of
his own tumultuous feelings. He couldn't quite decide

if what he felt for Grace Barton was admiration, respect, the beginnings of love—or all of that, and even more.

He had had plenty of spare time to ponder those feelings, with no answers.

All he could be certain of was that he had grown progressively more reluctant to leave as he had seen and learned more of the reticent Miss Grace Barton.

He glanced at Mercy, who was bending over her sewing in the chair nearest the hearth. Grace sat at a small desk close to the window, laboring over bills and household accounts by the light of a lamp. The glow from it surrounded her head like a halo, and made her hair appear a coronet. She did indeed look like an angel. An angel of hope.

Not for him, perhaps. Not after the life he had led. The women, the gambling, the drinking, the lies. The way he had antagonized his family.

His family. He could not recall ever sitting in such comfortable domesticity at Barroughby Hall, not even in his childhood. Always, there had been the discomfort of knowing that Adrian resented him for taking his father's attention, and that Adrian despised the mother Elliot loved, simply because she was not Adrian's mother, who lay dead in the churchyard.

As for his own mother—her presence had not necessarily been one to demonstrate happy maternal joy. She was as vain and spoiled as he had ever been, and one of the first memories he had was of her criticism when he had gotten dirty playing with some puppies. He had walked into the hall just as a party of fashionable guests had arrived.

"How could you!" she had cried, as if his state were a personal affront or an insult of the highest magnitude.

Mercy set down her sewing and stood up with a weary sigh. "I believe it's time I went to bed," she said, and Elliot realized she did look very tired, although she had done nothing more strenuous than peel potatoes today. "Good night, Mr. Elliot. Good night, Grace."

"Good night, Mercy. I shall be up shortly." As Mercy went out, Grace scrutinized her sister as if she were a doctor examining a patient. She reminded him of the surgeon at Barroughby, John Mapleton, who always looked at Elliot as if expecting to see boils or cankers or some other skin eruption, no doubt hoping to see an outward and visible sign of an inward and spiritual corruption.

Elliot made no move to leave, although he usually retired when Mercy did. He knew his own weaknesses well enough to realize that he might be tempted to try to seduce Grace if they were alone, and because of his respect and gratitude, he was determined not to do anything that might give her cause to regret his presence.

But he must caution her against Donald Franklin, so tonight he would try to find the appropriate words that would enable him to do so without forfeiting her good opinion.

Grace turned her attention to him, and he wondered if she was going to ask him to leave. Naturally, and most frustratingly, her expression told him nothing.

"Does your ankle hurt very much?" she asked matter-of-factly.

"It's getting better," he replied. "I daresay I'll be able to trudge into Barton soon."

She sighed, and he couldn't tell if it was with relief, or not.

"Good," she said flatly before returning her attention to the papers before her, giving him an answer he had not been anxious to hear.

He knew, of course, that his presence in their house was socially unacceptable; nevertheless, her lack of objection to his departure was rather depressing. He told himself it was simply that he wasn't used to such a reaction from any young woman.

He cleared his throat, ready to ask how well she knew Donald Franklin. Instead, he said, "Who is Lieutenant Brown?"

She swiveled to look at him. "He is the nephew of the Hurleys. He visited here a short time ago."

"And the Hurleys are?

"You would call them the harpies," she replied without so much as a hint of a levity.

"Oh, the most notorious gossips in Lincolnshire," he said. "Is the nephew anything like the aunts?"

Her lips moved in what might have been the start of a smile, but only for an instant, and her eyes remained annoyingly inexpressive. "No, he is not. He is a very charming, handsome young naval officer."

There was a certain tone to her voice that made him say, "Am I to understand that you do not approve of charming, handsome, young naval officers?"

Or lords, either, he wondered with a surprisingly personal curiosity.

"My opinion is of no consequence," she replied.

Not to Lieutenant Brown, perhaps, but it certainly was to him. "You do not approve of Lieutenant Brown, then," he observed cautiously.

"It is not for me to approve of him or not," she said. "Mercy likes him, not I."

For reasons that didn't bear close examination, Elliot was delighted to hear that. "Let me guess," he said lightly. "He is an irresponsible sailor who you fear has a woman in every port, and your lovely, innocent sister has fallen under his spell."

"I hope not!" she replied with unexpected fervor, and he realized, with some shock, that he had distressed her.

Well, well, well, perhaps here is a reason for the strain in the household. Mercy has fallen in love with a man of whom Grace does not approve.

And Mercy was so lacking in subterfuge, that must be the talk of the town. No wonder Grace sought to avoid the notorious gossips.

He almost chuckled. Such anguish over such a small problem! Why, compared to what he had done—

Any temptation to laugh died. If Grace feared censure over her sister's innocent love life, what would she think of the stories that could be told about *him?* She would never want to associate with a man of his reputation, let alone...

What? There wasn't going to be any future between

them, once he managed to apprise her of Franklin's true nature.

He realized Grace was looking at him and, for once, there was an obvious expression in her eyes. Unfortunately, it was one of wary suspicion. "How did you hear about Lieutenant Brown?"

He gave her his very best contrite look. "I tried to hobble away like a good little boy when the notorious gossips arrived. Regrettably, my ankle hurt too much. I was forced to remain near the stairs." He smiled mournfully. "I'm sorry I was naughty, but I didn't have much choice."

She regarded him impassively. "Oh."

Good heavens, was this woman *completely* immune to him?

Maybe it was better if she was. "They can have little enough to criticize about *you*," he remarked.

To his surprise, Grace blushed.

Likely she was unused to compliments.

"It must be something about the English weather that engenders that particular type of elderly spinster," he continued.

"I do not believe their 'particular type,' as you call it, is unique to our country," Grace remarked, whatever embarrassment she had felt obviously gone. Still, there was a certain rancor in her tone.

"You do not sound at all fond of them," he observed.

"They do not like me," she confessed with that unexpected ruefulness that sometimes crept into her voice and was all the more charming for its infrequency.

"I find that hard to believe," he said truthfully.

She shrugged her slender shoulders with a sensuously graceful gesture that instantly reminded him of why he had avoided being alone with her before. If his ankle didn't make any sudden movement painful, he would have bounded from his chair and kissed her.

He was considering risking the pain and possible consequences when she continued. "I fear I am too dull for their liking."

"Dull?" he demanded incredulously.

She flushed, the color slowly blooming on her satiny cheeks. "I am afraid they think me a cold, unfeeling creature, decidedly lacking in emotion."

"Then they are *fools!*" he replied decisively, and he did get to his feet.

He took two steps toward her before that warily suspicious look returned to her eyes, and he halted. "You are wise to keep them at a distance, I daresay," he said, thinking any remark better than a tense silence.

"I believe their lively interest in their neighbors comes from too much time and too little to occupy it," she said as he limped toward the mantel. "And surely this sort of leisure activity is not confined to England."

"I must admit that you are right," Elliot replied as he leaned against the cold stone surrounding the hearth. "I have traveled a great deal, and I fear I've seen notorious gossips in many places."

Her eyes flared with interest, and now it didn't seem to matter that he was standing closer to her. "You have?"

"Yes."

"Where?"

"Europe, for the most part," he answered, sensing with a pleasurable thrill that much of Grace Barton's customary reticence was disappearing. "Canada recently."

"Canada? That must have been exciting." Her eyes glowed as she asked him, excitement on every feature.

There was another type of excitement he would have given everything to see at that moment. However, he wasn't about to risk destroying the intimacy he had established, so he stayed where he was. "If one enjoys rustic conditions, freezing cold, unbearably humid heat, mosquitoes and a distinct lack of civilized company."

She frowned with disappointment.

"Europe, on the other hand," he continued, "is full of marvels."

How easily he could imagine showing Grace the beauties and antiquities of Europe's great cities. Paris. Berlin. Vienna. Rome.

He would show her more: the delights of the small villages of France, the chalets of the Alps, the castles along the Rhine, the sunny Italian countryside.

"To be so free to go where you will," she whispered, gazing at him with yearning in her soft brown eyes.

He took a step toward her, ready to tell her he would take her there, and anywhere else her heart desired.

She looked away from him. "Do you have business interests abroad?" she inquired coolly.

Disappointment, dismay and regret washed over him. If only they had met under other circumstances. If only he had not led such a dissolute life, for there were other parts of Europe he had seen, other parts that now he wished he had never known existed.

"Mr. Elliot?" she prompted.

"Yes, yes," he lied quickly. "I had family business there."

"They must be getting worried about you," she remarked.

"Who?"

Her eyes narrowed ever so slightly. "Your family. Would you like me to write to them for you?"

"I am quite able to write," he replied, thinking there would be no harm in writing a bogus letter and purposefully misdirecting it. After all, he had perpetrated worse frauds on other young ladies. "They will not be anxious about me yet. The day of my return was always somewhat vague."

That, at least, was no lie.

"I will write the letter," he continued, "and you may address it, so that the notorious gossips will never suspect."

She smiled, more than ample reward for his subterfuge, and nodded her agreement. "Very well."

"Once again, I must thank you for your kindness," he said, his tone carefully formal.

She rose slowly. "Until the morning, then, Mr. Elliot," she said quietly before she moved gracefully toward the door.

He had a sudden vision of Grace Barton in his large, canopied bed at Barroughby Hall, with her hair spread out on the white satin pillow, her body naked beneath the sheets as she waited for him.

"I trust you won't require any assistance," she remarked, glancing back at him over her shoulder, her inscrutable brown eyes regarding him steadily.

"Thank you, no. I can manage the stairs."

"Good night, Mr. Elliot."

"Good night, Miss Barton."

He didn't watch her leave. He didn't follow her to the stairs and upward. Instead, he sat and sighed while staring unseeing at the empty grate, feeling as if he had been holding his breath for the past several minutes.

What was the matter with him? Why was it so difficult for him to be alone with her? He had been alone with plenty of women, but none who made him feel so ashamed of his past. None who made him wish with all his heart that he had been a better man.

None who made him wonder if he could change his ways, and be worthy of her one day.

Oh, such speculation was rank foolishness. He was what he was, and she was only a simple country lass who had no notion of the ways of the aristocracy. He was no worse than many another he could name, and certainly he was far better than Donald Franklin.

Why couldn't he simply tell her what he knew and be done with it? It wasn't as if he should protect her, as Adrian had tried to protect him. He knew what a thankless task that would be.

Elliot shook his head, as if by doing so he could

rid it of unwanted and unnecessary comparisons. He had to go, and that was all there was to it.

After all, there would always be other women.

Grace waited anxiously in her room until she heard Mr. Elliot make his slow progress up the stairs and into his room. She heard the door close and the latch fall into place, then glanced nervously at Mercy, who was thankfully asleep.

What had just happened downstairs?

What had been happening ever since she had found Mr. Elliot beside the road?

It was as if her life had been a placid stream before, and was now a series of turbulent rapids, with the news of the raise in the rent, finding Mr. Elliot, Sir Donald's proposal, and being told of Mercy's predicament.

More recently, she also felt as if she were in a whirlpool of emotions, her own spinning out of control. All because of Mr. Elliot.

Why? Because he was handsome and charming? She had met handsome and charming young men before, specifically in the person of Lieutenant Brown, and those qualities held little appeal for her, coupled as they so often were with vanity, arrogance and overweening pride.

Not so with Mr. Elliot. It was as if he were completely unaware of his personal attributes, and his charm as natural to him as breathing.

Was it because he might be the answer to one dilemma, if he could fall in love with Mercy? Perhaps—although now, alone with her thoughts, she allowed herself to acknowledge that if Mr. Elliot excited her, it was because he seemed to like *her* better. He didn't appear to find her customary reticence troubling, nor did he feel the need to exert himself to get a reaction from her, as some men did, with often ridiculous results.

It was as if he liked her simply as she was, added to the thrilling notion that he seemed to prefer her company to Mercy's.

This in itself was unusual, for once men discovered that Grace was somewhat unresponsive to their overtures, they generally abandoned her for Mercy's company, to Grace's relief.

Of course, what Mr. Elliot thought of her wasn't important. It couldn't be important, not when so many other unsettling troubles perplexed her.

Tonight, when he had remained after Mercy had retired, Grace had thought to use the opportunity to try to find out something about their unexpected guest, because no matter what she *thought* she felt, she couldn't quite rid herself of the idea that a marriage between Mercy and Mr. Elliot would go a long way toward helping their situation.

Instead, she had found herself revealing far more of her thoughts and feelings to him—and he a near stranger—than she ever had to another soul. Why, she had told him things that even Mercy didn't know, about her dislike of the Hurleys and her poor opinion of Lieutenant Brown.

What was the point of lying to herself? she demanded silently. She *wanted* him to understand her. She *wanted* him to like her.

More than that, she wanted him to love her. In every way it was possible for a man to love a woman.

Although she had never experienced such extreme emotions before, she recognized her own lustful desire. Every time he spoke, every look he gave her, every moment she was with him, she found herself imagining what it would be like to be in his arms. In his bed.

Now Grace could understand how Mercy could have acted so immorally. If she had felt as Grace did in Mr. Elliot's company, it was not so surprising that she might act upon those feelings.

And perhaps it was no wonder then that Mercy seemed somewhat immune to Mr. Elliot's charms. Grace could well believe that after a night in Mr. Elliot's arms, she would never want another man for her husband. No doubt Mercy felt the same way about Lieutenant Brown.

When he had talked of his travels, it had been all she could do to keep from begging him to take her with him on his next adventure—when she hardly knew him! It was only by forcefully reminding herself that he hadn't simply appeared by magic in Lincolnshire, that he must have other ties and claims on his life, that she had managed not to.

Yet, somehow she didn't think those ties so very strong. He had not suggested notifying his family, nor did he seem at all anxious to do so now.

As at other times and despite his apparent jovial manner, tonight there had been moments of constraint, as if he were not being completely truthful....

So what did that matter?

It would be better if this confusing, bewildering man would leave.

No. Not leave. Not just yet.

She must remember Mercy. Mercy was in need of a husband.

For all Lieutenant Brown's dashing ways and handsome uniform, he had nothing of the appeal of Mr. Elliot. Surely, given time, Mercy would see that, too.

Time? There was little time left. Mr. Elliot would soon be gone.

As Grace forced herself to imagine Mercy as Mrs. Elliot, she knew that was not what she wanted to happen. She could admit, in the darkness of her bedroom, that she would rather live in exiled shame with her sister than see Mr. Elliot marry anyone else.

Across the hall, his bedsprings creaked.

He was in bed. Perhaps in his nightshirt.

Perhaps naked.

She wouldn't think about that. She would only wait a little longer, until he was surely asleep. Then she would lock his door, as she had done every night he had been here.

It was the wise thing to do, really, even if he did have a sore ankle.

A little nagging voice told her she wasn't locking him in; she was locking herself *out*.

After a time, she opened the door cautiously. She heard no sound from the other bedroom, and so she tiptoed across the hall.

She hesitated outside the closed oak door. All she had to do was put the key in the lock and turn it, and yet…and yet.

What would happen if she didn't lock it, but opened the door instead? What would he do if she slipped into his room, and then into his bed? Would he be shocked? Horrified?

No, he wouldn't, she thought as she recalled the way he had looked at her downstairs. He had regarded her in a way that had made her hot and anxious and full of a need that she couldn't suppress.

A way that told her he would welcome her in his bed. He would enfold her in his arms and kiss her.

Not tentatively, like a lad. Or with the selfish lust of a man like Sir Donald—

Sir Donald. Her lip curled with disgust and she hated him for intruding into her thoughts.

Yet she might have no choice but to marry him. All her playing with numbers and figures below had shown her that she had no alternatives, other than throwing herself and her unmarried, pregnant sister on the mercy of charitable institutions. They had barely enough money to see them through a month at a time, and nothing at all to spare.

If she had to marry Sir Donald, would anyone begrudge her one night of bliss in the arms of a man like Mr. Elliot? Would it matter that she was no longer a virgin if she married Donald Franklin? Was that considered part of the bargain, or could she not have this one night to remember and savor for the rest of her life?

She slipped the key into her other hand and placed one hand on the latch.

Then, cautiously, she opened the door and entered Mr. Elliot's bedroom.

Chapter Eleven

Grace could make out the familiar shape in the bed, for the moon provided enough illumination. She could see his blond head resting on the pillow. The breadth of his shoulders. The length of his legs.

Hesitating, she tried to tell herself to turn around and leave before he discovered her, to find the strength to return to her room.

She could not. Instead, she went toward him.

Suddenly, in one fluid and surprising motion, he threw back the covers and rose hastily. "Miss Barton! What is it?" he whispered urgently as he grabbed his trousers, yanking them on. "Is somebody inside the house?"

Unable to speak, her heart pounding in her breast, her pulse throbbing through her body, aware that he had been completely naked, she swallowed hard and shook her head while he began to do up his trouser buttons.

"Then why...?" he began, looking at her intently. His words hung suspended in the air for a long moment as they gazed at each other in the moonlight, until he crossed the room and pulled her into his arms.

His kiss was everything she knew it would be. Passionate heat burned between them, and with wild abandon, she gave herself over to the sensations filling her as his mouth pressed against hers. His tongue thrust between her lips, and his fevered caress pulled her into a vortex of desire and need that she couldn't have resisted if she tried.

Then, just as suddenly, he pushed her away. "My God!"

"What?" she gasped, bereft, abandoned, frightened by the horror of his tone. "What is it?"

"Get out," he said between clenched teeth.

She blinked back sudden tears of shame.

What had she done, coming in here? What must he think of her? "I'm...please," she whispered. "I thought...I meant..."

"Get out!" he repeated harshly.

With a choked sob that broke Elliot's heart, Grace rushed from his room, closing the door behind her.

Elliot stared at the ancient oak, so ashamed and upset and full of unfulfilled desire he could scarcely think except to blame himself for what had just happened.

Was there something about his face or his manner that announced to all the world the kind of man he was? Was it so obvious that he would take a woman into his bed without a question or a care?

Dear God, he was like a curse, destroying the virtue of all who came near him, no matter how much he tried to prevent it.

He sat heavily on the rumpled bed that smelled of lavender, like Grace. When he had held her in his arms and tasted her tender lips, that scent had been on her skin. Her soft, warm, tender flesh that he wanted so much to touch...

He had to leave. He had to get away, before he abandoned himself to the desire he felt and no longer had the strength to keep away from her.

And if he needed any evidence to prove that he would be forced to continue in the mould he had carved for himself, tonight had provided it. He could never change.

His just reward, no doubt. The final judgment for his sins.

The next morning, as Grace stood in the kitchen, she watched the black barouche coming up the lane, driven by a liveried servant, and with a familiar figure seated inside.

She felt a curious sense of detachment at the sight of Sir Donald Franklin come to call. It was as if, after all the riotous sensations that she had experienced last night, she had none left for today.

Or at least, no emotions she could name, except one.

Shame. Shame for her conduct. Shame for her feelings. A deep, burning shame that would increase tenfold when she saw Mr. Elliot again.

What could she say to him? He had not yet come downstairs for breakfast, and she wasn't sure how she could even face him, after her lewd and immoral act of entering his bedroom in the dead of night, no matter how delightful his kiss, or how much she had thought he wanted her. Obviously she had been wrong about what he felt for her. She had been carried away by the strength of her own desire, and a victim of her own weak surrender to those passions.

"What does *he* want?" Mercy demanded from the scullery, where Grace could see her glaring out the small window.

"I'll go and ask him," Grace answered, grabbing her straw bonnet from beside the door.

Given the current state of her emotions, a visit with Sir Donald might be preferable to facing Mr. Elliot, at least until she was more in control of herself; nor did she wish to witness Mercy being rude to their landlord, which would not help their situation one bit.

Therefore, she opened the kitchen door and stepped out into the yard.

"Good morning, Miss Barton!" Sir Donald called out when he saw her, and he tipped his sleek top hat. "I have come to invite you for a drive on this lovely morning."

"You are up and about very early, are you not?" she inquired politely.

"No man can rest when elections are looming, my dear. However, I have decided to enjoy a brief drive—for my health, of course—and must insist that you stop working and join me."

His health? He was rather unfortunately robust, and she suspected this drive had another object. Nevertheless, she said, "Very well, Sir Donald."

Watts, Sir Donald's driver, opened the door to the barouche, then assisted her inside. His look was undeniably curious, and she knew he must be wondering what this visit indicated.

That couldn't be helped and indeed, Watts's opinion was of little import.

Grace took her place beside Sir Donald, who moved conspicuously closer. As he did so, she tried not to think about Mr. Elliot any more. Unfortunately, the complete contrast in the men made that extremely difficult. Mr. Elliot was attentive, diffident, a true gentleman. The vain, pompous and arrogant Sir Donald was certainly *not* a gentleman, a fact becoming progressively more incontrovertible as his hand moved closer to her knee.

As Watts lifted the reins and the carriage began to move, Grace shifted away from her companion. He, perhaps aware that she was on to him, raised one hand to meditatively stroke his plump chin. "Have you come to a decision yet?" he asked quietly, leaning only slightly closer. "I have been most anxious."

"I, um, I...I have not."

"Oh." He leaned back and away from her, and when he spoke, his voice was as peevish as a spoiled child's. "I have been very patient. I must leave for London tomorrow, and was hoping to have your answer before then."

Grace chewed her lip with genuine distress. Her first and strongest response was what it had been when he had asked for her hand in the cow shed: an unequivocal refusal. She didn't want him as her husband. Even her vivid imagination was unable to conjure a remotely pleasant vision of the rest of her life as this man's wife. She would be no more to him than his house, or his carriage or his hounds, simply another item purchased for show. Yet she would have to bear his children. Share his bed.

As much as she wanted to refuse, however, there was no denying the fact that circumstances—Mercy's pregnancy in particular—might very well force her to marry this man.

What viable alternative was there that would see Mercy and her child safe and healthy? None. Better she should marry against her inclination than force Mercy to endure poverty and humiliation.

Surely Sir Donald would be willing to pay for Mercy's visit to an "elderly relative." They would have to keep her condition a secret from him until the wedding, of course.

Afterward Mercy would probably never be allowed to return, at least not if she wanted to bring her child, and Grace knew that Mercy would never abandon her offspring.

She choked back a sob that sprang to her lips. Never to see Mercy again. Never to see Mr. Elliot again. To have only Sir Donald, and the Hurley sisters and Mrs. Banks for company.

And the other villagers, too, she reminded herself. She was not completely friendless.

Yes, she was.

If only she possessed that facility for making friends easily! If only she did not find it so difficult to reveal her feelings! Then things might have been so very different.

Or they might have been the same. Look how she

had tried to show her feelings last night, only to be rebuffed. Better to reveal nothing. To risk nothing.

Gritting her teeth, Grace leaned a little closer to Sir Donald. "I do appreciate that my hesitation is not welcome, Sir Donald," she said, "but you can surely appreciate that your…compliment…was so very unexpected! I was flattered and overwhelmed.

"But there are not just my own wishes to be consulted. I am responsible for my sister, too."

Her words seemed to mollify him somewhat, for he smiled with some smug satisfaction as they came to a fork in the road. Both ways led to the village, one directly past the Hurleys' house, and the other a more easterly, circuitous route through a wood, the very way Mr. Elliot must have gone when he had gotten lost.

When she had found him and saved him.

It wouldn't do to remember that day, or the ones after, she told herself, and she turned her thoughts to the best road to take in this most practical of instances. As for the road her life would take, she wished a fairy godmother would alight beside the carriage, tell her that there was a pot of gold awaiting her at home, and that she need make no more momentous decisions, ever.

That would not happen, of course, and the fork drew closer.

Although Grace was quite convinced that the Hurleys were not only sure she would be Sir Donald's wife, but had probably already decided who should be invited and what food would be served at the wedding supper, she was not anxious to be seen out driving in his barouche. After all, some kind of miracle might happen, if not the fairy godmother kind, and she might be spared the necessity of marrying him. "Perhaps we should take the eastern road," she suggested.

Sir Donald eagerly barked the command, then turned to her with such a wide, pleased grin on his fat face that Grace immediately regretted her choice. Unfortunately, it was already too late, and they were rapidly approaching the wood.

She kept her focus on the trees rather than having to look at Sir Donald, and it was then that she saw the man leaning against a tree, his battered hat tipped back to reveal a face in need of washing, and a meditative expression as he watched them approach. Indeed, he was staring at them in such a rude, impertinent way, Grace was made even more uncomfortable.

"See that rogue there?" Sir Donald said huffily, gesturing unnecessarily. "When I am the member of parliament for this riding, I shall set about ridding our village of such miscreants. No doubt he should be in jail, if not deported!"

"He isn't doing anything illegal," Grace felt dutybound to point out, although she couldn't rid herself of the notion that Sir Donald might, for once in his life, be absolutely correct.

Then she decided to take this moment of apparent interest to note that several villagers had expressed concern over the number of vagrants passing through Barton. "I'm sure, though, that most of them are simply trying to make their way in the world without disturbing anyone,'' she finished.

"They're all lazy Irishmen," Sir Donald replied coldly. "They should be sent home after the harvest, but they won't go."

"I believe that is another thing that troubles many of the villagers," Grace said. "This practice of bringing in cheap labor—how are the local villagers to earn any money?"

Sir Donald looked angry for a moment, for he had to know that his own practice of hiring people from outside Barton and the surrounding area to work on his manor was a sore point with many villagers. Then, to Grace's surprise, he smiled at her. "As my wife, you would, of course, be able to advise me on such matters. Why, you might even be able to convince me to lower the rents. A pretty woman can often compel a man to do things he would never normally condone."

Was this a bribe for her hand in marriage? How naive did he think she was? His wife would hold little sway over him, especially when it came to anything involving his money. She would merely be some kind of trophy to him, to show at balls and parties, and to bear him children. Nothing more.

"Are you sure it does not trouble you that I am not of sufficient rank?" she asked.

"Your discernment does you credit, my dear," Sir Donald answered. He reached out and took her clenched hand in his own hot one.

Nothing would have given Grace greater pleasure

than to yank her hand from his and slap his leering face, but she restrained herself.

"Your beauty is your qualification for moving in the highest social circles," he continued in what Grace supposed he thought was a seductive tone. Instead, he sounded like some kind of simpleton. "And your family name is quite as good as anybody's."

It was certainly better than *his,* at any rate, and Grace tried to find some spark of determination in that. However, it only served to remind her how Mercy had disgraced that venerable name, and how others would be merciless in their derision when they found out.

If they found out. If Grace could not find the money to get Mercy safely away.

"Others have made unequal matches these days, and it hasn't harmed their standing," Sir Donald mused, still suffocatingly close to her. "I don't see why it should be any different in my case."

Because they probably married for love, Grace thought despondently. Then she realized that if she could keep Sir Donald talking, he might be less inclined to do anything except talk, especially as the trees grew thicker and the light grew dimmer.

"Oh, it would be so reassuring to know such things!" she exclaimed. "But unlike you, I am not privy to the doings of the higher classes. Barton is so far out-of-the-way, you see."

He nodded with regal condescension. "Naturally, I do not expect you to know the people I associate with, but this will change once we are married." It was all

Grace could do not to squirm when he looked at her. "Let me think of specific examples."

He let go of her hand to stroke his chin again, and Grace realized this was a habitual motion with him, and one that would surely drive her mad after a day or two. She seized the opportunity to quickly clasp her hands together in her lap.

"Well, there is Lord Paris Mulholland," Sir Donald said pensively. "Everyone thought he had a good chance of marrying into the royal family if he wanted to, he was so charming. Instead, he married the daughter of a dancing master or an artist or something equally ludicrous. In spite of that, his friends do not cut him.

"The Duke of Barroughby married the daughter of a very minor earl, and people are making fools of themselves to be included in their invitations. Hester Pimblett certainly wasn't well-known, and she's not even very pretty."

"Why, this is what I mean, Sir Donald," Grace said plaintively. "I have no idea who you're talking about."

"A very strange family, the Fitzwalters," Sir Donald continued. "The duke is a rather glum fellow, although women like him well enough. Good-looking, of course, but in a nasty sort of way, I always thought. His half brother—he was the charming one. And as for women!"

"He was a great favorite of the ladies?"

Sir Donald snorted an assent. "But a most debased scoundrel. He's been missing these five years."

"Missing?"

"Just up and disappeared, nobody knows why. All kinds of wild rumors, of course. Myself, I think the young rascal finally got murdered. He did keep the most unsavory company. Or else he did away with himself. Personally, I think the duke got tired of paying for his younger brother's mischief and had him...dispatched."

"Dispatched where?"

Sir Donald gave her a patronizing look. "To the devil, I suppose."

"You think he had him *murdered?*"

"He wouldn't be the first to rid himself of such a troublesome family member in that manner," Sir Donald noted in such a dispassionate tone Grace could easily picture him doing the very same thing.

He began to lean toward her again.

"I find all this so fascinating," Grace said with a smile as she inched away. "Do go on. Did you know him?"

Sir Donald shrugged. "I was great friends with Lord Elliot until he became so decadent I refused to see him anymore."

"Really?"

"I couldn't sully your delicate sensibilities with a description of his immoral activities," Sir Donald said loftily. "However, women were usually involved, to their detriment. Beautiful women, to be specific."

"And he a duke's brother!" Grace exclaimed with what she hoped was the right tone to indicate she was profoundly impressed by Sir Donald's social connections while finding his tale completely captivating.

And as if she didn't suspect Sir Donald could tell a biographical tale or two when it came to attempting to seduce women. There had been more than one story from maids who were dismissed from his service that implied Sir Donald expected a servant's duties to extend beyond the usual.

Apparently she had succeeded in her object, for Sir Donald's chest visibly expanded and he smiled with satisfaction. "Yes, his lordship and I were great friends. I met him at the Duke of Chesterton's. Marvelous old chap, that. Quite the hospitable host."

Sir Donald shook his head sadly. "The duke's brother was a reckless, foolish young man, if truth be told. Why, many's the time I said, 'Elliot, one of these days that handsome face of yours won't help!' and he'd just laugh and smile that lopsided grin of his and say, 'My charm will see me through! I haven't met a woman yet who was immune to me!'"

Lopsided grin? Elliot? Surely, Grace thought wildly, surely these were mere coincidences. A turn of the lips, a similar name—what did that signify?

Besides, their Mr. Elliot had been the perfect gentleman. It had been *she* who had acted immorally, not him.

"Confoundedly handsome man he was, too. I daresay if he's not dead, he's probably living with a woman, or in a brothel."

Of course she was being ridiculous, Grace told herself, if she could think their Mr. Elliot was this lascivious rascal of a lord. Her imagination had simply flown to a foolish conclusion. Whatever would a missing duke's son be doing in Lincolnshire? It was hardly a place to hide.

Unless he found two lone women to take him in. To feed him and house him and fall in love with him...

"I met the duke only the once. Stuck-up, conceited—what's the matter?"

Grace dared not say what was running through her mind, that Mr. Elliot moved, spoke and acted like a man to the manner born. "I...I was wondering what I would do if I ever met a duke," she stammered, saying the first excuse that came to mind. "I would probably make a fool of myself."

Sir Donald shook his head. "No, you wouldn't," he said. "You would do me credit. But I wouldn't let you near the Fitzwalters. They have an eye for beauty, and if Elliot ever did turn up, I'd be sure to keep you away from *him*. The fellow has no morals. No woman is safe around him."

"This Lord Elliot—he disappeared, you said before?"

"Yes. Five years ago. Nobody knows why, but knowing Adrian, I can make a good guess."

"They were only half brothers?"

"Yes. Lord Elliot's mother was the old duke's second wife. He said Adrian never liked him just because he didn't like his stepmother, or even the idea of a stepmother." Sir Donald shook his head. "Lord Elliot always had a good explanation for his troubles. Whether it was the truth or not, well, I'd not like to gamble on it."

A glib tongue, too.

Surely Lord Elliot and Mr. Elliot couldn't be the same person. She trusted their Mr. Elliot completely. Had she not been the one to enter a bedroom uninvited? Had she not left Mercy alone with him?

She had left Mercy alone with him!

Could it be that he was clever enough to make her think he cared for her, when Mercy was his true object? Could that be why he ordered her from his room, because he cared for another?

"The duke hated Elliot," Sir Donald continued with no prompting. "Always did. They probably quarreled again. It wouldn't surprise me to find out the duke killed him and buried his body in the garden." Sir Donald gave her a strange look. "All this interest in Lord Elliot—I could get jealous, if I didn't think the young fool was dead," he said, smiling in a mirthless manner.

"It seems you know so many gentlemen," Grace said absently.

"I would rather know *you* better."

Grace would have moved farther away, if she could have. Regrettably, she was pressed uncomfortably against the side of the carriage as it was. "Oh, there is nothing so very interesting about me."

"I think you should let me decide that."

Grace's only response was a weak smile.

"I would do my best to keep you safe from such men," Sir Donald murmured. "It would be my pleasure."

Grace stiffened, and when she spoke, she didn't keep her displeasure at his proximity from her voice. "You would protect me, is that it?"

"I would protect my wife."

"Would you?" she asked coolly.

"Yes!"

Suddenly, and to her horror, he crushed her in his strong embrace and pressed his hot, damp lips against her mouth.

Chapter Twelve

Grace pushed Sir Donald away, her anger and dismay adding to her strength. "Sir Donald!" she cried, wiping her lips with the back of her hand. "You forget yourself!"

"In your arms, I do forget myself!" he said excitedly. "Miss Barton, say you'll be my wife!"

Grace didn't answer Sir Donald's impassioned proposal as she moved to the opposite seat, as far away from him as possible, and as close to the driver. Watts was Sir Donald's employee, but surely he would come to her aid if Sir Donald tried to attack her more forcibly. After all, Watts was from Barton, and his glance back to see what was happening had held a hostility it was well Sir Donald didn't notice.

Feeling somewhat safer knowing Watts was there, she tried to calm down. "Please take me home," she said.

"Miss Barton, forgive me!" Sir Donald pleaded. "I was too impetuous. I was carried away by my feelings! You are driving me mad with yearning. Please say you'll be my wife."

"I would appreciate it if we could return without delay," she replied, keeping her tone as neutral as possible under the circumstances.

"But Miss Barton, you must understand—"

"I *understand* that I want you to take me home at once!" she said sternly.

"Oh, very well," he grudgingly conceded. "Watts, take us back to Barton Farm."

"Yes, Sir Donald," Watts replied, wasting no time in obeying the order, even though it meant a somewhat difficult turn.

When Elliot carefully limped his way into the kitchen that morning, he was absolutely determined to leave that very day. After last night, he couldn't stay.

He was a weak, immoral rogue, and he didn't know how much longer he could keep away from Grace. He wanted her so much! More than he had ever wanted a woman, but she was the last woman who would want him, Lord Elliot Fitzwalter, cad, cheat, seducer of women.

What she wanted was Mr. John Elliot, a gentlemanly victim of a robbery.

He supposed it was inevitable that one day he would be made to pay for his sins, but he could never have imagined the extent of the anguish that price would exact.

Yet how many women had suffered as he did now, because of him? How many hearts had he broken?

Too many. If only he had known...

He halted abruptly on the threshold. Mercy was

standing at the kitchen window, wringing her hands
with dismay as she watched a carriage depart.

She turned toward him when she realized he was
there. "Did you see him?" she demanded, her face
pale, her chin trembling.

"Who?"

"That man in the carriage. He is Sir Donald Franklin, our landlord."

"Ah."

Elliot sat at the table. His ankle was starting to
throb again, but that was nothing compared to the
pain he felt at the realization that Grace Barton was
virtually alone in that lout's carriage.

"He's a terrible, terrible man!" Mercy cried, coming toward him, the very flounces of her skirts shaking with agitation. "She should not speak to him!
Why did she go in his carriage?"

"He invited her, I suppose," Elliot said, trying to
sound composed, and hoping his apparent attitude
would induce some calm in Mercy.

As he spoke, he realized that she looked exhausted,
and there was something else. Something about her
that he thought he ought to recognize.

"You should have stopped her!" Mercy declared
passionately.

"Me?" Elliot asked. He wished he could have.
"You may recall that I am to be kept hidden."

Mercy began to pace, and every time she passed
him, Elliot found himself staring at her, first her glow-
ing face, then her midriff. How was it that such a
slender young woman came to have such a plump—

Then it hit him, like a bolt of lightning on a cloudless summer day.

Mercy Barton was with child. That would explain her weariness, the paleness, the thick waist, that quality to her complexion that he should have recognized soon enough, given that he had encountered his share of pregnant paramours, his own and those of his friends.

He might have guessed sooner, had Mercy not seemed so…innocent.

And had he not always associated that slight alteration of features as a sign of impending doom. Too many women he had known had used that as an excuse to demand more money, or better lodging, or even as a means for blackmail. Never marriage, though. He was careful enough not to pick women who would demand marriage, with that one notable exception.

Clearly Mercy Barton was not the paragon of virtue she seemed. Who was the father? The mysterious Lieutenant Brown, no doubt.

What about Grace? Did she know? Was it possible that she did not? Perhaps, if Grace trusted her sister completely, as she surely did.

She trusted *him*, after all, and he was far less to her than a sister, no matter how much he wished it could be otherwise.

If Grace did know, that would explain the strain between the sisters, for their perilous situation would be disastrously different. They would need more money, and have fewer opportunities.

Add to that the shame. People like those two old

harpies would make the Bartons' lives a misery if they remained here.

Yet Grace had given him sanctuary. Her decision now seemed unbelievably generous and kind, and un-repayable.

Even worse, he could easily imagine how Donald Franklin might make use of their potential disgrace.

Grace might decide to do anything to insure that her sister didn't suffer. No doubt Franklin could afford to send Mercy far away, where her pregnancy could be kept secret.

"Sir Donald is a loathsome *beast!*" Mercy declared forcefully.

"What evidence have you against him?"

Mercy flushed bright red, yet said nothing.

"Perhaps he only sounds wicked to country-bred ladies," he suggested, anxiously hoping there was knowledge to back her charge, and not simply prejudice.

She shook her head rapidly, then drew up a chair and sat close beside Elliot, her wide gray eyes gazing at him steadily. "I don't have any evidence," she said, immediately disappointing him. "I just know it—you can tell by the way he looks at her! *You* would never look at a woman like that, as if she were a slave to be bought or sold."

Elliot wished he could say she was right, that he had never gazed upon a woman solely as an object for his amusement. Unfortunately, he couldn't. Nor was he a gentleman, in the truest sense of the word.

"Why, you should have seen the way he was looking at Grace in church—in *church!*

"I'm sure he's going to ask for her hand, if he hasn't already, and I'm so worried that she'll think she'll have to accept, because of...because of the rent."

And your condition, he finished in his thoughts.

Surely there was *something* he could do.

As he looked at Mercy, so worried and anxious and pretty and pregnant, an idea came to him.

A feasible, horrible idea. A way to help them that would break his heart.

Grace might be tempted to marry Sir Donald because she was bound by sisterly duty to take care of Mercy.

Mercy's unmarried state would lead to shame and disgrace for both the Bartons.

There was one solution that would solve both those problems: If Mercy were married, Grace would be free of the responsibility of looking after her sister, for that would fall to Mercy's husband. If Mercy had a husband, Grace's dishonor would be lessened.

Who better than he to marry Mercy Barton?

Neither one of them was virtuous. He had provided more than one husband with a child not his own, so perhaps it was only fitting that he raise another man's child. It would be far more disturbing to allow Grace to bear Donald Franklin's offspring.

He didn't love Mercy, but what did that matter? He did not deserve the love of a decent woman like Grace. He had not earned such happiness.

Mercy seemed to regard him as a friend, not a potential suitor, no doubt because she still harbored hopes for the timely return of Lieutenant Brown.

A small stumbling block, he thought bitterly. He had wooed and won other men's women before, always successfully.

He reached out and took Mercy's hand gently in his as she waited anxiously beside him.

When she turned toward him, startled, he gave her the look that had won many a reluctant woman's heart. "You are so sweet," he whispered, raising her hand to his lips and brushing a kiss across it.

She yanked her hand away as if his lips had been hot coals, and a shocked expression replaced the surprise in her gray eyes. "Mr. Elliot!" she cried, hurrying to the opposite side of the room. "What are you doing?"

This extreme reaction was rather unexpected and a little unnerving, given his previous conquests. However, having made his decision, he was not about to give up.

"I am paying you a compliment," he replied with another winning smile. "I am trying to tell you how much you inspire my admiration."

"*I* inspire your admiration?"

He smiled more and spread his hands in a gesture of supplication. "Surely you cannot doubt it."

"But I don't want your admiration!"

"I can't help the way I feel," he murmured, hating himself for the fraud he was perpetrating, but unable to think of any better way to help Grace. "You are so lovely."

"I am in love with another man!" she cried, backing up until she hit the door, with a desperation in her eyes that warned him to come no closer.

Still, such a declaration had never stopped Elliot in the past, and he told himself not to let it impede him now. Mercy needed a husband, and he needed to prevent Grace from marrying Donald Franklin. "Mercy, my darling, I need you," he lied, using the words that had always guaranteed success. "I can't live without you. I..."

He could not bring himself to say he loved her. Try as he might, as necessary as it was to a successful end to his plan, he could not. "Please, I want to marry you."

"Marry me?" She stared at him as if the idea was one too terrible to contemplate.

"Yes." He went down on one knee, following the prescribed formula. "I know I have been acquainted with you but a little while, yet you will make me the happiest of men if you will accept me. Please, will you do me the honor of becoming my wife?"

"Mr. Elliot, you must stop!" she protested, a little more feebly, he thought, and although he knew he should be pleased, he wasn't. He was only...satisfied.

"I don't love you!" she said, with astonishing firmness that was more like her sister than herself as she crossed her arms over her chest. "I'm in love with someone else!"

Elliot decided he wouldn't play the naive young suitor. "The father of your child?" he asked softly, rising from his humiliating position.

Her eyes widened. "Who...who told you? Grace?"

"Nobody told me. I can see for myself, and so will other people, soon enough."

She turned pale and looked about to faint, so he

quickly led her to a chair. "Sit here." He fetched a glass of water and made her drink it.

"How long have you known?" she asked, gazing up at him woefully, all her previous rectitude gone.

"Not long. How far are you?"

"Nearly three months, I think."

"Soon you won't be able to hide it."

Mercy looked at him with an anguished expression. "I've added to our troubles immensely, I know. If I wasn't with child, I could have gone to stay with the Hurleys. They offered me a home." She glanced down at her stomach. "Obviously, that is quite impossible, under the circumstances."

She sighed heavily. "Grace doesn't have the faith in Adam that I have. I *know* he will come back and marry me, just as soon as he is able. I am not at all afraid for my future."

Elliot wished he could believe that she need not be. Unfortunately, his experience told him otherwise.

"It's Grace I'm worried about. I know she's worried about what we're going to live on. I'm so afraid she'll do something rash, like marry Sir Donald, just to save me. But there is no need to save me!"

Suddenly she regarded Elliot with a shrewd, calculating expression. "Doesn't that trouble *you?*"

Startled by her unexpected perception, he didn't answer.

"I think it does," she said slowly. "I think it troubles you very much. I think that's why you've asked me to marry you!"

"Whatever do you mean?" he asked, unable to meet her steady gaze.

Mercy leapt to her feet and stood directly in front of him. "You do like Grace more! I *knew* it! Oh, this is wonderful!" she cried, clasping her hands together rapturously. "You must tell her at once! The moment she returns!"

Elliot rose and walked toward the window, looking out over the tranquil farmyard. "I cannot tell your sister what isn't true," he said quietly.

"What?" Mercy demanded, facing him with her hands on her hips. "You *do* care about her, don't you?"

"I am grateful for her assistance and—"

"I've seen the way you look at her."

He glanced at Mercy out of the corner of his eye, and his lips twisted into a sardonic grin. "It would be better if you could say something about the way she looks at me."

Mercy's eyes grew light with merriment, and a smile made her dimples appear. "She cares for you a great deal, if I am any judge."

Elliot refused to accept Mercy's romantic, hopeful assertion. "How can you be sure?" he asked, some of his very real desperation creeping into his voice.

"I just am."

That was not much of an answer, Elliot thought with a disappointment as great as his desire.

"Besides, you must love her. She is so beautiful, and good, and kind!"

He gave her another wry smile. "Then why must she love me?"

Mercy answered him with all seriousness. "Because you are handsome and good and a gentleman."

"If I am handsome and enjoy a certain position in society, those are accidents of birth. But I have not been a gentleman for many years, and I have only recently truly learned what it means to be good, by living here."

"I don't believe you!" Mercy cried.

"Your sister would."

"But she is always ready to see the bad side of things!"

"The only thing I want to know is, does she see the bad side of Donald Franklin?" he replied.

"Yes, of course she does. She doesn't even like him. That's why she absolutely cannot marry him.

"But he doesn't matter now," she continued excitedly, "because you can propose to Grace, and she will marry you, and I will marry Adam, and Sir Donald can do whatever he likes about the rent!"

This whole conversation was taking on a completely dreamlike quality, but whether delightful or a nightmare, Elliot wasn't sure. "Do you truly believe your sister would accept me, even if I thought myself worthy enough to ask for her hand in marriage?"

"Oh." This seemed to be a stumbling block that Mercy had not considered.

Then she brightened again. "She *must* be in love with you by now. You've been here nearly a week. *I* fell in love with Adam after an hour, so surely Grace has had ample time. And she went to so much trouble to get you here...." Despite her bravado, her words trailed off and her face grew doubtful.

Now it was his turn to scrutinize her. "Have you

been hoping this would happen all along? Is that why you were so insistent I stay?"

Mercy blushed as she nodded defiantly. "If Grace marries you, everything will be fine."

"And to think I assumed it was my charm and good looks that made you urge her to let me remain," Elliot replied sarcastically. "You seem to have this all worked out. How do you know that, if we were to marry, I can support your sister?"

"You are rich."

"What?"

"Or your family is. I can tell by your clothes, and your voice, and your manner."

She had assumed. They didn't know. "As much as I admire and respect your sister—"

"There! You *are* in love with her!"

He held up his hand to silence Mercy's sisterly enthusiasm. "As much as I admire and respect your sister, I do not love her," he said, and even as he said it, he knew it was the greatest lie of the many he had told.

He did love Grace Barton, as much as any man could. He wanted nothing more than to spend the rest of his life with her, yet he had ruined any chance of that before he had even met her, by living a life that was a shameful disgrace. How he wished he had heeded Adrian's warnings now!

"You will," Mercy said confidently. "You must! She's beginning to fall in love with you, if she isn't already. A sister can tell these things."

"I think you are letting your imagination run away with you."

"Oh, no, I'm not at all imaginative. Ask Grace."

"Be that as it may," Elliot said, a hint of frustration in his tone, "I do not love her. Nor am I rich enough to marry her. I was once able to afford good clothing, but that was some time ago. I have few prospects."

"You asked me to marry you, with those same few prospects," Mercy reminded him.

He stared at the ground. She was quite right; nevertheless, he wasn't about to tell her that he was more sanguine about her acceptance because of her pending social disgrace. "I hadn't had time to think things through."

"Why *did* you ask me?" Mercy demanded.

"I wanted to...to..."

"To help Grace by alleviating my disgrace," she finished triumphantly. "You see, you do love her, and I think offering to marry me is a noble, if foolish, way to show it."

Elliot rubbed his forehead and tried to think clearly. His emotions were so torn between hope that Mercy was right about Grace caring for him, and dismay that Mercy might simply be seeing what she wanted to see, he felt as if he were caught in a whirlpool. "I suppose I should be delighted you're not angry with me."

Mercy smiled warmly. "How could I be? You were only thinking of Grace. Whom you must and shall marry!" she finished happily.

Elliot did not reply. He had nothing to offer Grace besides himself, and his shameful past.

"Ask her when she returns. I shall go upstairs and you may speak with her alone for as long as it takes."

"No!"

"You will not ask Grace to marry you?" she asked quietly.

"No."

"And you will leave us? What if she marries Sir Donald?"

"Before I go, I will pay a call on Donald Franklin and convince him to keep the rent as it is," he said.

"He will listen to you?"

"I can be very persuasive, Miss Mercy."

She looked at him for a long moment, then nodded reluctantly. "What will you do now?"

"I suppose I'll go on my way to London."

"Will you take me with you, then?"

Elliot regarded Mercy with a puzzled frown. Hadn't she just said, quite forcefully, that she was in love with another man?

"In a very short time, as you have pointed out, I won't be able to keep my condition a secret. I have been planning to go to London to have the baby, if Adam didn't come back before I was due. But I'm already starting to show, so perhaps I should leave now. I would be grateful for your escort."

"What about Grace?"

"I don't want her to be tainted by my disgrace, so she must stay here as if nothing out of the ordinary is happening. We shall tell everyone I've gone to visit one of our second cousins."

"You seem to have this all planned," Elliot remarked.

"I've been thinking about it for quite some time. If Adam returns while I'm away, Grace will be here to direct him to me, too. If we ask anyone else to do that, soon everyone will know that Adam is more than a mere acquaintance, and I would rather not be the subject of any more gossip than necessary. Or Grace, either."

Elliot had to agree with her. "Do you know anyone at all in London?" he asked, recalling the many things that might happen to a pregnant, unmarried young woman in that city.

"No," Mercy admitted.

"Then I believe you should reconsider. London isn't safe for a lone woman," he replied.

Mercy chewed her lip worriedly. "But no one will know me there."

"You cannot go to London without someone to take care of you, and you know that would worry your sister."

"If I stay here, I will shame her." Mercy straightened her shoulders. "If you think London not a good choice, then I will go someplace else."

There was one place he knew she would be well cared for, and where, if he was willing to forget his pride, he could get enough money for Grace's needs, too.

He had no pride left. Not anymore. The only thing he had left was the family he had abandoned.

Hester and Adrian would surely be willing to help her, even if Elliot wasn't the father—perhaps especially then. He knew in his heart, no longer shackled by arrogant conceit and foolish pride, that they would do so because he asked it of them.

He also knew now that everything Adrian had done had not been to upset him or make him feel inferior and beholden, but because of his brotherly love, the kind of love Elliot had seen Grace bestow on her sister. If only he had understood earlier that protection could be a sign of love, and not control, he would have been a happier man. "Will you come with me to my family's home? You will be welcome there."

"What will they think when you appear with me?" Mercy asked softly, trepidation in her eyes.

"They will think the worst, at first, until I explain the situation." Convinced now that was the road he must travel, Elliot accepted it. "Adrian will give me money if I give him a good reason, and saving Grace from the greedy clutches of Donald Franklin is one of the best reasons in the world."

Suddenly Elliot had a hopeful vision of himself returning to Barton Farm like a knight in shining armor, only instead of a lance, he would have pounds sterling.

Mercy looked doubtful. "Grace won't take your money. She will say it's charity."

"I won't give her any choice."

Mercy's eyes widened, and then she nodded her acceptance. "When should we leave?"

"Tomorrow."

"Tomorrow?" she asked weakly.

"Yes. The sooner, the better." For his sake, as much as hers. The longer he stayed, the more difficult it would be to say goodbye to Grace.

"Then I had better go pack my things." Mercy surveyed the kitchen slowly, her gaze finally coming to rest upon him. "I don't want to go," she whispered. "What will I do without Grace?"

He didn't answer as she turned and left the room, because he was wondering the same thing.

Both the inhabitants of the kitchen at Barton Farm were so immersed in their conversation, neither of them saw the thin, pockmarked young man peering in the window, who quickly ducked and ran away.

Skurch hurried to his gang's hiding place, nearly tripping over his own feet in his eagerness to report what he had seen. Bob would be pleased, and they hadn't been cowardly fools to stay with him. They were in a way to get a lot more than ten pounds now!

He ran on through the woods, barely pausing to notice the pile of brush and stones that hid Wickham's body. *He* was the fool, thinking Boffin wrong.

He quickly gave the call of a fox to tell Treeg it was a friend before he came out of the underbrush and flopped onto the ground beside the smoking fire, gasping for breath and unable, for a moment, to respond to Treeg's demands to know what the bloody hell was the matter.

Before Skurch had recovered sufficiently to speak, Boffin appeared across from the clearing, strolling toward them. He saw Skurch and quickened his pace.

"What's goin' on?" Boffin demanded, squatting beside Skurch. "Seen a ghost or summat?"

"No ghost," Skurch panted. "*Him!*"

"What 'im?" Boffin demanded.

"It was 'im, I tells ya. Stayin' with them two women, like you said he would."

"He come out?" Treeg asked eagerly.

"Naw." Skurch smiled proudly. "I was watchin' the house like I was supposed to, and I thinks to meself, Skurch, old son, we could be hidin' in the woods like a bunch o' savages for days lest you do summat. So I crept up t' winda when the pretty one went off in the carriage with the fat fool."

Boffin regarded Skurch with excitement in his dark, narrow eyes. "You're sure it was 'im?"

Skurch nodded. "Certain as I am that I am asittin' here."

Boffin leapt to his feet. "I knew it—find a pretty girl, you'd find *him!*"

The other two exchanged pleased looks. "What'd we do now?" Treeg asked.

Boffin grinned as he meditatively scratched his armpit. "Well, that's an interestin' question. Go to his brother the duke and get paid for telling what we know, or go to Lord Elliot hisself and get paid to keep quiet?"

Chapter Thirteen

As Grace and Donald Franklin rode in silence, she ignored her corpulent companion and turned her thoughts to what he had told her about Lord Elliot Fitzwalter.

Specifically, she was trying to convince herself that they had not been harboring a missing nobleman, and one with a reputation for seduction at that, which would mean she had been completely wrong about him.

Unfortunately, the silence did not continue, for Sir Donald's profuse apologies broke out anew and there was a true sense of alarm in his tone. He seemed genuinely upset that he had been so impetuous and rude and lascivious, as if he really cared to have her good opinion.

Why did he want her?

The answer was rather quick to hand. He wanted her for his wife because she represented what he lacked: an old, respected family name, and try as she might not to acknowledge it, she had a pretty face.

Pretty enough for him, although Mr. Elliot didn't

seem to find her attractive. According to Sir Donald, Lord Elliot enjoyed seducing pretty women.

Therefore, she concluded, Mr. Elliot could not be Lord Elliot.

As they turned down the lane to Barton Farm, Grace breathed a sigh of relief, until Sir Donald suddenly and with what looked like true remorse took hold of her hand.

"Miss Barton," he said plaintively. "Please let me say again that it is only my affection and impatience that made me act like such a brute today. I...was carried away by your beauty and sweetness. Please say you'll forgive me."

"I forgive you, Sir Donald."

He was apparently encouraged, although her tone was distinctly noncommittal. "Then, please, let me assure you again that I most ardently desire to have you for my wife."

"I know the power of your feelings."

He looked rather uneasy, as well he should. He cleared his throat and leaned a little closer, his expression more truly desperate than Grace would have believed possible.

"I'm sorry to have to insist, Miss Barton, but I must have an answer, today."

"Why?"

If he was seriously determined to be her husband, he might as well discover now that she was not going to be completely submissive.

"Because," he began hesitatingly before continuing in a rush, "because the election is a month away and I must have your answer before I see Lord Denburton in London.''

So that was the man behind Sir Donald's bid for parliament. Grace had heard of him, for Barton was not that much of a backwater that they wouldn't have heard of the man said to control not just Lincolnshire, but parts of several other counties, too. No wonder Sir Donald was so anxious to do as Lord Denburton commanded.

"Please, Miss Barton, marry me!" he pleaded, his manner selfishly desperate and so completely repellent that her first impulse was to tell him she wouldn't marry him if he were the last man on the earth.

But then what of Mercy? What would become of her sister if they had no home, no money, no friends, no prospects? They might wind up in a workhouse or almshouse, far from home, sick and hungry. What would be Mercy's chances of having a safe childbirth and healthy baby under those conditions?

Terrible, as Grace well knew. Mercy and the baby both might die.

Yet what of love?

What of it, indeed? Love would not feed or clothe them, or give them shelter.

Grace raised her eyes and looked at Sir Donald's dark, fat face. "Yes, Sir Donald, I will marry you."

Donald Franklin's eyes flared with pleasure. "That's marvelous! My darling." He kissed her hand passionately, and his touch made her flesh crawl.

She tried to submit to his action. She was going to be this man's wife, condemned by her own consent.

Heaven help her.

But she couldn't endure his touch. Not now. She simply couldn't, not until she was bound by the laws of man and the church. "Sir Donald, please! We are not married yet!" she protested.

Thankfully he stopped. "Not yet," he replied significantly. "You have but to name the day."

"I—"

"It must be before the election," he mused, ignoring her completely.

"Very well," Grace said. He would not want her once he discovered Mercy's pregnancy, so it would be better to have the ceremony over and done with as soon as possible.

She felt a curious sense of detachment regarding this necessary subterfuge, and certainly nothing approaching guilt, perhaps because she knew she was going to have to live with the consequences for the rest of her life.

"I will tell Lord Denburton of our engagement at once. That should satisfy the old buzzard."

The driver stopped the carriage and she was very glad when Watts opened the door. "Goodbye, Sir Donald," she said, struggling not to betray her despair.

"Oh, farewell, my dear!" he said jauntily. He grinned broadly, looking like a happy toad. "I shall call on you when I return from London."

Grace made a smile in response. He waved his hand, a movement she did not return.

After the carriage had gone down the lane, Grace swiveled slowly on her heel and, taking a deep breath, began to walk toward the kitchen. It was going to be very difficult to tell Mr.——her sister, what she had just done.

But not nearly as difficult as marrying Sir Donald Franklin.

Elliot knew he should stay out of sight as the carriage stopped in the farmyard, but he waited near the window nonetheless. He had to see Grace and Franklin together, so he would know what to say, and what to do.

Franklin looked somewhat healthier than Elliot recalled, but there was no mistaking the man's dark, heavy features, or the leer that lurked about his lips when he looked at Grace. If Elliot's ankle had been sound, he would have bounded from the room that very instant and challenged Franklin to a duel, based solely on that look.

"Farewell, my dear!" Franklin called out with all the impertinence Elliot could have expected from him. "I'll call on you when I return from London."

Elliot wanted to strangle the throat that had the audacity to address Miss Barton as "my dear."

Then Grace opened the door and stepped inside, and Elliot had to face her.

What could he say to her after last night? How could he begin to explain the self-loathing he had felt when he ordered her from his room?

How pale she looked! And exhausted, as if she had been fighting a battle.

Yet how beautiful, too, in her familiar plain gown, her large brown eyes showing such patient endurance, suffering—and something else, something that he might have seen on a martyr's face as she stood waiting for the flames.

"What did he say to you?" Elliot demanded, inwardly promising that Donald Franklin would rue the day he was born if he touched so much as a hair on Grace's head.

She colored and her lips became a narrow frown while suspicion darkened her features.

"Mr. Elliot," she replied coldly, in a way that made his heart sink with despair.

Mercy was wrong. Grace didn't love him.

"Where is Mercy?" she inquired, her tone as frigid as a gale in the North Atlantic.

She knew. She knew who he was and what he was.

He wanted to howl with anger and frustration. Franklin must have seen him, or else she had told him of their visitor, and he had revealed his identity. Yet why had Franklin not come into the house, if that was so?

She was waiting for an answer. "Your sister is upstairs packing her bags," he said, assuming as matter-of-fact an air as he could. Perhaps her change in manner had nothing to do with him, and everything to do with Sir Donald.

"Packing her bags?" Grace asked, moving further inside the room. "Why?"

"She is leaving with me tomorrow."

Grace stared at him, aghast. "Leaving...with you?"

"I know this is a shock to you, but let me assure you, she will be quite safe and well cared for," he said, willing her to believe his sincere words.

"By you, I suppose?"

He told himself not to be insulted by her disparaging tone. "No, not by me. I'm going to take her to my family's home."

"You mean the home of the Duke of Barroughby?"

"Yes." He strolled toward the mantel and leaned upon it. "Might I ask how you found out who I am? And when? Do I owe Sir Donald Franklin for your edification?"

Still watching him warily, she crossed toward the table. "Indirectly. I guessed, from things Sir Donald told me today."

"Then you didn't tell him about your uninvited guest?"

"Heavens, no!"

He bowed slightly. "Better for all concerned, Miss Barton. We wouldn't want to cause more scandal."

"No, we wouldn't." She continued to regard him with a look he couldn't read and then her chin began to quiver. He would have spoken more kindly then, had she not raised that same chin defiantly in the next instant and said sternly, "What kind of proposal have you made to my sister?"

"Despite what you may have heard of me, it was an honorable one. I asked her to be my wife."

Grace's chest constricted. She couldn't breathe, couldn't think.

But wasn't this what she had wanted, Mercy safely married, her baby with a father? And her own freedom, from worry as much as Sir Donald Franklin.

Why then did she suddenly feel death might be

preferable to his announcement, for Mercy's agreeing to leave with him must signify her acceptance.

She wanted to moan with despair or scream with anguish. Instead, she slowly removed her gloves and crumpled them in her hot palms.

"Unfortunately, she declined my hand."

"What?" Grace gasped, her gaze darting to his face as she tried to read his inscrutable eyes. She sat heavily in the nearest chair. "She refused?"

"Yes, she refused. It seems she continues to love the father of her child."

"You know that, too?" Grace asked incredulously. "Did Mercy tell you?"

"You apparently know my reputation. Do you doubt that I couldn't tell for myself?"

"Yes, I do know something of your reputation, and so you know why I would not allow her to go anywhere with you."

His gaze faltered. "If one can believe Sir Donald."

Then he raised his brilliant blue eyes and regarded her steadily. Shamelessly. "You helped me when I was in need, and now you must allow me to repay you by helping your sister. Despite what you may have heard, I promise you I will treat your sister with the utmost care and respect. You and I both know she cannot remain here much longer."

"I...I don't need your help," Grace said, attempting to sound composed. "I can look after Mercy."

He cocked his head as he looked at her suspiciously. "How? All by yourself?"

"I am going to marry Sir Donald. I have told him so."

"Oh, Grace, no!" Mercy cried, suddenly rushing into the room. "You mustn't." She turned to Elliot. "Mr. Elliot, tell her she mustn't. I will go away. You needn't be ashamed because of me. Mr. Elliot has said—"

"This man is Lord Elliot Fitzwalter," Grace said flatly.

"*What?*"

"He is a rogue, a womanizer, a gambler. He took advantage of us, and I don't want you to go with him."

"He lied?"

"Oh, don't be so naive!" Grace exclaimed, completely frustrated by Mercy's innocent romanticism, and full of anguish. "Yes, he lied."

Elliot ignored Mercy's shock and spoke only to Grace. "I did lie, and I have been an irresponsible cad."

He regarded her intently, willing her to see his sincerity in what he was about to tell her. "It is because of what I have been that you must believe me when I say you cannot marry Donald Franklin, because for everything you have heard of me, I could tell you many more things infinitely worse that he has done. You would be better off in the poorhouse than married to him."

"Listen to him, Grace," Mercy said fervently. "I could never forgive myself if you married that man because of me!"

"Why should I believe you?" Grace demanded, disregarding her sister. "How can I be sure you aren't lying to me now?"

"Because I ask you to," he said quietly, and then he held his breath as he waited for Grace to respond.

His only hope now was that she believe him enough not to marry Franklin, and trust him enough to let him help her sister.

She regarded him with those lovely, inscrutable eyes. "Will you promise me that my sister will be safe in your care?" she asked softly.

"Yes."

"And what you say about Sir Donald is true?"

"I would swear to it on the Bible."

Grace slowly nodded her head. "Then I won't marry him, and Mercy may go with you."

At this sign of her trust, Elliot felt hot tears spring to his eyes, which he blinked back. He had been weak all his life; now, he must be strong.

And then a new idea came to him, born of love. Could he not become worthy of Grace's love? Was there not some way he could redeem himself in the eyes of the world, and Grace Barton?

Even as his mind raised the questions, his heart vowed that it would be so.

It *must* be so!

Mercy hurried to her sister and embraced her ecstatically. "Oh, Grace, thank heavens! I knew that odious man had designs on you and I have been so worried!"

She said other things of a similar nature, which Grace did not hear as she looked at Elliot Fitzwalter over her sister's shoulder.

"I must finish packing," Mercy announced suddenly, and she quickly hurried out of the room.

Leaving Grace and Elliot alone.

Grace swallowed hard, and finally, her practical nature reasserted itself. "How are we to get you and Mercy from Barton without causing gossip?" she asked, gesturing for him to sit and telling herself she was doing the right thing by trusting him.

Surely she couldn't put much credence in anything Sir Donald said, and surely she could have faith in this man, who had had ample opportunity and a willing victim for seduction, yet had not attempted to do so.

He remained standing. "I shall leave here first, and walk to Barton," he said evenly. "If you will lend me enough money, I will purchase a passage on the coach to Lincoln. Mercy can also purchase a ticket for the same coach. Once she and I reach Lincoln, we can take the train to Barroughby, and from there, hire a carriage to take us to Barroughby Hall."

"What will your brother say when you arrive so unexpectedly?"

"I daresay he'll be shocked," he said with a lopsided grin that made her heart ache.

"Are you certain—?"

"Mercy will be welcome, and I'm sure Adrian will be relieved to see me." His grin became wryly self-mocking. "Mama will likely be delirious with joy."

Grace tried to smile in response, but her heart was too heavy.

"Rest assured, I would not propose this course of action if I were not fairly certain of the outcome," he said, his voice softly consoling. "Granted my half brother and I have had our differences, but I think he will be prepared to overlook them if I grovel sufficiently.''

''Will you? Grovel?''

''I shall apologize for all my past transgressions.''

Grace waited for him to say more. To ask her to come with him. To say that he would miss her. To say that he would come back to her.

To tell her that he loved her.

Instead, he turned on his heel and abruptly left the room.

Chapter Fourteen

Elliot walked as quickly as he could down the road toward the village. It wouldn't be too difficult to find Franklin's house, for surely someone at the inn or on the road could point the way.

Now that the Bartons knew who he was, he didn't particularly care who else saw him, especially since he was leaving.

Around him, the varied green of the leaves of the blossoming trees rustled with the slight breeze that held the merest hint of the sea and fens. The Bartons' garden bloomed with a simple loveliness he would not soon forget, and the underbrush along the lane was dotted with the subtle white, pinks and blues of wildflowers.

How could he have thought Lincolnshire miserable country? He would miss its rustic beauty when he got home to the manicured lawns and trimmed shrubberies of the gardens at Barroughby Hall, although not nearly as much as he would miss Grace.

He hadn't gotten very far when he heard a crash in the underbrush like a wounded deer stumbling about, and then a short, stocky man stepped out of the undergrowth in front of him.

Elliot halted abruptly and stared at Boffin, not gone at all, but very much present.

He had completely forgotten the man's existence.

"Well, well, well, if it ain't my lord," Boffin said. "Hey, lads! Hurry up. 'Ere 'e is, come out to meet uz!"

Other men appeared, one young and pockmarked, the other older. All were ragged and filthy.

Three to one. Not the best of odds.

Nevertheless, Elliot stood his ground, his hands clenched at his side. "Well, and good morning to you, Boffin," he said, affecting a good-natured tone. "I didn't expect to see you again."

"I daresay you didn't," Boffin replied, strolling toward him as his companions gathered behind him.

"If you're after your ten pounds, I'm afraid you've caught me at rather a bad time. I'll have to write you a cheque. I don't suppose you or one of your charming friends has some paper?" His gaze swept over the miscreants behind Boffin. "No? Then pardon me, I have an errand to attend to."

"Oh, no, you don't, my lord!" Boffin stepped in front of him, barring the way.

"There! You've done it again!" Elliot declared, putting his hands on his hips.

"Eh?" the skinny young one said, obviously puzzled.

"You've called me 'my lord,'" Elliot said in a bemused tone. "You must be mistaking me for someone else."

The ruffians behind Boffin glanced at each other, and the younger one licked his lips nervously.

"You're Lord Elliot Fitzwalter," Boffin said. "I seen you in London."

"Recently?"

"No. Six years back, before you disappeared!"

"My dear fellow!" Elliot exclaimed, placing one hand on his chest in a gesture of surprise. "As flattered as I am to think that you believe me an aristocrat, I assure you, I am not this Lord Elliot Fitzwalter, but David Fitzgibbons of Cambridge. Would I be dressed like this if I were a nobleman, and would I have to gamble to make a living?"

The men behind Boffin began to mutter. Their leader glanced at them sharply. "It's 'im, I tells ya! Don't be fooled by his talk!"

Boffin stalked up to Elliot. "You ran off and nobody's seen ya. Not your brother the duke. Not your mother. That's why you're dressed in those clothes and got to cheat at cards to get money!"

"And I suppose those two young ladies are not my cousins?" Elliot addressed the other men, his tone skeptical and sarcastic. "They just found me, a complete stranger, and took me into their home? They've let me stay with them for no other reason than the tenderness of their hearts? Nor am I related to the local constable, who might find it fascinating to hear about the men lurking around here."

The young man started to back away.

"It ain't 'im," the older man muttered. "Sounds like a toff, I grant ya, but the rest don't make sense. You're wrong, Boffin."

"I ain't!" Boffin came even closer, and Elliot began to feel the trickle of sweat down his back. He was still outnumbered three to one, although the others looked to be thinking twice about bothering a man who could be a relative of the constable. "Get me some money, or I'll tell your brother where you are!"

Elliot smiled, for Boffin's words were no threat to him, not since he had decided to return home. "You may tell this alleged brother of mine anything you like, and see if he believes you—provided a duke's servants would even let men such as yourselves inside his manor house."

"Give over, Bob," the younger man whined. "He ain't the one."

Boffin's eyes narrowed and his jowls quivered with rage. "If he ain't Lord Elliot Fitzwalter, I still mean to have my ten pound, if I have to strip him naked and sell his clothes!"

He lunged for Elliot, not appreciating that a man who has spent considerable time in gaming dens might have learned a thing or two about defending himself. Before Boffin knew quite what hit him, he was lying on the ground, flat on his back and with a bloody nose. He tried to get to his feet, but fell back down, unconscious.

Elliot faced the man's companions. "Anyone else care to try?" he offered.

The young one made a run for him, but Elliot was ready and soon he, too, was sprawled on the ground, likewise unconscious. By the time Elliot looked up, the other fellow had disappeared into the trees.

Elliot had no wish to leave Boffin and his crony

on the loose. Therefore, he pulled off Boffin's rope belt and tied the men's hands together. "That should hold you until the law arrives," he muttered, tightening the knot.

He looked around, but there were no signs of the other man.

Elliot had no delusions about honor among thieves. The other fellow would not wait for his cronies to revive. He would be long gone by the time these two came around.

Elliot straightened, brushed off his clothes and continued on his way.

Donald Franklin grunted and looked up from *The Times* when his butler Remington knocked on the open door of his study. Like all the rooms of Sir Donald's home, this one was large, stuffy and overdone. "Well?" Franklin demanded querulously.

"There is a gentleman asking to see you, Sir Donald," Remington said with great deference. "I explained that you were about to leave on a journey to London, but he was most insistent."

Franklin tossed the newspaper aside. "What gentleman?"

"He declines to give his card, Sir Donald."

His master let fly with a particularly vivid and obscene curse. "Then he's no gentleman and he can go to the devil."

"Donald, ever the same charming fellow, I see," Elliot remarked, ignoring the horrified butler and strolling into the room.

Franklin jumped to his feet. "What the—Fitzwalter!"

"In the very flesh." Elliot elegantly sat in the chair recently vacated by the surprised Franklin.

"Get out and leave us alone," Franklin ordered the butler gruffly, and the man seemed only too happy to obey. When he was gone and had closed the door, Franklin stared at his unexpected guest. "What are you doing here?"

"What, no delighted exclamations of joy at my return? No tender lamentations for my pitiful clothes? I was hoping for a rather better reception from such an old and dear friend."

"You haven't changed much," Franklin muttered. "Where have you been?"

"Oh, here and there. Around and about," Elliot replied with a grin.

"How did you get here?"

"Would you believe I found a magic lamp and rubbed it and—no, I see you wouldn't. In that case, I shall simply say that the innkeeper of The Three Crowns was good enough to provide me with the necessary directions."

Then Elliot frowned. "The point is, I'm here now, and I find myself in a somewhat embarrassing situation."

"That's nothing new," Franklin replied, regarding Elliot suspiciously.

"Nor for you," Elliot said, and there was a hint of menace in his voice that wasn't lost on his unwilling host. "I've heard some very interesting things about you, Donald."

"What things?"

"I understand you're thinking of standing for member of parliament for this riding."

"So what's that got to do with you?"

"Nothing much. I don't care what you do—provided it doesn't harm any friends of mine, or my family."

Franklin raised his eyebrows. "You were never much for family."

Elliot waved his hand in a gracefully dismissive gesture. "Five years gives a man plenty of time to think. Now, about your political aspirations—"

"They've got nothing to do with you," Franklin repeated harshly.

"Not specifically, no." Elliot glanced down at his hands as if examining his fingernails. "I also heard you're thinking of getting married."

"I don't know where you get off barging into my house and—"

His words ended with a gasp as Elliot lunged from the chair and grabbed Franklin by the throat, his expression murderous. "Don't you, dear Donald?" he said through clenched teeth. "It just so happens that the woman you propose to sully with your idea of holy matrimony is a friend of mine, and I simply cannot allow such a disastrous event to take place." Elliot let go when he realized Franklin's lips were turning purple.

Franklin rubbed his neck as Elliot moved back. "I'll have the law on you!" he croaked.

"Will you?"

Franklin's angry and frightened gaze faltered. "I

should. That'd be one scandal your brother wouldn't help you out of!''

Elliot regarded the man steadily. "Speaking of scandal, there are plenty of interesting stories I could tell your neighbors about the man who wants to represent them.''

"You wouldn't dare!''

"Why not?''

"Because I could tell a pretty tale or two about *you!*''

"I am not running for parliament,'' Elliot noted coolly.

"And what's Grace Barton to you, anyway?'' Franklin demanded. "A former lover?''

"You're disgusting, Franklin. The fact that you could even think that of her shows that you are an ignorant, debased imbecile.''

"What do you care if I marry her or not? Don't tell me Lord Elliot Fitzwalter's suddenly gone all chivalrous?''

"I wouldn't consider the why of it, if I were you, Franklin. You would strain what little brain you possess. Let it suffice that I have an interest in what happens to Grace Barton, and I will not allow you to marry her.''

"*Allow* me? You won't *allow* me?'' Franklin demanded. "Who do you think you are, to come into my house and order me about like some kind of lackey?''

"I am Lord Elliot Fitzwalter, second son of the Duke of Barroughby. I know all about your illustrious career in brothels, gaming rooms and opium dens, and

I will gladly tell everyone and anyone what I know if you persist in this plan to marry Grace Barton, and run for parliament.''

Franklin turned pale, but his mouth was a determined line and his eyes were full of hate. ''You know because you were there, you arrogant, stinking aristocrat! I'll tell everyone what I know about *you!*''

''Go ahead. I have no political ambitions. Indeed, you should recall that I have no ambitions at all.''

''Except to get between Grace Barton's legs, I'll wager!''

Elliot didn't bat an eyelash. ''Say anything like that again, and I will gladly kill you.''

Franklin stumbled toward the mantel, his hand fumbling for the bell rope. ''Get out! Get out of my house!''

Elliot held out his hand placatingly and smiled. ''Donald, my dear fellow, calm yourself. You're getting very overwrought.''

Franklin hesitated and regarded Elliot with suspicion. ''You've just threatened to kill me, and you think I'm only being *overwrought?*''

''I don't think it unnatural for a man to get a little annoyed when you insult a woman he admires, especially when his designs are strictly disinterested. Really, Franklin, she's quite lovely, but certainly not the type of woman I want in my bed. Why, she'd be far too timid. I'm rather surprised you'd think of bedding such a female.''

Franklin relaxed a little. ''As you say, she's lovely. And she's from an old and respected family.''

"But why marry at all? I'm surprised you would even consider it. You always liked...variety."

"Lord Denburton recommends it."

"Lord Denburton is still prowling about, is he?" Elliot regarded Donald Franklin studiously. "How old a man is he now? He must be seventy-five if he's a day. Surely getting a bit old to be pulling strings."

"He's still got lots of pull, believe you me, Fitzwalter."

"And to think, he's my beloved godfather. I must look him up when I get home."

"He's your godfather?"

"Indeed. And I really think you should reconsider running for public office. Why, you'd always have to be looking over your shoulder, in case someone else we both know decides to tell stories." Elliot's expression and tone grew grave. "If you give up that preposterous idea, I will promise never to reveal what I know about you."

Franklin would have had to be an idiot not to understand the import of Elliot's words: give up Grace Barton and running for parliament, and Elliot Fitzwalter would keep quiet. If he didn't, any chance of political office would be ruined anyway, and quite possibly any hope of further advancement, for there was much Elliot could tell that would insure that Franklin was spurned by honorable men everywhere. "Oh, very well," he grudgingly conceded. "I won't marry Grace Barton, and I won't run for parliament."

"Excellent! I knew you would eventually see reason. Oh, and there's also the matter of the rent on the Barton Farm."

Franklin sighed wearily. "What about it?"

"I also think you should reconsider the raise you've proposed. I must say, it's excessive, and I'm sure upon further consideration, you'll agree." Elliot's lips turned up into his lopsided grin, only this time, his grin was as much of a threat as any words could be.

"I'll go bankrupt!"

"Oh, I hardly think so."

Elliot moved toward the door with the languid grace that Franklin had always envied, as he had envied Fitzwalter's position, wealth and women, although never had he hated Fitzwalter as much as he did now. "Donald, I bid you adieu. It's been delightful seeing you again, old fellow."

With a disgruntled frown, Franklin nodded and reached for the bellpull. "Remington, show this *gentleman* to the door," he ordered with immeasurable scorn when the butler appeared.

Elliot smiled, bowed politely and turned to go, pausing on the threshold to look back and say, "Oh, and by the by, if you'd care to begin earning the respect of the locals, you might send someone out to the road near the Bartons' farm. They'll find two ruffians there who deserve to be jailed for assault. They had the unmitigated gall to try to attack me this morning."

Donald Franklin's only response was an unintelligible, angry grunt.

The next morning, Grace folded the last garment and closed Mercy's small trunk. "Is that everything?'' she asked, trying to sound as if Mercy left home every day.

In truth, they had never been away from each other for more than a day, and Grace knew this parting was, in a sense, forever. Mercy was leaving both childhood and Barton behind, literally and figuratively, and not just temporarily.

Even if Lieutenant Brown returned, and he and Mercy married, his career would take Mercy far away.

If Lieutenant Brown did not return, Grace would have to give up Barton Farm.

Yet it wasn't only Mercy whose presence she would miss, she reflected with a weary sigh. Hopefully, when the time came for her to join Mercy at Barroughby Hall, she would be able to think of Lord Elliot as nothing more than an unexpected, rather unsuitable guest who had repaid their kindness in kind. She should be able to look him in the eye and converse intelligently, as she had not been able to yesterday, when he had returned.

She had been so troubled and distressed, she had scarcely been able to utter a word. She didn't even ask where he had gone.

He had likewise been silent, and Mercy, too, had spoken little.

''Yes, I think I have everything,'' Mercy replied softly. She reached down for her valise, but Grace took it. ''I'll carry this.''

''I wish you were coming with us,'' Mercy murmured. ''I'm going to be so lonely without you!''

''I will miss you, too,'' Grace said with a rueful

smile that hid a heavy heart. "Of course, I can always visit the Hurley girls if I want company."

Mercy smiled and sniffled simultaneously. "I promise I will write every day," she vowed, her eyes starting to shine with tears.

"I promise to reply every day," Grace said with a forced levity. "Now we had better have our breakfast. I wouldn't want you fainting on the road."

"I'm sure Lord Elliot wishes you were going with us, too."

"*I'm* sure he agrees that this is the better way," Grace replied.

After all, he had not asked her to go with them. He had not even implied that he wanted her company. "Someone has to stay to look after the house and garden. Besides, what would happen if Lieutenant Brown came back and nobody was here to tell him where you'd gone?"

"*When* Adam comes back, explain why I couldn't wait here for him."

"Mercy," Grace said hesitantly, "what if he never comes back—or at least, not to marry you?"

Mercy didn't meet her gaze. "If he dies before we can be married—the only thing which would prevent that from happening—I will do my best to raise his child." She looked at her sister and smiled tremulously. "With your help, Grace."

Grace swiftly and fervently embraced her sister.

"Promise me you'll come when it's time for the baby," Mercy whispered, choking back a sob. "Promise me!"

"I will," Grace vowed solemnly, her own voice far from steady.

"We had better get some breakfast before we get too maudlin," Grace said after a moment, drawing back and speaking briskly, although with a suspicious huskiness. "I had better rouse Lord Elliot."

"Just think, he was a nobleman all the time," Mercy reflected tearfully while she wiped her eyes as Grace stepped across the hall to knock on the door.

"My lord!" she called out when she got no answer. "He must be still asleep," she remarked to Mercy. "My lord!"

She put her hand on the door and cautiously opened it, to see that the room was empty. "He's... he's gone!"

"Gone?" Mercy gasped, hurrying to her side and staring into the vacant room.

Grace leaned against the door frame. What did this mean? Why would he promise to help, and then disappear?

Then she saw the paper on the bed and rushed to pick it up.

It was a note, and a quick glance at the bottom told her it was from him. Mercy stood beside her, and together they read Elliot's flowing script.

Dear Miss Barton,

How cold and formal! Grace thought, although perfectly proper. Yet how much she would have preferred something gentler, something that told her she was as important to him as he was to her.

Allow me to thank you once again for your generous hospitality, which I hope to one day repay in kind. It is my wish that you feel free to come to Barroughby Hall at any time in the next several months to visit your sister. Please rest assured that you will be welcome.

"You must come, Grace!"

Grace did want to be with her sister, but dread was beginning to take the place of happiness. What if she had totally misinterpreted Lord Elliot's behavior toward her? After all, he had rebuffed her. Maybe he didn't even like her. Perhaps he looked that way at all women.

It was not unlikely that once he was back where he belonged, he would consider her nothing more than a tenderhearted stranger who had taken him in. A little flirtation on his journey home.

How could she bear to see him again, knowing that she loved him, and fearing that he did not harbor a comparable feeling for her? It would be terrible—almost as terrible as saying goodbye to him today was going to be.

Also, I wish to assure your sister that she may stay at Barroughby Hall for as long as she likes. I'm quite certain my brother and his wife will be delighted to have her.

As we decided last night, I have gone on ahead to Barton, so that no suspicion of our friendship will give the notorious gossips opportunity for tales.

Friendship. How pale a word it was—and how correct her assumption had been.

Disappointment threatened to overwhelm her, and she might have started to cry, if Mercy had not been standing beside her. As it was, it merely took a monumental effort not to.

Once again, allow me to give you my humble and sincere thanks, and to wish you all happiness.

Grace gave Mercy a sidelong glance, to behold her sister staring at the paper with a very puzzled frown. "It is...not a very *loving* letter," Mercy said quietly, with obvious dismay.

"No, it isn't," Grace replied.

"I thought—"

"We should eat our breakfast," Grace said shortly. She was in no humor to discuss this letter, or anything else with Mercy.

She needed to save every ounce of her energy, so that she would be able to bid a calm, composed farewell to Lord Elliot Fitzwalter when they met at The Three Crowns.

Before he went away, back to his aristocratic life with his aristocratic friends, taking her beloved sister with him, and leaving her all alone.

Once again, Elliot trudged along the lonely road to Barton.

It had been his intention to take his leave in person; however, as he had lain in that bed for the last time, awake and restless, recalling how awkward it had been when he had returned from Franklin Hall, he knew that he could not bear the idea of parting from Grace again in the intimacy of her home. Better by far to nod a cool farewell from the coach window, where he wouldn't be tempted to blurt out his love for her, or his determination to make himself worthy to be her husband.

After all, he had only Mercy's word to go on that Grace might already love him. Maybe she did—he hoped she did!—but he was nonetheless determined to woo her properly, once Mercy was safely looked after and he had found some means to earn a living independent of his family.

He would ask Adrian to provide him with some capital, then he would go to London. He had many friends, with many businesses, and he thought he might be able to use his natural attributes in some business capacity, if one of them would give him the opportunity.

Yet therein lay another reason he dare not voice his hopes to Grace.

He might fail.

Chapter Fifteen

Grace kept a close watch over Mercy as they slowly walked toward Barton. The coach didn't depart for Lincoln until after the noon hour, so it wasn't the rate of their progress that brought the worried frown to Grace's brow.

It was concern over Mercy's state of health, for the day was warm and the way tiring, as well as the undeniable realization that if anyone cared to really scrutinize her younger sister, they would notice that her waist was not as slim as it used to be. Indeed, it was easy to believe that inquisitive busybodies like the Hurley girls would guess the reason at once.

"Are you very tired?" Grace asked softly, setting down Mercy's small trunk and valise that she had insisted upon carrying. "We could rest a little."

"I'm all right, Grace," Mercy replied. Then she smiled wanly. "Although I'll be happier once we're safely past the Hurley house. Hopefully, they won't be at home."

Grace nodded her agreement. "Or they will be too busy gossiping with a visitor to see us pass."

"Yes!" Mercy replied fervently.

Unfortunately, they soon found out that this was not the case, for the moment they drew abreast of the large stone abode, with its painfully neat garden behind a low stone fence, Myrtle Hurley came out of the door as if she'd been shot from a cannon. Miss Ethel followed dutifully behind, likewise swiftly. They both wore bonnets and carried baskets, and Grace could only hope they intended to work in their garden.

"Good morning, my dears!" Miss Myrtle called excitedly, waving at them as she bustled down the flagstone walk toward the road. "Are you going into town?" she asked breathlessly. "How very *fortuitous!* So are *we!*"

"Morning!" Miss Ethel echoed. "Most fortuitous!"

Grace suspected that if they had planned to go into town, it had only been after seeing herself and Mercy, for Miss Myrtle's bonnet strings showed signs of hasty tying, as did her sister's.

Mercy exchanged a weary glance with Grace as they halted, and Grace noticed that Mercy drew her light shawl over her chest and stomach.

"Why, what's *this?*" Miss Myrtle declared in her sweet singsong voice when she opened the gate, stepped into the road and saw the baggage. She halted so abruptly, her sister collided with her.

"Ethel, take care!" Miss Myrtle admonished in a brief aside as she continued to gaze at the trunk and valise as if she had never seen baggage before. "Are you going somewhere?"

"Mercy is going to visit our second cousin in Bath," Grace lied smoothly.

"*I* didn't know you have a second cousin living in Bath," Miss Myrtle accused with another smile.

"Didn't know," Miss Ethel seconded.

"It is not a close connection, but she has extended the invitation, and Mercy is pleased to go."

"But surely there is no need for dear Mercy to leave Barton *now,*" Miss Myrtle said with a knowing smile. "The rents are not going to change, after all."

This time Grace couldn't hide her surprise. "They're...they're not?"

"No, my dear." Miss Myrtle stepped toward Grace and took her arm, turning her toward town. She began to walk, barely giving Grace time to pick up the baggage. "Mrs. Banks came to see us on the way to market this morning. Really, it is a most *bizarre* business!"

"Bizarre!" Miss Ethel echoed, and Grace glanced back to see her take charge of Mercy.

"What happened?" Grace asked.

"It seems, my dear, that a young man came to Franklin Hall yesterday and *demanded* to speak with Sir Donald."

"Who was he?" Grace inquired, although she knew perfectly well. That was where Lord Elliot had gone, and he must have persuaded Donald Franklin to keep the rents unchanged.

If only she could thank him before he went away— but she had to pretend she didn't know him when they met him at the coach.

Miss Myrtle's fishy eyes had grown even wider.

"That's part of the mystery! He wouldn't say. He didn't even have a visiting card! Really! *What* are manners coming to!"

"I'm surprised Sir Donald agreed to speak with him," Grace observed.

"So were *we*. We were even more surprised to hear that Sir Donald is going to *Europe*. At once. For his *health*."

"I...I beg your pardon?" Grace said, dumbfounded.

"Yes, my dear. Whoever would have guessed he was sickly! Still, Mrs. Banks was in *quite* a state about it."

Miss Myrtle's gaze became eagerly curious. "But we assumed you knew *all* about it, my dear, especially when we heard the wedding is called off."

Grace's knees went weak with relief. Although she had been prepared to speak to Sir Donald herself, she was delighted not to have to do so.

For which she could also thank Lord Elliot, no doubt.

"This must be *most* unsettling for you, my dear!"

"Why?" Grace demanded, rather ruthlessly enjoying the discomfort that appeared on Miss Myrtle's face.

"Well, that is, we had heard—"

"A rumor, and nothing more," Grace concluded for her.

Unfortunately, it took more than a snub to quiet Myrtle Hurley, or allay her suspicions.

"Oh, you can tell *us* all about it," she said sympathetically.

There was no one in the world Grace would be less likely to confide in; nevertheless, she had to remain in Barton for some time, so she would be foolish to make the Hurleys her enemies, especially when Mercy hoped to be married to their nephew. That was going to be an awkward enough situation, without Grace making it worse.

By this time, however, they were mercifully near the inn where the coach would be stopping before taking on new passengers and journeying to Lincoln. Grace eagerly scanned the cobbled street, and spotted Lord Elliot, gracefully lounging near the entrance to the stable. He straightened slightly when he saw her, too, and smiled, but only for an instant before turning away to watch the coach horses being changed.

"Why, look!" Miss Myrtle declared, nodding toward Lord Elliot. "That might be the fellow there who spoke to Sir Donald! He was a *handsome* man, Mrs. Banks said. He looks like *quite* the rogue to me."

"A *rogue!*" Miss Ethel echoed decisively.

"Do you suppose he means to go in the coach?" Miss Myrtle continued. She stopped and turned toward Mercy. "I think you should reconsider going, if *he* is to be a fellow passenger."

Mercy shook her head. "Our cousin is expecting me. I'm sure I'll be quite safe."

By now they had reached the yard of the inn. "Good day, Miss Hurley, Miss Ethel," Grace said firmly, finding it increasingly hard to abide their presence and not to acknowledge Lord Elliot's.

"It is really too bad Grace isn't going with you,"

Miss Myrtle criticised. "So *dangerous* for a young lady to travel alone!"

Mercy smiled weakly. "I shall be fine." She paused a moment, then said, "If your nephew comes to visit, please tell him I said hello."

"Oh, we will!" Miss Myrtle said. "But we don't expect him before next spring, if then. He is so very indispensable to the admiral!"

That was the last straw for Grace. *"Goodbye!"* she said, and she took Mercy's arm as forcibly as Miss Myrtle had taken hers and escorted Mercy into the inn.

Very well aware that Lord Elliot was still outside.

"Goodbye, dear Miss Mercy!" the twins called out in unison, and with some genuine feeling. "Take care! And when you get to Lincoln, be sure to sup at the Cock's Crow! They serve the best—"

Grace closed the door firmly and realized Mercy was quietly weeping.

"You will stay here until Adam comes, won't you?" Mercy pleaded in a whisper after Grace had fetched her a drink of water. "I couldn't tell his aunts where I was going. I have to count on you—although I wish so much you were coming with me...." Her words trailed off into a pitiable sob.

Grace wanted to cry, too, but that would only upset Mercy more. "I will stay here, but I must come to Barroughby before the baby does," she said, attempting to smile.

"What if Adam—"

"Then I'll leave him a note with his aunts."

"They'll read it!"

"I know. If he's not back by then, it won't matter what they think."

"They'll be so nasty!" Mercy raised her tragic eyes to look at Grace. "I'm sorry, Grace."

"Adam will come in time," she said, willing herself to believe it, and to make Mercy think she believed it. "If he is delayed, we shall find another place to wait for him."

"Grace, you are so good to me! The best of sisters!" Mercy said, uselessly wiping her eyes, for her tears were falling in earnest.

Grace smiled tremulously and swallowed hard. "I think the coach is ready," she said, listening to the shouts outside.

She rose slowly. She didn't want to say goodbye— to Mercy, or to Lord Elliot.

Mercy stood, too, and stopped her weeping, drying her eyes once again before she put her hand in Grace's. Together they went outside.

Lord Elliot was where he had been before, leaning against the wall near the stable.

How handsome he was, and how calm—while she felt like the Spartan boy who had let himself be torn to ribbons rather than reveal he had a fox cub beneath his tunic.

Then, to both her delight and chagrin, Lord Elliot strolled toward them. "Taking the coach to Lincoln?" he asked, and he glanced at the road before returning his gaze to them.

Grace half turned and caught sight of the edge of Miss Myrtle's skirt. Which wasn't moving. They were standing there watching them! It was too mean and too terrible!

"Yes, I am going to Lincoln," Mercy said with remarkable composure.

"It is a fine day to travel," Lord Elliot remarked.

When would she ever hear such another voice, Grace thought with despair. He made the most banal remark intriguing.

Then, suddenly, Grace didn't care what the Hurleys, or anybody else, thought. She had to thank him for saving her from a disastrous marriage, even if it had been nothing more to him than repayment for their hospitality. She moved as close to him as she dared and, with her back to the Hurleys, spoke very quietly. "Thank you for talking to Sir Donald yesterday."

"Delighted at the outcome," Lord Elliot replied lightly. "He came to understand that to marry you would not be in his own best interest. The man always was a coward." He glanced down at her. "He is not the only one."

Grace's heart started to hammer in her chest as she wondered what he meant. How could she ever find out? This was hardly the place for an intimate conversation, and he was leaving.

"I...I should know how you managed it, in case he should try something similar again. When you have gone."

Lord Elliot's steady gaze faltered. "Ah, yes. When I am gone," he said softly. He raised his blue eyes to look at her again. "I told him I would let several influential people know about his past if he did." His expression grew pensive. "The one good thing to come from my own disgraceful career."

There was something hiding in his blue eyes, but she couldn't put a name to it. It might be only gratitude and regret, but it might be something more.

Unfortunately, there was no time left. The horses had been changed, and the coach driver fastened a steely gaze on them. "You comin' or not?" he bellowed, to which both Mercy and Lord Elliot nodded.

Lord Elliot stepped forward to open the door for Mercy, who quickly embraced Grace. "I'll miss you so much!" she whispered, starting to cry again.

"God bless you, Mercy!" Grace murmured, letting go and watching Mercy disappear into the coach, so that only Lord Elliot was standing near her. He didn't say anything, nor did she as they looked at each other.

Ask me to go with you, she pleaded silently. *Ask me to be your wife.*

Without a word, without a sign, he stepped inside the coach, the driver cracked his whip, and the coach rattled down the street.

Grace watched the carriage turn, her eyes on Mercy's frantically waving white handkerchief.

"Well, my *dear!*" she heard Miss Myrtle say behind her. "This is all very strange. Very strange indeed!"

"Strange!" her sister echoed.

Grace turned to them with such a silently forbidding expression they wisely backed away. Then she mutely marched past them and toward her home.

If she had never felt so alone in all her life, and if she dreaded an empty future with a permanently broken heart, that was only for her to know. And if her cheeks were wet with tears, she didn't want anyone to see.

Hester Fitzwalter sighed as she prepared to enter the drawing room of the Dower House. She was feeling very tired with this pregnancy and would have preferred to remain at home, but the dowager duchess had not been well of late, and Hester felt duty-bound to make her daily call.

Not that she had any hope of any change in her step-mother-in-law's attitude toward her. The dowager duchess continued to blame Hester for her beloved son's long absence, and not without some cause.

Yet Hester could no more have married Elliot Fitzwalter than she could have become queen, not if she were to be true to her heart. She loved Adrian Fitzwalter, and his half brother had never stood any chance of changing that, no matter how eloquently and desperately he had pleaded with her to become his wife, for Elliot had never truly loved her. At first, he had simply wanted to upset his brother by pursuing her. Later, his motives were less certain, and his proposal had held something of a selfish sincerity—but no love.

She had often wondered, in the years since his angry and abrupt departure, if he had found another woman to love him, and for him to truly love, in a way that would allow Elliot to be the man he was capable of becoming.

They might never know.

With a sigh, and resolving to be as pleasant as possible, Hester opened the door and entered the room. As usual, the duchess sat by the window that had the best view of the long drive to Barroughby Hall, and as usual, the duchess sat stiffly straight, in a pose of great expectation.

The older woman didn't move or turn from her post of observation as Hester came into the room. "Good morning, Your Grace," Hester said softly.

"He has sent no word?" the duchess demanded.

Hester tried not to sound as weary of that question as she was. "No, Your Grace."

"You are pregnant again," the duchess remarked coldly.

"Yes, Your Grace."

"I suppose you and your husband delight in breeding a pack of boys to take away Elliot's birthright," the duchess muttered.

Hester bit her tongue. There was no point in arguing with the duchess. There never had been, and although there was animosity in her tone, it was nothing compared to what Hester had endured in her first days as the dowager duchess's companion. It was as if living in daily anticipation of her son's return had drained most of the venom out of her.

"Where is Adrian?" the duchess demanded.

"He took David riding," Hester replied.

"You will spoil that—" Then the duchess half rose from her chair, her clawlike hand extending toward the window. "It's...it's...!" she cried feebly, her other hand clutching at her heart.

Fearing the woman was taken ill, Hester hurried to

her side, putting a supportive arm about the elderly woman's narrow shoulders. "Your Grace, what is it?" she asked as she reached for the bell the duchess kept by her side to summon her maid.

The duchess threw off Hester's arm with surprising strength as she straightened. "My boy! My Elliot! My darling boy has come home!"

Hester followed the duchess's staring gaze out the window, to see a plain closed carriage coming up the drive. There was absolutely no way in the world to tell who was inside, or even how many passengers it bore, and many people came to Barroughby Hall.

Fearing the duchess was having some kind of fit, Hester rang the bell more vigorously. "Please, Your Grace, sit!" she pleaded, glancing at Barroughby Hall as if she could summon her husband with her mind. "I shall see who it is."

The duchess ignored her. "It is my son!" she declared. "A mother *knows!* Get out of my way, Hester!"

"Your Grace, please!" Hester didn't move, hoping the duchess wouldn't try to get past her. She glanced again out the window as the carriage stopped and a figure disembarked.

Then Hester stared at the familiar man standing before Barroughby Hall in the same languid attitude she well remembered.

The duchess pushed Hester out of her way, lifted her skirts and hurried from the room. Hester quickly followed.

Lord Elliot Fitzwalter had returned at last.

Chapter Sixteen

Elliot stared at the ornate facade of Barroughby Hall.

Little had changed in the five years he had been away. The house was as uninviting as it had ever been, the windows as much like disapproving eyes as he recalled.

But while this building had not altered, he realized that *he* had, and he knew that was truly why he had returned. He was not the same selfish, spoiled creature he had been the night he left, vowing never to come back. Indeed, now he could finally admit to himself that his decision to leave Canada had nothing to do with ennui, or disgust with that country; he had been homesick, for this place and the people who lived here. The servants who had known him all his life. His mother.

Even Adrian.

"Is this your home?" Mercy whispered from her place at the window of the carriage, her voice full of awe.

Elliot turned around. "Yes." He saw the trepidation in her big gray eyes and grinned. "Don't worry. They'll be kind to you here. I promise."

"Elliot!" A female voice cried his name from somewhere in the distance. He looked past the house, toward the rise where the Dower House had been built about a century ago. Over the smooth, brilliantly green lawn came a dauntless figure he recognized at once, hurrying toward him with her black bombazine skirts blowing out behind her.

"Mother!" he cried in response, and he began to run toward her, relieved and delighted that she was alive and well, for despite his words to Grace, he had feared it would be otherwise.

"Elliot!" his mother called out again, slowing down for the last few steps as he reached her. She fell on his neck, weeping. "My boy! My own precious boy, home at last! I knew you would come! I knew it!"

"Mama," he whispered, "I'm glad to be here. I should never have stayed away so long."

For a long moment, he held her to him. She had annoyed him and aggravated him and spoiled him and had chosen to stay here rather than face an unknown future with him, but she had done the best she could, and he had repaid her poorly.

Then he saw another person over her shoulder, another woman coming toward them across the lawn, at a more sedate pace.

Hester—little changed from the way he remembered her, except to look even more content than any woman he had ever met. She exuded peace and calm and patience. Nevertheless, his heart began to beat with something akin to panic when she halted.

What if she did not want him here? She was Adrian's wife; she had the power to send him away. It would be no more than he deserved, yet if he was forced to leave again, with no resources, how much longer it would be before he could become worthy of Grace's hand!

"Lord Elliot," she said, and then she smiled. "Welcome home."

All was forgiven. He saw it in her gentle eyes, heard it in her soft voice, and felt it in her smile.

He gently disengaged his mother's arms, although she kept a firm hold on his arm, and stepped toward her. "Hester. I'm happy to see you. Marriage seems to agree with you."

Her hand went to her stomach, and Elliot realized that Mercy was not the only pregnant woman close by. How happy Adrian must be!

As if in response to his thoughts, two people rounded the corner of the house.

It was Adrian, and a little boy with dark hair and serious eyes so like his brother's, Elliot surmised that Hester was not expecting her first child. Doubly blessed was Adrian, with a living son. "Elliot!" he gasped.

Removing his mother's clinging hand, Elliot took a deep breath and faced his brother staunchly. "Hello, Your Grace," he said with a bow, using the most formal of titles, wondering what, if any, greeting his older sibling would give him.

Adrian regarded him silently for what seemed a

very long, still moment, his dark eyes inscrutable, his mouth neither smiling nor frowning. "I wondered what all the commotion was," he said softly.

Then, to Elliot's great joy and infinite relief, Adrian smiled and extended his hand as he came closer, the little boy trailing behind with a puzzled look on his face. Adrian accepted Elliot's proffered hand, and then—miraculously!—pulled him into a warm embrace. "I'm so glad you've come home."

Hester's young son tugged at his mother's skirt. "Who's that man and why is Daddy crying?" David demanded.

Hester smiled at his curiously questioning face. "That is your Uncle Elliot," she said, her voice considerably less than steady as she struggled not to cry, too. The sight of both his parents in tears would surely be too much for her little son to take with his usual equanimity.

"The one I'm named after?" the viscount asked.

"The very one."

Elliot David Phillip Fitzwalter walked regally toward the two men, who were wordlessly grinning at each other as they both swiped at their cheeks, removing any trace of unmanly tears.

"How do you do?" he demanded of this previously unknown uncle, in his childish voice but with all the arrogance of an aristocrat. "I'm named after you!"

Elliot bent down toward the little viscount. "Named after me?" he asked, casting an incredulous glance at Adrian.

"I am Elliot David Phillip Fitzwalter, Viscount

Sommerfield,'' the child announced. ''Mama says you're my Uncle Elliot.''

''She's right, and I'm very proud to be so.''

The dowager duchess, who had waited for this day for so long, was not about to let any brotherly sentiment take precedence for any length of time. She quickly claimed Elliot's arm again. ''Come inside, Elliot, and tell us where you have been. What have you been doing? Why didn't you write to me?''

''I've been in Upper Canada,'' Elliot explained as he moved toward the carriage.

''Canada!'' his mother exclaimed in horror. ''I thank God you didn't freeze to death!''

Hester took hold of her little boy's hand and wondered if Elliot was going to give the carriage driver directions about his baggage. To her surprise, she instead saw Elliot hand out a very pretty young woman, who smiled shyly at them all.

''Mama, Adrian, Hester, may I present Miss Mercy Barton? Miss Barton, my mother, the Dowager Duchess of Barroughby, my brother, the Duke of Barroughby, and his wife.''

Miss Mercy Barton. Not his wife, then.

Mercy Barton dipped a curtsy and blushed furiously. ''How do you do, Your Grace?'' she whispered to the imperious dowager duchess. ''Your Grace? Your...''

She paused in embarrassment when she came to Hester, who quickly came forward even as she puzzled over this woman's relationship with Elliot. ''Please, call me Hester,'' she offered.

To suggest the use of her given name was a shocking breach of decorum which the dowager duchess would have been sure to remark upon under less remarkable circumstances, but Hester wanted to put this young woman, and Elliot, at ease at once.

"Then you must call me Mercy," the young woman replied shyly.

"I'm hungry," the little viscount announced, obviously immune to the import of the events transpiring around him. "Is it nearly time for tea?"

"Indeed it is," Adrian said. "Come, let us all go inside."

The dowager duchess assumed pride of place, and, still holding Elliot's arm, led the way inside. Adrian glanced at Hester, then held out his arm for Miss Barton. "If you will allow me," he said gallantly.

"I shall lead you in, Mama," David declared to Hester, assuming what in his four-year-old eyes passed for a very sophisticated air.

Hester smiled and nodded. She took a moment to tell the driver that a footman would come for the baggage, while Miss Barton timidly laid a small hand on her husband's strong forearm. As Hester watched them turn to go inside, she saw something that added yet another surprise to this most surprising day.

Unfortunately, it was something that made her doubt that Elliot had changed so very much, after all.

After a tea that had been one of the most awkward in Elliot's existence, given his mother's attentive stares, his brother's questioning looks, Hester's concerned graciousness and Mercy's silent timidity, Elliot stood beside the hearth in the study of Barroughby Hall. He had stood thus many times in his life, waiting, with a nervous anticipation that he had been determined to hide, for Adrian to pass judgment on him. To tell him again what a wastrel he was, to warn him that he had better change or he would regret it. And then, when all the recriminations were over, to reveal how he had managed to "save" Elliot again.

He hadn't always dreaded this room. When his father was alive, he had enjoyed coming into the cozy darkness of the mahogany paneled study, with its old, comfortable chairs and worn Aubusson carpet. It smelled of his father then: of tobacco and brandy, and tweeds damp from rambles on the estate. Here there had been no sense that he had to be perfect, for his mother's sake, because he was her son. Here, there was no black-browed, black-eyed Adrian exuding jealousy or condemnation. Here, he had been content.

All that had changed when his father had died and Adrian had taken his place as the head of the household.

Well, he had done nothing wrong this time, despite Adrian's worried frown, and he was no longer waiting for Adrian to speak. "Mercy Barton is a friend, and nothing more," he announced when Adrian arrived and closed the door softly.

Adrian raised one dark eyebrow in a gesture Elliot remembered well. It conveyed skepticism as nothing else could. "Apparently a good one, if what Hester suspects is true."

"What does Hester suspect?"

"That the young woman is pregnant."

Elliot knew he should have guessed the shrewd,

observant Hester would figure that out. She had managed to guess the true nature of Elliot's resentment for his brother after a relatively short period of acquaintance. "She is," he admitted. "I am not the child's father."

"Oh?" Again, that eyebrow spoke volumes.

"No, I am not. The father is a young naval officer named Lieutenant Adam Brown. If you were to ask Miss Barton, she would confirm that, and also that we didn't meet until she was two months gone."

"If that is the case, why is she here with you?"

"Because she is pregnant and unmarried, and I thought we could help her."

"We?"

Elliot sighed. This was not going to be as easy as he had hoped. "You and Hester, then. In my circumstances, I have little to offer."

Adrian strolled toward the table holding the brandy decanter. "Might I ask what those circumstances are?"

"Why not? You're asking everything else."

Adrian's hand hesitated as he lifted the crystal stopper of the decanter. "You can hardly be surprised by my curiosity."

"No, not at all. If anything, I'm surprised that my arrival has been greeted with such equanimity."

Adrian poured two drinks. "Five years is a long time," he answered. "Plenty of time to think." He glanced at Elliot. "As I believe you'll agree."

Elliot approached him. "Yes, it is. And yes, I've done some thinking—but more in the past few weeks than in the rest of those five years."

Adrian gestured for Elliot to sit, and when he did, sat opposite him, in their father's chair. "Hester thinks you've changed."

"And you?"

Adrian didn't meet Elliot's gaze. Instead, he took a drink and stared into the brandy. "I would like to believe her assessment."

"But?"

"But it's been five years, and never once did you write, not even to your mother. Do you know how you have made her suffer?"

"Since I am her son, I think I have a better idea of that than you."

"Then why not write?"

"Because she chose your money over me, as I'm sure you recall."

"She's an old woman, and what you did was cruel."

Elliot felt the old enmity rising in him and forced it away. "Adrian, I'm not going to argue with you over what I've done in the past. I was wrong. I was a fool. I wasted time and money. I hurt the people who loved me. I admit to it all." He looked down at the brandy snifter in his own long, slender fingers. "And I am suffering for it. Will that not satisfy you?"

"You have not asked after Elizabeth Howell, either."

Elliot had dreaded this. Of all the shameful things he had done in his life, this had been the worst. While what he had done had been cowardly, he had not acted without some cause, and he reasoned it was time he told Adrian the whole story. "I know you think of me as a callous Casanova, seeking to deflower young virgins, but that isn't strictly true. All the women I pursued made it rather obvious that they had no true desire to maintain their virtue. Even Elizabeth Howell.

"I also know you think I simply seduced and abandoned her, and I won't deny the seduction, but it was quite mutual. She practically cornered me at more than one party and assembly and...and I was too weak to say no." Adrian frowned, but Elliot held up his hand to silence him. "I am not blaming Elizabeth. I surely led her on, feeding my own stupid pride and vanity. I just want you to understand that I'm not...I'm not like Donald Franklin."

Adrian gave a brief nod, and although his brother's face remained impassive, Elliot took that as a sign to continue. "After Elizabeth and I had made love..."

He paused, ashamed anew of what he had done, and even of the words, now that he knew what real love was. "Afterward, the first thing she said, quite proudly, was, 'Now I have had a Fitzwalter.' I was going to ask her what she meant, but I didn't because...because of the wild look in her eyes. I mean, Adrian, it was so disturbing, that look. Triumphant and peculiar!

"But that wasn't the worst of it, because she started to cry and mutter to herself. Then she began to weep and tear out her hair, as if half-mad with guilt for what she had done, yet proud of herself, too. I tell you, Adrian, it was something quite out of my experience, and I'll confess that I was terrified. I was sure she was mad—I think she was mad when I first met her, but I was too selfish to see it.''

Adrian's eyes widened. ''Then maybe what she said to me when we danced the first time I met her wasn't so naive, after all. She said...'' He paused. ''The implications were so vulgar, I was sure she didn't know what she was saying.''

Elliot sighed. ''I told you, she wasn't well, even then. Anyway, I wasn't sure what to do. I did my best to calm her down.

''Rather surprisingly, she quieted at once. I mean, immediately—something that also seemed odd. Then, she demanded to know when the wedding was to be.

''I tell you, Adrian, I've not often been as afraid as I was that night. I'll never forget those eyes of hers as long as I live! She seemed possessed, and so desperate for an answer, I named a day, any day. That seemed to calm her again, and she fell asleep. I left at once.

''I was so shaken I didn't want to go home. I went to my club, had several brandies—and yes, I know that was a stupid thing to do—and I tried to think what to do next.

''All I knew for certain was that I was certainly not going to marry her. I didn't even want to see her again. I never guessed her brother would believe that *you* had seduced her and challenge you to a duel.''

''He only knew it was a Fitzwalter, and he assumed it was me.''

''I'm sorry he shot you.''

Adrian smiled sardonically. ''So was he, but he was only being a brother.''

Elliot nodded thoughtfully. "I know that now, Adrian. I...I didn't understand then that protection could mean love. I didn't know anything about love—not really—until I saw how Hester loved you, and how you cared for her.

"How I hated you both in those days, because you made me see what I did not have. I wanted so much to hurt you, and Hester, too. I acted like a jealous, depraved monster!"

"Yes, you did," Adrian replied evenly.

"And then I spent five years trying to convince myself that love didn't matter, or that what you felt was foolish." Elliot sighed wearily. "Oh, God, Adrian, I was the fool, not you!"

"We have all done things we regret."

Elliot managed a rueful grin. "You are not even going to allow me to wallow in my self-pity, are you, brother?"

"No," Adrian replied, a shrewd expression in his dark eyes. "I believe you have done enough of that already."

Elliot nodded and continued with his story, determined to tell Adrian everything. "Anyway, I made my way home. The next day, sick as a dog and desperate, I decided to...well, you know what I did. What I always did. I ran away."

"Is that why you left Canada, too? What were you running from then?"

"Nothing—well, not exactly. I thought I was leaving behind the cold and the heat and the insects and the colonials. I know now I was running *to* something. I was running home."

"Obviously, you were somewhat delayed, at least long enough to encounter Miss Barton."

"I was on my way to Lincoln when I..." He hesitated again, tempted to hide some of the more embarrassing aspects of his recent history, then plunged on truthfully. "I was trying to elude some gamblers I had cheated. I was drunk and I fell off the horse I had stolen. The next thing I knew, I was in a cow shed. Miss Barton had found me and dragged me there."

"What?"

"Don't tell me you're shocked."

"Not with your behavior, I'll admit. I'm surprised that young woman could drag a man more than three feet."

"It wasn't Mercy Barton. It was her sister, Grace—and yes, it was most surprising. But Grace Barton can be a very determined woman."

He set down the brandy and began to pace, a sign of agitation that was a family trait, as Adrian well knew. Elliot hesitated a moment, then regarded Adrian steadfastly. "When I discovered that two women living alone had rescued me, I managed to persuade them to allow me to stay with them while I recovered." His tone became sarcastic and self-recriminating. "I repaid their kindness by giving them a false name and using their home to hide in—although I must say I *thought* Boffin and his men would be long gone by then."

"They weren't?"

"No, as I discovered later, when they tried to blackmail me."

"My God, Elliot, what *have* you been doing?"

"I want you to understand, Adrian, that I'm not proud of what I did, or the man I was. Then I discovered that Donald Franklin was after Grace." He shuddered at the memory.

Adrian sat up straight as the poker beside the hearth. *"Donald Franklin—!"*

Elliot nodded. "Yes. Believe it or not, my dear old friend actually wanted to marry her."

"I think I can infer from your tone that he reconsidered?"

"Yes," Elliot answered. "But before that, I suggested that Mercy, whose pregnancy I had discovered for myself, marry me, to prevent that marriage and spare any further embarrassment to her sister."

"What the devil were you thinking?" Adrian asked. "Do you love her?"

"No, I don't. You will also be astounded to hear," he continued ruefully, "that she absolutely and unequivocally refused. It seems her heart belongs only to Lieutenant Brown, the father of her child."

"Thank God for that!"

"Yes," Elliot answered briefly. "So then I suggested she come here until the baby is born."

"That was kind of you."

"Wasn't it, though?" Elliot said. He tried to laugh.

"Where is this Lieutenant Brown?"

"Gibraltar, I believe. Grace fears he doesn't mean to marry Mercy at all. He seems to be a bit of a bounder, and if he is, then I wouldn't entertain any hopes, either." His expression grew bitter again. "I should know." He smiled, but there was certainly no joviality in his eyes. "May Mercy stay here until the baby is born?"

"Of course." Adrian looked at his brother, thinking about the way his voice softened when he spoke of "Grace." "Why didn't her sister come with you?"

"I...I didn't ask her. She would have refused, anyway. Somebody had to stay to look after their house, and she would want things to appear as normal as possible. And they both thought someone should be there in case Lieutenant Brown *does* return."

Adrian looked at Elliot, who for so long had been a scourge in his life. "You're in love with Grace Barton." It was not a question, because Adrian had no doubts.

"I don't know," Elliot mumbled in protest, but by then Adrian was on his feet, directly in front of him.

"Yes, you do. Listen to me, Elliot. I, of all men, know how love can change a man. Something has happened to make this alteration in you—and the realization has scared you to death."

Elliot walked away, staring out the window. "You seem very sure of your opinion. As always."

"Only because I've felt the same way myself."

"What's this?" Elliot asked ruefully, once more facing his brother. "The dark Duke of Barroughby admitting he was afraid?"

"I was terrified."

"I'm glad to hear it," Elliot said with a relieved grin, while Adrian grew more serious.

"You love her very much, don't you?"

"More than I ever thought possible," Elliot confessed softly.

"What do you intend to do about it?"

He smiled wanly. "I want to ask her to marry me."

"Why haven't you?"

"She's only known me a week. Mercy thinks I have a chance, but I won't ask Grace until I have something better to offer her than..."

"Than yourself?"

Elliot nodded.

Adrian looked pensive and sympathetic. "Elliot, I was terrified Hester wouldn't want me because of my reputation, undeserved though it was. I understand the despair of remorse." His eyes became apologetic. "Now you can understand why I was angry with you. I thought *your* actions were going to rob me of Hester." His voice grew quieter. "Then I feared that I didn't deserve her anyway, because of that stupid thing I had done in university."

Elliot shook his head slowly. "My problems are different from yours, as they always have been. You had caused a fire and hurt your friend, but it was an accident. The rest of all your dishonor was based on rumors and taking the blame for *my* misdeeds.

"But unlike you, my reputation is *deserved.* I have led a decadent life, and so now, I don't deserve a decent woman like Grace Barton. At least, not yet."

"Did you ever think to ask Miss Barton how she felt about that?" a feminine voice demanded.

They both turned toward the door, which they hadn't heard open, to see Hester on the threshold, an annoyed frown on her usually calm face.

Chapter Seventeen

Hester marched into the room, closing the door firmly behind her.

"You Fitzwalter men are all the same!" she said forcefully. "Adrian almost ruined our happiness because he *assumed* that I would respond in a certain way to his proposal. You *assume* that Grace Barton will not want you, without even giving her the chance to speak."

"Hester," Elliot said, stinging at her rebuke, "you don't know Grace. You weren't there. *I* was."

"You were not the only two people at Barton Farm," Hester noted, coming toward him with a slightly less angry expression on her face. "I have just had a very illuminating conversation with Miss Mercy. She tells me that she is absolutely convinced that her sister loves you."

For a moment, joy filled Elliot at the confirmation, before reality intruded. "Mercy believes it because she hopes it is so."

"Oh, Elliot!" Hester said sternly. "Give the woman credit for knowing her own sister!"

"Grace Barton never told me she loved me."

"When did she have the chance? What did you expect? A declaration?"

He thought of Grace's sudden appearance in his bedroom. At that time, and ever since, he had blamed himself for her uncharacteristic behavior.

Now, as Hester spoke, he began to hope there was another explanation: that Grace's action *was* a declaration, of love.

"Did you tell her of your feelings?" Adrian asked.

"No," he muttered, fearing that had been a grave mistake. "I didn't think I should. I have nothing to offer her, except myself."

"Mercy apparently thinks that's more than sufficient, and is quite sure her sister would accept you."

"Mercy Barton in a romantic," Elliot reiterated, willing himself to be sensible. "She also wants Grace to be married, and I was the most available candidate."

"This doesn't sound like the arrogant Elliot I know so well," Adrian remarked. "You *are* in love with Grace Barton."

"I know that!" Elliot snapped. "And I know that I'm not good enough to marry Grace Barton!"

Hester regarded him steadily. "Yes, you are," she said softly. "Not just because of what you have said, but because of the way you have said it. Nothing could have convinced me more."

"Very well," Elliot said sardonically. "Let us assume Grace loves me, and I love her. What are we to live on? Air?"

"You are a lord. You have—"

"A title, and little else. I remember very well that our father left everything to you, Adrian."

"I can give—"

Elliot shook his head. "I don't want gifts."

"You want Grace, don't you?" Adrian demanded, exasperated.

"He needs self-respect, too," Hester added quietly.

"Hester's right. It's not just to Grace that I need to prove I am not a worthless being. I have to prove it to myself." He took a deep, calming breath. "I'm a gambler by nature, Adrian. I'm good at it—and that takes more than luck. I understand people, their little quirks and expressions that tell me when to bet, and when to wait. It has occurred to me that this might prove to be a valuable skill in business."

"You want to engage in trade?" Adrian asked, dumbfounded.

Elliot said, "I know our father wanted our name to be respectable above all else, because I used that knowledge to my own advantage many times. However, I don't think there's anything dishonorable about being in business, if one conducts oneself honestly.

"Therefore, what I propose is this—if you will give some capital to begin, as a loan, I will take it, at a suitable rate of interest. I will somehow establish myself in business, and if I succeed, I will return to Barton and court Grace Barton as a would-be husband should."

"What will you consider a success?" Adrian asked, and Elliot knew he feared some outrageous answer, like a Mayfair mansion and servants and other extravagances.

"Enough to support my wife and perhaps...children. To have a home. Nothing more."

"How long do you propose to wait for this success?" Hester asked.

"I will give it a year."

"She is to wait a year, with no word? You would abandon her?"

Elliot flinched at Hester's choice of words, thinking of the last woman he could be said to have abandoned. "Unfortunately, I'm not sure whether the change in my character is permanent, much though I hope it may be. Time may be the only way to tell.

"If Grace truly loves me, she will not be so quick to abandon that love. I can only hope that the next time I see her, I will be worthy of her." He grinned, once more the charmingly handsome Lord Elliot that all his friends would recognize. "I would not take it amiss if Mercy were to write to her sister about me, or to tell me the news from Barton from time to time when I come home."

"Come home? You are going to leave again?" asked Hester.

"I should make my own way in the world, don't you think?" Elliot answered. "I will go to London, and try to make my fortune in the very best fairy-tale manner."

"What is going on here?" the dowager duchess demanded, marching into the room as if no time at all had passed since Elliot last visited there. A closed door had never been able to keep her out. "Elliot, my dear boy, you've been closeted with Adrian far too long. It's nearly time for dinner.''

"I'm sorry, Mama. We had business to discuss.''

"Business? What business?''

"*My* business. Don't you think your charming son would cut a dashing figure at the Royal Exchange?''

"At the Royal Exchange?'' the duchess replied, aghast, as she sat upon the very edge of a chair and regarded him with astonishment. "Elliot, this is nonsense.''

"No, this is necessity,'' he replied.

"Necessity?'' The duchess turned a cold glare onto her stepson. "What does he mean, necessity? Your father did not mean for you to turn him out, penniless.''

"I know that full well,'' Adrian said, but before he could go further, Elliot sat beside her, took her hand in his and looked into her eyes.

"Mama, I need to make a new life for myself. Adrian is going to help me get started, but I must and shall be independent. That is what I've always wanted—''

"To leave me?'' she gasped. "Again? Oh, Elliot, I couldn't bear it!''

He held her hand and stroked it gently. "Mama, I won't run off like the bitter, selfish rogue I was, if that is what you fear. I must go to London to make my way but this time, I shall write often. I promise. And when I am a success, you can come and visit me.''

"With your wife?''

This time it was Elliot who looked astonished as

he stared back at her. "Wife? Have I said anything about a wife?"

"Miss Barton insists that you are going to marry her sister, although I must say I fail to understand why you have brought *her* here to meet your mother, instead of the intended bride."

"It's a long story, Mama, and as you say, it is nearly time for dinner."

"Dinner can wait," the duchess declared imperiously. "I want to know all about Grace Barton."

Adrian and Hester exchanged glances. "If you will excuse us, Your Grace, we had best see to David. We shall wait dinner for you, if necessary."

"Of course you will. Now, my son, tell me everything."

Elliot looked at his brother, who made a small, resigned shrug of his shoulders. Hester, too, was not going to help. Instead, they both left the room.

Reluctantly, Elliot did his best to explain what had happened between himself and Grace Barton, and when he was finished, he waited for her to declare that no mere farmer's daughter, no matter how ancient and respected her family, was good enough for her beloved son.

"You love this woman?" the duchess demanded when he was finished.

"Yes, I do."

"You believe she loves you?"

"I think so. I hope so."

"You will go into business for her sake, forswearing your noble heritage?"

"Mama, please, I—"

The duchess held up her hand. "Enough." She reached out and took his face tenderly between her palms, her eyes glistening with unshed tears. "My boy, if you love this woman, and she has the wisdom to see your merit, you have my blessing."

She let go, cleared her throat and, somewhat miraculously, seemed to sit up even straighter. "I always thought you would be wasted on an aristocratic wife, who would surely neglect you and waste her time on balls and other frippery. You need a decent, dutiful woman who will be justly aware of the honor you do her. This Grace Barton—you did say she was beautiful?"

Elliot tried not to smile, although he was vastly relieved at the way his mother's thoughts were tending, even if her reasons were not the most gracious. "Yes, Mama, extremely beautiful."

"Thank goodness for that. I can live with the talk of Lord Elliot throwing himself away on a poor girl of little background. Indeed, it sounds so charmingly romantic! However, I couldn't endure them to say you were lacking in taste."

"She's intelligent and practical, too."

"Intelligence and practicality in a woman is commendable. She reminds me of myself."

Elliot had to stifle a delighted chuckle. His mother was intelligent, given that the cultivation of her mind had been sorely neglected from her childhood onward, but practical? His mother had never had a practical thought in her life—unless she, too, had undergone some drastic changes during the past five years. As he looked at her, he doubted that very much.

The dowager duchess rose majestically. "As far as I am concerned, Elliot, I shall be delighted to meet Miss Barton at any time of your choosing."

"I'm glad you approve, Mama."

Holding Mercy's latest letter loosely between her fingers, Grace sighed and leaned out the open window, which overlooked the garden and yard. The summer was over, and autumn was at its height. Very soon she would be leaving Barton to go to Barroughby Hall, and Mercy.

With another sigh she blamed on her continuing worry over the absent Lieutenant Brown's failure to return, she reached out to pluck an ivy tendril that was working its way along the frame.

The way Lord Elliot Fitzwalter had worked his way into her life. Into her heart.

Try as she might to pretend she was distressed about Mercy's troubles, this was one of those moments when she knew that there was another, more personal, reason for her despair.

She still persisted in wondering if Lord Elliot would return, at least to see how she was faring now that Sir Donald had gone to Europe. He had seemed to care for her, yet he said nothing before leaving, and she had begun to wonder if she was only imagining that yearning look in his deep blue eyes.

Unfortunately, the only visitors she had were the ever-inquisitive Hurley girls, with their questions and pointed looks, and the well-meaning Reverend Percy-Pembleton, whose slow, thoughtful manner of speaking was enough to drive Grace to distraction.

She sat on the edge of the sill of what she still thought of as Elliot's window. The day was a warm one for the beginning of October, and a fragrant breeze blew over the nearby hills. Her garden had bloomed lavishly, no doubt because she had had plenty of time to devote to it.

She had hoped she would get used to being alone. Rationally, she realized that there was absolutely no help for it. Mercy could not have remained in Barton as her pregnancy advanced. She would have faced an embarrassment of pointed looks, suspicious stares and whispered innuendo, especially on the part of the Hurley sisters—as *she* had, based on considerably less evidence than Mercy's physical changes would have been.

Word had gotten out that Sir Donald had indeed intended to marry Grace Barton until another, unknown man had appeared. The wedding had been called off. Although the exact connection between the three people remained a mystery, the stranger was variously identified as Grace's lover, secret brother or a blackmailer. Some even thought the man might have been an agent of Lord Denburton, who perhaps hadn't approved of the match between Sir Donald and Miss Barton.

Grace said nothing. What would be the point? She couldn't say who the man was without having to explain how she knew Lord Elliot, and it really didn't matter, anyway. Unless Lieutenant Brown married Mercy, she would be leaving Barton herself in a little while, probably forever.

Given Lieutenant Brown's continuing absence,

Grace could only be glad Mercy had gone to Barroughby Hall, although Mercy was apparently still clinging to the hope that Adam Brown would return and marry her.

Unfortunately, the Hurleys were very voluble about their nephew's future. They were quite sure, based upon his letters, that he would soon be engaged to the admiral's daughter, and very likely to become an admiral himself on the strength of that connection.

Naturally Grace said nothing of this in her letters to her sister. Even her practical nature recoiled at the thought of destroying Mercy's hope, although she did tell Mercy that Lieutenant Brown's absence seemed likely to be prolonged.

Once again she began to read Mercy's latest letter. The Duke and Duchess of Barroughby were proving to be most kind and hospitable hosts, and Mercy was hopeful that Grace would soon come to Barroughby for the birth of her child. The duke and duchess were most anxious to make her acquaintance, too, or so they said.

Grace told herself that she only wanted to wait until it was closer to Mercy's time before shutting up the house and abandoning her garden. Even at that time, she would miss some of the harvest. Although this was not nearly as important as Mercy and her child, it was not something to dismiss entirely, for financially, their difficulties were not completely resolved.

Even more troublesome, however, and the true reason for Grace's delayed departure was the idea of seeing Lord Elliot again. Mercy's letter stated that he was expected to return to Barroughby Hall soon, after spending his summer in London.

Grace was afraid to meet him again, and afraid that she had been a sentimental fool.

It was just as well Mercy didn't say much about Lord Elliot. She mentioned him occasionally, and it was clear the breach between the brothers had been mended.

Grace had told herself again and again that it would be better if she could forget him, except for the kindness he had extended to her sister. There could never be any relationship of a serious nature between them. He was a lord, she a farmer's daughter. They moved in completely different social spheres. Surely he had other obligations.

Social obligations, such as dancing at balls with other, more eminently suitable young ladies.

Grace glanced down the lane again and a sudden movement caught her attention. Ever since that pair of ruffians had been apprehended not far from Barton Farm, she had been nervous whenever a stranger appeared, especially when it turned out that a third man had been murdered. For a little while, the trial, which resulted in one man's hanging based on the other's confession, had even managed to silence the speculation about the Bartons.

When a man came striding toward Barton Farm, therefore, Grace's first reaction was to jump back from the window.

Then she realized, as she watched him, that there was something familiar about this man, with his

tawny brown hair and rolling gait, carrying a duffel
bag slung over his shoulder.

Grace gasped, for the man walking so jauntily
down the lane as if he had not a care in the world,
was Lieutenant Adam Brown.

Chapter Eighteen

Grace stood frozen to the spot as a wave of emotions swept over her. First was the simple surprise of seeing Lieutenant Brown in her lane, when she was so used to thinking of him in far-off Gibraltar. The second was relief. The third was hope. Yet, under it all, she was also extremely angry with him for abandoning Mercy to her fate and then strolling down the lane as if nothing at all had happened since the last time he had come to call.

It was the anger that propelled her down the stairs and through the kitchen, where she threw open the door just as he opened the gate.

Lieutenant Brown looked little changed, except that his skin was noticeably tanned, and he wasn't wearing his naval uniform.

"Miss Barton!" he called out cheerfully.

"Lieutenant Brown," she answered coolly, telling herself being angry would not help at all. "You have returned."

As he halted and set his duffel down, a wary look

came into his brown eyes. "Indeed I have. I hope I find you and your sister well."

"You find *me,* but Mercy is not at home."

"Where...where is she?"

"She had to go away," Grace said. "Won't you come in, and I'll tell you all about it."

Looking as stunned as a man who has been knocked to the ground unexpectedly, he accepted her invitation, sitting in the chair beside the hearth that she indicated. "She is well, is she not?" he asked anxiously.

His expression was so fearful and so upset, Grace began to forgive him. "She was well when she wrote to me two days ago."

"Where is she, then? I must go to her."

"Yes, you must." Grace ran her index finger over the top of the table and gave him a sidelong glance. "When you do, is it your intention to ask for her hand in marriage?"

Lieutenant Brown flushed. "I suppose I should ask for your permission," he said with an unexpected shyness. "You are the head of the household, after all."

"What would you do if I declined to give it?"

Lieutenant Brown's mouth dropped open so that he looked like one of the many fish he might have encountered at sea. "I...I beg your pardon?"

"I said, what would you do if I declined to give you permission to marry my sister?"

Lieutenant Brown rose abruptly, his chair scraping loudly across the floor. "I would go to Mercy and ask *her* for her hand."

"She would agree?"

"Of course she would! We love each other and nobody's going to stop us from getting—" He hesitated when he got a good look at Grace's relieved face. "You aren't going to deny it, are you?"

"No, I'm not. I simply wanted to assure myself that your affection was genuine." Grace regarded him steadfastly. "In fact, given the circumstances, I must insist that you marry her."

"Given what circumstances?"

"Given that when you left, she was pregnant with your child."

Lieutenant Brown flopped back onto his chair. "What?"

"She's having a baby, in about a fortnight's time."

"A baby?"

"Your baby."

"In a fortnight?"

"Yes, or thereabouts."

Suddenly he jumped to his feet. "Why didn't she tell me?"

"She didn't know herself, until you were gone."

"Why didn't she write to me?" he demanded of Grace angrily, as if she had somehow prevented Mercy from corresponding.

"She wouldn't because you were not properly engaged. Why did you not write to her?"

"She asked me not to," he said, and then a look of sudden comprehension crossed his suntanned brow. "I thought she wanted to wait until she could tell you of our plans. It did seem to be taking her a long time to write to me, but she is so sweet and shy,

I thought... I should have seen—noticed from the change in her expression—that she wasn't sure of her standing in my heart! Oh, I am an imbecile!''

Demonstrating great forbearance, Grace did not voice any agreement.

"Oh, dear, sweet, foolish Mercy!'' Lieutenant Brown went on, shaking his head and laughing. "I told her I loved her, and would forever. I thought she understood that I meant I wanted to marry her. I suppose I should have gone down on bended knee and said it properly.

"Why, I've already resigned my commission, so she wouldn't have to leave Lincolnshire when we're married because I knew how she loved it here, and I've got myself a job with my cousin in Grantham. But she could have written me!''

"I think she was afraid of what your aunts would say if they found out you were corresponding.''

He nodded. "And they would,'' he said sardonically. "Yes, that I understand—but I wish she had told me somehow.'' Then he lunged for his duffel bag. "It doesn't matter now, as long as she's safe and well. Where is she? I will go to her at once!''

"She is at Barroughby Hall.''

"Barroughby Hall? Where is that?''

"The town of Barroughby, in Hampshire. It is the home of the Duke and Duchess of Barroughby.''

"Very good. I shall take the coach to Lincoln and the train from there to Hampshire.'' He went to the door, then hesitated and turned slowly toward her, his eyes narrowed with a suspicious wariness. "Barroughby, you said?''

"Yes."

"How did she come to make the acquaintance of the Duke of Barroughby?"

"We, um, we met his brother, Lord Elliot."

Lieutenant Brown's duffel hit the floor. "Elliot Fitzwalter?" he asked in a strange voice. "I thought he was dead."

"He is very much alive. He arranged for Mercy to go to Barroughby Hall."

"Oh, no!" Adam Brown murmured, then he glared at Grace. "You've put Mercy into that man's hands?"

"Yes, but you don't—"

"No," he said harshly, "*you* don't understand. I've heard many things about Elliot Fitzwalter, from other officers, seamen and even the proprietors of certain wharfside pubs. He is *notorious*—a womanizer, a gambler, a rogue of the worst stripe!"

Grace faced Lieutenant Brown boldly. "Perhaps he was all those things once, but I assure you, Lieutenant Brown, that I have every faith in my sister's safety and care under his protection. I might also point out that you are hardly in a position to criticize, having left her without any kind of formal understanding. I have heard you have apparently been enjoying the attentions of a certain admiral's daughter, so it could be that Lord Elliot is not the only one who could be called a rogue."

"But I—"

"Be that as it may, Mercy's letters give no indication that she is being in any way mistreated or in any danger at all from Lord Elliot Fitzwalter, who has not been at Barroughby Hall these past several months.''

Lieutenant Brown was clearly not convinced. ''Miss Barton, Lord Elliot Fitzwalter is a very charming, very handsome, very shrewd and conniving fellow, if half the things I've heard about him are true. You and Mercy—well, you've never associated with men of his kind before, and while you are intelligent and clever, he could very well have fooled you into believing he was the gentlest, most sincere man on the face of the earth, all the while planning...''

Before Grace could answer, before she could say that she still believed Mercy perfectly safe, he continued. ''Why don't you come with me to Barroughby? If she is well, I'm sure she misses you, and if she is not, then she will need you.''

Grace hesitated, torn between her desire to see Lord Elliot and Mercy, and her fear that she would find that Lord Elliot did not care for her.

Then something happened that took the decision from her hands, for a carriage came rumbling swiftly down the lane.

Grace and Lieutenant Brown hurried into the yard as the driver yanked the horses to a halt. A well-dressed, middle-aged man disembarked. ''Miss Barton?'' he inquired, running his gaze over both of them.

''Yes!''

''The Duke of Barroughby has sent me to fetch you. Your sister has need of you. Please, if you will be so good as to read this, it should confirm what I am telling you.''

Grace snatched the paper from the man's outstretched hand and tore open the ducal seal.

The note was not from the duke, but written in Mercy's own hand.

"What does it say?" Lieutenant Brown demanded, leaning over her shoulder.

Grace read the few words quickly. Mercy had written that she had started to labor more than once, and although the process seemed to have stopped each time, the midwife had said that the baby would come any time. Mercy's letter pleaded with Grace to come at once.

"I must go to her without delay. I'll get a bag!" Grace cried hurriedly before rushing into the house and frantically throwing a few of the most necessary items into a valise.

Something was very wrong. The false labors, the brevity of Mercy's note, the desperation in her tone, the early birth. And as with any birth, the baby was not the only one at risk.

"Oh, dear God," Grace murmured, closing her eyes for a brief moment. "Please, help her! Please, let her be all right!"

By the time Grace ran back downstairs, her cloak half on, her bonnet clapped on her head and her valise in her hand, the duke's man had gotten back into the carriage, which had been turned around. Lieutenant Brown was standing exactly where she had left him.

"I must come with you," he said urgently.

Grace hesitated. What right did he have to come

with her now? Had he not forfeited any claims by his long-delayed return?

Then she saw the desperate yearning in his eyes and knew she couldn't deny him. She nodded her acquiescence, and not just for the sake of that look. Mercy would want him, and she couldn't deny Mercy, either.

Not now, when she knew all too well the agony of longing.

She tossed her valise to the man, who caught it deftly, and climbed inside, reflecting that it was just as well she wasn't putting herself in the sole care of this stranger, although if anybody saw her leaving like this, more rumors would surely fly.

That reminded her of something, and she glanced back at Lieutenant Brown, who was nearly in the carriage. "Should you not take leave of your aunts?"

"To hell with my aunts!" Lieutenant Brown cried, banging on the side of the carriage to alert the driver the moment he was seated. "Mercy needs me!"

In another instant, they were on their way.

The journey to Barroughby seemed longer than it was, made even more wretched and tedious by Adam Brown's constant talking and questioning.

First, he wanted to know all about Mercy: how she had been since he had last seen her, if she was upset, if Grace thought she still loved him. He explained several times about the admiral's daughter, who was a fine woman, but certainly there had never been anything between them except friendship, as the admiral's daughter was in love with another officer currently at sea. He condemned himself for not proposing properly, or writing to Mercy, propriety be damned.

Like a child, he kept asking how much farther, and bemoaned each delay. Grace's nerves were so strained that more than once she wanted to shout at Lieutenant Brown to shut up and leave her alone.

Nevertheless, she tried to reassure him, to the best of her ability, for she could not completely exonerate him. When all was said and done, both he and Mercy should have known what might happen by their passionate activity. Both of them should have insured that they understood the nature of their relationship; in Grace's mind, both were equally responsible for what had befallen them.

Besides listening to Lieutenant Brown's constant stream of talk, and worrying about Mercy's current plight, Grace also had the anticipation of meeting Elliot Fitzwalter to contend with. She was tempted to ask their escort, who introduced himself as Mr. Taylor, the duke's steward, if Lord Elliot was at Barroughby.

Instead, she found herself tongue-tied, fearful of any response he might give her. If Lord Elliot was there, she would have to worry about meeting him; if he was not, she would wonder if he might soon arrive.

She thought of subtly asking Mr. Taylor about the duke's younger sibling, until he revealed that he had only been the steward at the Barroughby estate for the past two months.

Soon enough, however, they reached the town of Barroughby. When they got off the train, Mr. Taylor took them to a waiting barouche embellished with ducal arms.

"Not long now," he said kindly, and he was right.

Grace had expected a ducal seat to be something extraordinary, but no imagination could have prepared her for the splendor of Barroughby Hall. The estate itself was huge, enclosed by a stone wall that hid the wide expanse of lawn from curious eyes. The house was enormous, and as the carriage went along the winding drive, Grace decided she was glad she hadn't known that "Mr. Elliot" belonged to such magnificence. She would never have had the gall to drag him through the mud.

Under other circumstances, she would have found her arrival at such a place cause for timidity, too. However, her concern for Mercy destroyed any sense of inferiority she had, especially when she saw a man standing on the steps, apparently waiting for them.

He was tall, dark haired, dark browed, and there was a tension in his stance that made her stomach knot. What if they were too late?

The carriage had no sooner rolled to a stop than the man was at the door. "Miss Barton, I presume?" he asked, glancing at Lieutenant Brown for the briefest of moments.

"Yes. How is my sister?"

"She is in labor," he said, opening the door and lowering the step himself. "She will no doubt feel better now that you are here."

"Which way?" Grace demanded as she exited the carriage. "Where is she?"

"Inside. A footman will show you the way."

Grace lifted her skirts and ran up the wide expanse of steps.

Meanwhile, the dark-haired man watched the other passenger get out of the carriage as quickly as Miss Barton had. "Lieutenant Adam Brown, late of Her Majesty's navy," he said, climbing over Mr. Taylor in his haste. "I'm engaged to Miss Mercy."

"Are you, indeed?" the man said with an aristocratic languor that didn't match the intensity in his deep brown eyes.

"Yes! Get out of my way!"

He, too, ran up the steps, not bothering to find out that the man he had spoken to so rudely was Adrian Fitzwalter, the sixth Duke of Barroughby.

"Mercy!" Grace cried, hurrying past the footman and rushing into the sumptuous bedroom.

She noticed little of the fine furnishings or draperies, or the cluster of people; her attention was focused solely on Mercy's pale face, nearly as white as the satin pillow on which her head rested, her brow dampened with perspiration. "Mercy!"

"Grace!" Her sister struggled to a sitting position, and an older woman, with a face as wrinkled as a walnut and skin of a similar hue, moved to help her. "I'm so glad you've come!" Mercy lowered her head and bit her lip even as she held out her hand for Grace to grasp. "I'm so glad!"

As relief that Mercy was yet alive flooded through Grace, she realized that her sister's clasp was far from strong. "Lie back, dear," she said softly, assisting her.

"I'm fine, really, now that you are here," Mercy whispered, never letting go of Grace's hand. Her face contorted as another pain assailed her, and her grip tightened for an instant. Grace glanced nervously at the woman she surmised was the midwife.

"Nearly time," the woman said matter-of-factly. "Everyone out, if you please."

"I will stay," Grace said firmly.

"And I," an unknown woman's voice added.

Grace turned to look over her shoulder and was surprised to see another pregnant woman in the room.

"That is the Duchess of Barroughby," Mercy whispered.

Before Hester Fitzwalter could speak, a man could be heard in the corridor outside. "I wouldn't care if the queen said I couldn't go in!"

"Adam!" Mercy cried, as the young man erupted into the room. He ran toward her, and she suddenly started to sob, great, deep choking sobs that told Grace more than words ever could that while Mercy had professed absolute confidence in her lover, she, too, had had her doubts.

How painful it must have been, all this time with no one but strangers about her! She should have forgotten the farm and come with Mercy, no matter how awkward or tense it might have been.

"Mercy, my love, don't cry!" Adam Brown said as he knelt beside the bed, tenderly brushing back a lock of sweat-dampened hair. "I'm here now. I won't leave again, ever. I promise."

Mercy nodded and wiped away her tears with a trembling hand. Grace heard a small sound, and discovered that the other woman in the room, the duchess, was also wiping her eyes. She gave Grace a wry smile and shrugged her shoulders sheepishly.

Grace thought she could like the duchess.

"Why didn't you tell me?" Lieutenant Brown asked in a whisper, tenderly kissing Mercy's forehead.

"I didn't want you to think you *had* to marry—" Mercy started to pant, a grimace of pain crossing her face.

"Out! Now! You, too," the midwife commanded Lieutenant Brown.

"Not yet," Adam replied sternly. He got down on one knee. "Miss Mercy Barton, will you do me the very great honor of consenting to be my wife?"

"Yes!" Mercy gasped, and then an anguished cry broke from her lips. "Hester!"

Grace watched helplessly as the other woman, a *stranger,* answered her sister's summons. Did Mercy begrudge her long absence? Had she forfeited her place at her sister's side by her absence and doubts?

Oh, she never should have stayed at home, troublesome emotions or not!

Hester leaned as close to Mercy as her condition would allow and listened as Mercy whispered to her. Lieutenant Brown, who was also privy to the conversation, began to nod enthusiastically.

Then Hester straightened and left the room without one word to Grace.

"Grace?" Mercy gasped.

"What is it?" Grace asked, moving swiftly to the other side of the bed, so frightened by her sister's weak voice and pale face that she forgot any of the Fitzwalters existed.

"Grace, would you be my maid of honor? Adam and I are going to be married."

"Of course, dear," Grace said. "Whenever you like."

Mercy's only response was a long, low moan.

Another carriage came rolling down the drive at breakneck speed. Before it had stopped completely, Elliot Fitzwalter jumped out and ran up the steps into Barroughby Hall. He halted in the foyer as a scream of pain filled the air.

"Oh, God!" he muttered, looking around in a panic. "Adrian!" he shouted. "Adrian!"

His half brother appeared in the corridor leading to his study. "Elliot! Come here—and quit shouting!" he said sharply.

When Elliot discerned the worried expression in his brother's eyes, his fear for Mercy's safety increased.

All the way from London, he had been imagining how Grace would feel about him if her sister died. Specifically, he was terrified she would blame him for taking Mercy away and robbing Grace of her sister for the last months of Mercy's life.

"How is Mercy?" he demanded as he followed Adrian into the study.

"She's not in any particular danger yet, I understand," Adrian said after quietly shutting the door. "The midwife is here. Hester told me she's concerned that the baby will be too small to survive."

"Dr. Woadly?"

Adrian's expression clouded. "He's getting old,

and he doesn't know much about childbirth, when all is said and done. Even your mother agreed with me on that. Mrs. Crocker has helped dozens of women give birth. I thought it best to fetch her instead.''

''I see.''

''I think Mercy will do better now that her sister is here.''

''Yes—I'm sure she will,'' Elliot mumbled, not meeting his brother's gaze.

Grace was here. Inside this house. He had only to go up the staircase and down a hall to see her.

''Miss Barton arrived with a Lieutenant Brown,'' Adrian remarked.

''Lieutenant Brown? The baby's father?''

''So I understand.''

Elliot glanced at his brother and managed to smile. ''Thank God for that. I'm glad her faith in him has been rewarded.''

There was a flurry of footsteps outside the door and both men started. ''I'll see what it is,'' Adrian offered. He was gone but a few moments. ''More water,'' he said with a sigh. ''Try not to worry. That's not uncommon.''

''I'm as nervous as if I were the father,'' Elliot said, hoping Adrian would accept that explanation for his trembling fingers and distracted manner.

''More, perhaps,'' Adrian noted. ''You didn't tell me Miss Barton was so beautiful.''

''I thought your days of admiring a lovely face were over.''

''I admire. Nothing more.''

''I know.''

Adrian strolled over toward the window and addressed his brother without looking at him. "I'm not surprised you want to marry her."

"Because she's beautiful? I promise you, Adrian, my feelings run deeper than that."

Adrian turned around, his lips twisted into a wry grin. "I know they do. I can tell just by looking at you."

"God, Adrian, now that she's here, I'm scared to death. What if Mercy dies? She might blame *me*."

"Calm down, Elliot," Adrian ordered. "I don't think Mercy will die. And I don't think you're giving Miss Barton enough credit to understand that you were trying to help them. Nobody forced Mercy to come with you, after all."

"Yes, yes, I know," Elliot admitted, rubbing his forehead in frustration. "I just can't think rationally where Grace is concerned, I suppose."

Adrian chuckled quietly. "Rationality has little place when it comes to love, I'm afraid."

"I'm glad you find my plight so amusing."

"Not amusing, per se. I speak so only from the lofty heights of my experience—as you shall, some time hence. Tell me, how goes the shipping business?"

For a time, the talk turned to Elliot's business affairs in London, but both men's minds were not really on the subject at hand, or even the discussion of love so recently concluded. Adrian was listening for sounds that would indicate trouble with Mercy's labor. Elliot was listening for that, too, and wondering what he would say to Grace when it was all over, whatever the outcome.

The door to the study suddenly burst open, and a

very pregnant Hester stood panting on the threshold. "Adrian!"

"What is it?" Adrian and Elliot demanded simultaneously, sharing one thought: disaster!

"Send for Reverend McKenna! At once! They want to be married."

Adrian gave one succinct nod. "How long before the baby?"

"Mrs. Crocker thinks an hour, perhaps two." Suddenly Hester's hand reached for the door frame and she bent over, a groan escaping her lips.

Adrian was at her side in an instant. "The baby?"

She nodded, her lips pressed tightly together for a moment before she spoke again. "The baby."

Adrian lifted Hester's arm around his shoulder. "Elliot, you know Reverend McKenna," he said. "Fetch him at once, will you? Tell him Lieutenant Brown has come, and there's to be a wedding."

"Can't that wait until—"

Adrian swept his wife up into his arms. "No! The wedding is to be *now*—before the baby comes."

Elliot nodded, understanding at once the necessity of the hasty marriage, if not how it was to be legally accomplished without a reading of banns, or a special license. Perhaps, he thought as Adrian carried Hester out of the room, actual legality was not the issue.

Perhaps the marriage ceremony was merely to ease a woman's dying.

Chapter Nineteen

"Reverend McKenna?" Elliot strode into the vicar's study without waiting for the maid to announce him.

The freckled, redheaded Scot rose and frowned when he saw who said his name. Elliot was no stranger to the young clergyman, although Elliot hoped that whatever else Reverend McKenna had heard about him, he would have heard the more recent, much more favorable news. "The duchess sent me for you."

The minister looked as puzzled as Elliot had been.

"She said there was to be a wedding," he explained.

"Has Lieutenant Brown come, then?" the vicar asked, a pleased smile replacing his previous expression.

"Yes. Just now. But it may be too late."

"If the baby hasn't yet come, it's not too late," the clergyman replied briskly, reaching for the small black bag that Elliot recognized as one used to carry necessary items when the minister visited a shut-in parishoner. "I've read the banns these past three weeks. A bit of a stretch of the legalities," he confessed as he adjusted his dog collar. "Still, I considered Miss Mercy a member of the parish. I've been expecting this call, if Lieutenant Brown came."

He headed for the door, where a maid hovered anxiously. "Tell my wife I won't be home for dinner."

Glancing back at Elliot with sympathetic eyes, he said, "Come, my lord. I gather no time is to be lost."

Grace looked up from wiping Mercy's brow as the door to the bedroom opened, and a red-haired man walked in. It took her a moment to appreciate that he was a minister—a thought which filled her with more fear, as if that were possible. Had they sent for him because of her sister's condition?

She glanced back down at Mercy, whose head rolled from side to side. Her pain was continuous now, and nothing Grace or Lieutenant Brown or the midwife could say or do seemed to ease it.

"Miss Mercy?" the minister asked in a Scottish lilt.

Grace was surprised to see Mercy open her eyes and smile, albeit briefly. "You've come in time," she murmured. "Adam?"

"Here, my love."

Mercy nodded in the direction of the clergyman, who put a small bag on a nearby side table. With swift movements he took out and put on a small stole, then opened his prayer book. Coming to stand near Lieutenant Brown, he began to read the marriage service.

Grace listened in stunned silence as Mercy and

Lieutenant Brown were married, even though Mercy could barely answer.

The moment they were pronounced man and wife, the midwife declared, "Right. Now, everyone out."

Grace didn't move, thinking that Mrs. Crocker couldn't mean her, but the woman did. *"Everyone,"* she repeated.

When Grace still didn't move, not willing to leave Mercy, the older woman smiled kindly. "It's time, and no distractions. Let us do our job.".

Grace nodded slowly and left the bedroom, following Reverend McKenna and preceding Lieutenant Brown, who stayed to press a kiss on Mercy's perspiring face.

They all went out into the hall, and then Grace wished she had stood her ground.

Lord Elliot was there, a short distance away, and he was watching her.

Grace didn't speak. She couldn't think of anything to say to him, nor was she going any farther from Mercy, especially as she listened to the muffled, anguished sounds from inside the room.

She was vaguely aware of Reverend McKenna's short, whispered conversation with Lord Elliot, and the clergyman's departure. She knew Lieutenant Brown was seated on a very ornate and very old chair not three feet away. He suggested she sit, but Grace couldn't do that, either.

Nor could she pace, as she wanted to. That would take her too close to Lord Elliot.

So, in agony of silence broken only by Mercy's stifled cries and moans, they all waited.

Once a maid came to offer them refreshments, but none of them wanted any. Another time, the duke arrived and spoke softly to his brother. Then he was gone.

After what seemed an eternity, but was really only an hour, a baby's cry pierced the silence. Lieutenant Brown jumped to his feet and looked at Grace, his expression both pleased and frightened.

Grace said nothing, her attention drawn to Elliot Fitzwalter, who walked slowly toward her.

The door to the bedroom opened, and the midwife stood there, a beaming smile on her face. "That's one of the healthiest babies I've ever seen. Lieutenant Brown, come see your fine and brawny son."

Adam Brown grinned like a monkey and bounded past the midwife.

Grace took a tentative step toward her. "Mercy?" she whispered.

"As well as a woman can be who has a baby that size and tries to keep him waiting for a clergyman to come," the midwife replied with another smile, standing aside a bit to let Grace see Mercy, who was holding her infant in her arms and smiling weakly at her husband. "She'll be fine."

"Oh, thank God!" Lord Elliot said as Grace sighed with relief and happiness.

She turned to go, only to come face to chin with Lord Elliot. "Aren't you going in to see her?" he asked quietly.

She tore her gaze from him and shook her head. "Not now," she replied in a whisper. "She should be with her husband."

"Then will you join me for a cup of tea? I'm completely exhausted."

Grace's first impulse was to agree, her next to decline.

"I shall not take no for an answer," Lord Elliot said kindly. "You look done in and I know how you must have been worrying about your sister. This time, you must allow me to do the nursing."

He was right—she *was* tired, as tired as the day she had dragged him to her home.

Before she could answer him, though, another maid bustled into Mercy's room and spoke briefly to the midwife, who said something unintelligible to Mercy and Lieutenant Brown, then hurried away with the maid.

"It's Hester," Elliot explained. "It seems this is the day for babies to arrive at Barroughby Hall."

A feeble "oh" was the only response Grace could make as he offered her his arm to escort her downstairs to the drawing room.

She didn't dare look at his face, and she tried not to notice the feel of his muscular arm beneath her hand. He hadn't returned to Barton in all these months, and she was a fool if she thought his manner to her had ever been anything other than a mild, habitual flirtation.

No matter how much she wanted it to be otherwise.

They entered the drawing room, a large, sumptuously furnished room that intimidated Grace nearly as much as her company. She wondered where to sit, what to do and what to say, while Lord Elliot gave a few brief orders to yet another waiting maid.

Then he sauntered into the room, and she would have thought him completely at ease, except for a slight hesitation in his manner. "Won't you sit down?" he said, gesturing at one of the many fine gold-and-green brocade sofas.

She did so, keeping her eyes firmly fastened on the marble top of the tea table in front of her.

"I hope your journey was not too difficult," he said evenly.

"No."

"You have been keeping well?"

"Yes."

He walked away, toward the tall, narrow windows. "Did the notorious gossips give you a difficult time?"

Now Grace could look at him, since his back was to her. "Not really. I've managed to avoid them as much as possible, and something else happened that took a little of their attention from me."

"Oh?" He glanced over his shoulder, an interrogative expression of his face.

"Yes." She swallowed hard, determined to sound composed and unaffected by his presence. "Two outlaws were apprehended near our farm. It seems there was another one, but the leader murdered him. At least, that was what the younger one said."

"What happened to them?"

"They found the body, so the leader was hanged. The other one is in jail in Lincoln, and likely to be there for some time."

"The leader—his name was Boffin?"

She looked at him with surprise. "How did you know?"

Lord Elliot turned and gave her a rueful look. "I apprehended him. Or rather, he and his men tried to apprehend me, and lost."

"You?"

He came a little closer, sitting on an ornate chair at some distance. "I cheated him at cards," he confessed quietly. "I didn't mean to put you or anyone else in danger, though. I was sure he wouldn't keep looking for me."

"You cheated him at cards?"

"Sir Donald told you I was a rogue."

Grace regarded him steadily. "I do not see a rogue. I see a man who did his best to help my sister and me, and to whom I am very grateful."

Elliot found it difficult to breathe properly. "I've been trying to reform," he said intently. "I've been working for a friend in the shipping business. Not as exciting as gambling, I confess, but it's not as dangerous, either."

"Oh?"

If only he could read her expression better! It was taking all his energy to sit in this chair and keep away from her, when he wanted nothing more than to gather her into his arms and kiss her. "It's delightful that Lieutenant Brown arrived at last."

Her gaze faltered. "It would have been better if he had never gone away."

"Yes," Elliot answered, wondering at her mournful tone, and if he was a fool to attach any significance to it. "He didn't know about Mercy, though."

She silently nodded her head.

"Just as I didn't understand the consequences of some of my actions," he continued. "I might never have understood, if I hadn't stayed with you and your sister. I have never seen...never witnessed...Oh, Grace, I owe you so much!"

She raised her lovely brown eyes to him and they were not inscrutable now. He could see the yearning there, a yearning that matched the longing in his own heart, and a tremulous fear, too.

Tentatively he rose and walked slowly toward her. "Do you know why I've really tried to reform?" he whispered, kneeling beside her and taking her slender, soft hand in his. "I've been trying to be worthy of you."

"Worthy of *me?*" she asked softly, her gaze searching his face. "You are a lord, I am only a farmer's daughter."

"I was a rogue, and you were my savior. Grace, I—"

Suddenly, and to Grace's great dismay, a tall, elderly woman, very straight of back and stern of mien, marched into the room. She halted abruptly.

"Elliot," she declared, her piercing, measuring gaze alighting on the couple before her. "Who is this?"

"Mama, this is Miss Grace Barton," Elliot said, dropping her hand and rising. Grace, too, hurried to her feet. "Miss Barton, my mother, the Dowager Duchess of Barroughby."

Grace dipped a curtsy and inwardly wished the dowager duchess to the farthest reaches of the earth.

"So, you are the woman my son loves."

Grace felt as if the room was starting to spin. "I...I beg your pardon?"

"Mama!" Elliot said, his hand suddenly clasping Grace's, warm and strong.

He didn't deny it. He didn't move away. He didn't leave her. Her heart began to beat with a joyful hopefulness that she simply could not subdue as she looked at him.

"Well, don't you?" his mother demanded.

Elliot looked at Grace and she saw the love shining in his eyes. "Yes, I do," he said softly, and for her alone. "Very much."

Grace suddenly and surprisingly burst into tears.

"What's the matter with her?" the duchess exclaimed as Elliot helped Grace to a chair.

"I'm...I'll be...it's just that..." Grace stammered, shocked and embarrassed at this emotional reaction, but really much too happy to care.

"You might have allowed me to tell her of my feelings myself, Mama," Elliot chided, addressing his mother while his gaze never left Grace's face.

"You wouldn't. You're too self-effacing."

This time, Elliot did glance at his mother over his shoulder. "Me? Self-effacing?"

"You didn't tell her before, did you?"

"No, you didn't tell me before," Grace said, smiling through her tears. "But neither did I tell him how *I* really felt."

"Mama...?"

The dowager duchess turned with a majestic wave of her hand. "I know when my presence is not desired. I am not in my dotage yet, Elliot," she said, gliding toward the door like a ship in full sail. "I shall leave you two young people alone." She paused and eyed Grace slowly. "I always knew my son would choose an exceptional bride."

"Mama spoke out of turn," Elliot said as his mother went out and closed the door.

For one horrible moment, Grace feared that she had been mistaken when she heard him say he loved her, until he knelt again and took her hand in his, regarding her earnestly. "I do love you, Grace. I've kept away because I wanted to make something of myself before I saw you again. To prove to you, and to me, that I was indeed a changed person."

"I thought you didn't come back because you didn't love me, that I was wrong to think... imagine...hope... I had behaved so badly that night, coming into your room—"

"I was horrified to think I had somehow corrupted you."

"You? You didn't do anything wrong."

"Neither did you," he said, smiling.

She frowned slightly. "I should have said something, but...but it has always been hard for me to tell even those I dearly love how I feel. Even when I want to. *Especially* when I want to, and—" she raised her eyes to him shyly "—especially you. I love you. I love you with all my heart."

"Grace!"

In that instant, she was in his arms, rapturously happy.

In the next, they were betrothed.

* * *

Several days before the wedding of Miss Grace Barton and Lord Elliot Fitzwalter was to take place, a frustrated and distracted Elliot entered the nursery of Barroughby Hall, where Grace, Mercy, Hester, Adam and Adrian were doting over the newborns, Lady Alicia Clara, daughter of the sixth Duke of Barroughby, and Charles Arthur Elliot Brown.

Elliot squatted to sit on a child's chair and ran his hands through his blond hair until it was almost standing on end. "Grace," he said, addressing her as she left cooing over Alicia and came toward him, "let's elope. We can be to Gretna Green in a day."

"Your mother?"

"She's insisting on inviting the whole House of Lords. It's too much—and most of them are half-dead anyway."

He heard Adrian's deep chuckle and looked at his brother, whose expression was decidedly unsympathetic. "I don't know why you find this so amusing," Elliot complained. "You're going to be footing most of the bill for the food."

Then he saw Grace's worried frown and wished he had kept quiet.

"To think I would live to hear the day you would ever criticize having money spent on you! The wedding's worth whatever it's costing just for this moment," Adam noted sardonically.

It was obvious his manner did not reassure Grace. "I think I would rather elope, too," she said. "So many aristocrats...and fine ladies...and the cost—"

Hester hurried to the bride's side, taking the hand that Elliot wasn't holding and patting it gently.

"Don't let these two fine fellows upset you," she said kindly. "Adrian is delighted to do this for you both. Besides, we have to show Elliot off."

"Egad! And I've tried so hard to become more than a decorative object," Elliot moaned.

"You're not a decorative object!" Grace protested.

"We all know that," Hester said. "Now we must show that to the world, or—" her voice became very serious and intent "—they might not believe he has changed."

Elliot had never considered his wedding in that light, his reasons having far more to do with marrying the woman he so deeply loved than any social demonstration.

Grace nodded, and she got that now-familiar, determined look in her eye. "Then we *should* invite them all."

"I'm outmaneuvered!" Elliot protested halfheartedly. He looked at Adrian. "You're sure about this, then?"

"Absolutely—and you know how stubborn I can be."

"Yes, I certainly do."

"That's settled, then," Hester said contentedly.

"Grace, can I tear you away from these children?" said Elliot, rising from his tiny perch.

"Of course," she replied, letting him lead her out of the nursery.

He paused at the top of the stairs where there was a tiny alcove lit by a small, round window, and drew her to him. "It isn't going to be easy, marrying into my family."

Grace smiled up at him with perfect contentment and love. "I like them."

"Even Mama?"

"She loves you very much."

"I was so contemptuous of that before I went away," he murmured.

"Staying here with your family, I'm hearing so many interesting things about you," Grace replied with a smile, leaning her head against his chest.

"What things?"

"Oh, just enough to appreciate how much you have reformed."

She felt his chest rise and fall with a deep sigh. "It's to your credit, you know. I would probably be sitting in some horrible, dingy tavern in London, cheating at cards for my next meal, if you hadn't rescued me, in more ways than one."

"You rescued me, too," Grace said softly, lifting her head to look into his blue, blue eyes. "Not just from my loneliness. If I hadn't found you, I might have married Sir Donald Franklin." She shivered involuntarily at that thought and his embrace tightened.

"Speaking of that wretch, who I gather has no intention of returning from France anytime soon, my godfather, Lord Denburton, has asked me if I could suggest someone to stand for member of parliament in the riding of Barton-by-the-Fens, based on my 'holiday' there."

"Lord Denburton is your godfather?"

Elliot grinned and inclined his head. "I think Adam Brown would do very well, if he is willing to settle in Barton."

"Oh, Elliot! How wonderful! Mercy and Adam can have the farm!"

"Excellent idea, since you'll be living with me," he added huskily, before his lips bore down on hers with a fiery kiss that Grace was in no hurry to stop.

Indeed, her own passion compelled her to return it in a manner that could only be described as wanton, until Elliot finally drew back and took a deep breath.

"My God, woman!" he said, grinning his lopsided grin and with a twinkle in his eyes. "I'm going to have to go away again, or I'll never be able to control myself until the wedding."

"You will just have to control yourself, my lord, because I will not allow you to leave me ever again," Grace said, trying not to smile and failing miserably.

"You sound just like Adrian."

"Is that so very bad?"

"Well," he drawled, once more pulling her close, "at one time, it would have been." He assumed a philosophical expression. "Since I've mellowed, I can endure it."

"Elliot?" Grace asked, even as he was bending to kiss her again.

"Yes, my love?"

He started to nuzzle her ear, and the sensations were so light and delightful, she almost forgot what she wanted to say. "Do you think your mother really will invite the whole House of Lords?"

"I wouldn't put it past her."

* * * * *

HARLEQUIN WOMEN KNOW ROMANCE WHEN THEY SEE IT.

And they'll see it on **ROMANCE CLASSICS**, the new 24-hour TV channel devoted to romantic movies and original programs like the special **Harlequin® Showcase of Authors & Stories.**

The **Harlequin® Showcase of Authors & Stories** introduces you to many of your favorite romance authors in a program developed exclusively for Harlequin® readers.

Watch for the **Harlequin® Showcase of Authors & Stories** series beginning in the summer of 1997.

If you're not receiving ROMANCE CLASSICS, call your local cable operator or satellite provider and ask for it today!

Escape to the network of your dreams.

Reach new heights of passion and
adventure this August in

ROCKY MOUNTAIN MEN

Don't miss this exciting new collection featuring
three stories of Rocky Mountain men and the
women who dared to tame them.

CODE OF SILENCE
by Linda Randall Wisdom

SILVER LADY
by Lynn Erickson

TOUCH THE SKY
by Debbi Bedford

Available this August wherever
Harlequin and Silhouette books are sold.

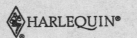

HARLEQUIN® Silhouette®

Let's Celebrate!

LOVE & LAUGHTER™

invites you to
the party of the season!

Grab your popcorn and be prepared to laugh
as we celebrate with **LOVE & LAUGHTER**.

Harlequin's newest series is going Hollywood!

Let us make you laugh with three months of terrific
books, authors and romance, plus a chance to win a
FREE 15-copy video collection of the best romantic
comedies ever made.

For more details look in the back pages of any
Love & Laughter title, from July to September,
at your favorite retail outlet.

Don't forget the popcorn!

Available wherever
Harlequin books are sold.

 ◆ HARLEQUIN®

Look us up on-line at: http://www.romance.net

LLCELEB

**HARLEQUIN AND SILHOUETTE
ARE PLEASED TO PRESENT**

Love, marriage—and the pursuit of family!

Check your retail shelves for these upcoming titles:

July 1997
Last Chance Cafe by Curtiss Ann Matlock
The most determined bachelor in Oklahoma is in trouble! A
lovely widow with three daughters has moved next door—and
the girls want a dad! But he wants to know if their mom needs
a husband....

August 1997
Thorne's Wife by Joan Hohl
Pennsylvania. It was only to be a marriage of convenience—
until they fell in love! Now, three years later, tragedy
threatens to separate them forever and Valerie wants only to
be in the strength of her husband's arms. For she has some
very special news for the expectant father...

September 1997
Desperate Measures by Paula Detmer Riggs
New Mexico judge Amanda Wainwright's daughter has been
kidnapped, and the price of her freedom is a verdict in
favor of a notorious crime boss. So enters ex-FBI agent
Devlin Buchanan—ruthless, unstoppable—and soon there is
no risk he will not take for her.

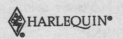

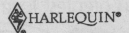 **HARLEQUIN®**

Not The Same Old Story!

 **HARLEQUIN PRESENTS®**
Exciting, emotionally intense romance stories that take readers around the world.

 *Harlequin Romance®*
Vibrant stories of captivating women and irresistible men experiencing the magic of falling in love!

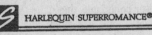 HARLEQUIN® *Temptation®*
Bold and adventurous—Temptation is strong women, bad boys, great sex!

HARLEQUIN SUPERROMANCE®
Provocative, passionate, contemporary stories that celebrate life and love.

HARLEQUIN AMERICAN ROMANCE®
Romantic adventure where anything is possible and where dreams come true.

HARLEQUIN® INTRIGUE®
Heart-stopping, suspenseful adventures that combine the best of romance and mystery.

 **LOVE & LAUGHTER™**
Entertaining and fun, humorous and romantic—stories that capture the lighter side of love.

Look us up on-line at: http://www.romance.net   HGENERIC